W9-BVE-835

M

Wood, Ted
Flashback

DATE DUE			
AUG 2 6 1992	MAR 1 9 1993		
SEP 5 1992	NOV 1 1993		
SEP 21 1992	NOV 1 9 1993		
SEP 29 1992	DEC 1 9 1994		
OCT 23 1992	DEC 2 6 1994		
NOV 2 4 1992	DEC 2 8 1994		
DEC 1 6 1992	JUN 5 1995		
JAN 2 5 1993	DEC 1 1 1995		
FEB 3 1993			
MAR 3 1993			

Mynderse Library
31 Fall Street
Seneca Falls, NY 13148

Flashback

Flashback

Ted Wood

CHARLES
SCRIBNER'S
SONS

NEW YORK

Maxwell Macmillan Canada
Toronto
Maxwell Macmillan International
New York   Oxford   Singapore   Sydney

For Bill, Beryl and all the rest
of the Aussie Woods

This is a work of fiction. Names, characters, places, and incidents either
are the product of the author's imagination or are used fictitiously.
Any resemblance to actual events or persons living or dead is
entirely coincidental.

Copyright © 1992 by Ted Wood

First American Edition 1992

All rights reserved. No part of this book may be reproduced or transmitted
in any form or by any means, electronic or mechanical, including
photocopying, recording, or by any information storage and retrieval
system, without permission in writing from the Publisher.

Charles Scribner's Sons   Maxwell Macmillan Canada, Inc.
Macmillan Publishing Company   1200 Eglinton Avenue East
866 Third Avenue   Suite 200
New York, NY 10022   Don Mills, Ontario M3C 3N1

Macmillan Publishing Company is part of the
Maxwell Communication Group of Companies.

Library of Congress Cataloging-in-Publication Data
Wood, Ted.
    Flashback/Ted Wood.—1st American ed.
        p.   cm.
    ISBN 0-684-19414-7
    I. Title.
PR9199.3.W57F54   1992   92-14127   CIP
813'.54—dc20

Macmillan books are available at special discounts for bulk purchases
for sales promotions, premiums, fund-raising, or educational use.
For details, contact:

Special Sales Director
Macmillan Publishing Company
866 Third Avenue
New York, NY 10022

10 9 8 7 6 5 4 3 2 1

Printed in the United States of America

CHAPTER 1

Five kids were standing around an old Ford Fairlane on Main Street. I weighed them up as I jogged out of the trees on to the dusty road surface of Main Street. After three years as police chief in Murphy's Harbour I know every one of the locals by sight, and most of the regular visitors. This bunch was out of tune with the town and I jogged over to the wall of the grocery store in my running shorts and T-shirt and pretended to stretch against the wall while I weighed them up.

They weren't sporting any gang regalia, colours or the same baseball caps worn backwards but the way they lounged on the fenders of the car, smoking, showed they had something to prove.

Only one was an individual threat, the biggest, he could have been twenty or even older, the same height as me, six one, about 175 useful pounds, boxer's muscles although his face was unmarked.

One of the others was carrying a baseball bat and he looked the most knotted up. He was around sixteen, fair hair and a neat little rat tail tickling his neck. One of the smokers said something to him and he said something hard and flat in return and they all laughed, yukking it up like actors. Then he made his move, along the front street in my direction towards a mongrel dog tied by its leash to a post at the other end of the store.

He picked up speed and cocked the bat and I sprang. He was five yards from the dog, I was ten but I covered the ground in four strides. The kid stopped when he saw me coming but drew the bat back and stood ready to swing. He figured I would halt, out of range, and use my silver tongue. Instead I took the two extra steps and straight-armed him in the upraised elbow.

He sprawled backwards, dropping the bat. I grabbed it before one of the others could. They were on the move, springing away from the car, closing on me, shouting. Then the big one held his hand up and they stopped.

'Pretty tough, shovin' people around?' He was doing his best to sound rough but he had an educated voice.

'I'm the chief of police here. What's your name?'

He ignored the question, cocking his head to his claque. 'Some pussy town you got here, chiefy, if that's how you dress.'

The rest of them had surrounded me, sniggering. I was glad I'd picked up the bat. I had to keep control or be swarmed.

I reversed it in my hands, holding it like a rifle and bayonet, butt towards him, and moved in on him, fast. He backed off, which gave me whatever psychological advantage there was but the others were still around me. 'In the car, son, and head out.' I told him, not raising my voice.

'Or what?' he sneered, but he licked his lips.

'I'm counting three.'

He looked around at his guys and nodded and they started inching in again.

'One,' I said clearly. They were four feet from me now, all around.

'Two.' He stood his ground.

'Three.' I reversed the bat and slammed the handle down on his toe. Not a recommended move. It did no more than embarrass him, making him swear and hop on one toe. But it worked, making it look like I didn't need to do more than humiliate him. I whirled, to face the next biggest. 'Get him in the car and out of town or you're next.'

He tried to stare me down for a moment, then took the other guy's elbow. 'Come on, Eric, the hell with this place.'

The guy shook him off and hobbled to the car and I

watched as he got into the passenger seat and sat there, glaring at me.

The other three scrambled into the rear of the car, one of them saying, 'You ain't seen the last of us.' Then the driver spurted away, spinning the car in a U-turn that tore a rut in the unpaved roadway and left a plume of dust as they roared back down the road towards the highway.

I heard a woman's voice saying, 'They were going to kill Ragamuffin.' It was one of our regular summer people bending over the dog which had roused itself at last and was standing, shaking off the dust it had gathered.

'Maybe not,' I said. Why sow anxieties? 'They're just kids.'

She's a fussy little woman, a widow in her seventies. 'Well, you sure showed them, Chief. Thank you.' She hoisted her grocery bag tighter under her arm and unwound the dog's leash from the post. 'Come on, Ragamuffin, let's go home.'

I glanced around the street. The usual crowd of youngsters was standing on the patch of dusty grass against the end of the bridge. It's the gathering place for teenagers, where the girls can giggle and the boys arm-wrestle and swear at one another in their newly broken voices. Occasionally I have to ask them to keep the music down to a dull roar, other than that they're harmless.

I went over to them and asked. 'Hi, did you know any of those guys?'

They didn't. Even the boys were glad to tell me that. Usually they're too cool to talk, letting the girls do it for them, but they were against the gang, strangers on their turf.

I nodded and left them, cutting my run short to go down to the police station which is south of the bridge, instead of crossing over and making my usual five-mile circuit of the water, both sides, both bridges. I wanted to let the other police know what was happening. Most of the towns hereabouts don't have police of their own, they depend on the Ontario Provincial Police, the OPP.

I called the Parry Sound detachment and alerted them, giving the licence of the Ford and a rough description of the kids. Then I checked the car's ownership. It belonged to a Walter Patton at an East Toronto address. I knew that Toronto has teen-gang problems so that didn't surprise me, but I wondered what they were doing this far north. Setting up a branch plant?

I hung up and sat for a moment glancing around my domain. Pretty good by the standards of cottage country. The office has a counter between me and the front door with a bench for the few people who linger long enough to sit down. There's the usual clutter of police posters and a rack of public information brochures on things like road safety and child abuse that nobody ever comes in to pick up. My side of the fence contains a desk with the original muscle-powered typewriter that was new when the office was built in the 'sixties. Behind the desk there's a stool that was once used by our civilian employee, the 'mister' in police slang. But he was let go a couple of years back when he got into trouble and the town's been too cheap to replace him since, so its seat is getting dull. Then there are a couple of grey filing cabinets, a teletype machine and, new this month, a Fax.

There were a couple of messages on the teletype. A wide load would be heading up the highway the following night. If possible, I should be at the highway entrance when it passed, routine. But the second one stopped me. George Kershaw, white male, forty-two years old, five-ten, had eluded the guard who had been sent with him on a day pass from Joyceville, a medium security jail. He'd skipped from Toronto, at the Skydome where he had been attending a baseball game. He was wearing a blue shirt and slacks, was unarmed but should be considered dangerous.

I tore the message off and clipped it on the board I keep

for special news. I knew he was dangerous. I'd been the
guy who locked him away, five years ago, in Toronto, where
he had held up a bank, shooting the manager and taking a
female hostage. My partner and I cornered him half an
hour later. He'd used the woman as a shield, threatening
to blow her away, his words, until I told him I'd shoot him
through the mouth and he'd be dead before he could react.
Then he shoved her away and dived, shooting at me but I
hit him first, taking the fight out of him, He'd sworn at his
trial that he would get me. A lot of them do that but I had
a hunch he meant it. And I've put a few guys in jail since
I've been here, so I was sure he knew where to come
looking.

That did it. I stuck the baseball bat under the counter,
on a ledge that contained a pile of accident forms and a
six-pack of empty pop bottles. Then I locked the station,
shoved the key back in the pouch on my shoe and headed
home.

Freda was watering the garden when I got back. Wearing
a big hat and the striped dress she had made for her pregnancy and usually referred to as 'the tent'. She was full
term now and had been flagging for the last couple of weeks
as the July heat picked up, but today she was full of energy,
spraying the tomato plants.

'You're back early. Have a good run?'

'OK, as far as it went, but there was a hassle in town.
Nothing serious, but I figured I should hold off on the
exercise until later.' I put my arm around her shoulder and
she gave me a quick kiss, buckling the brim of her hat
against my forehead. Sam, my big German shepherd, got
up from the porch and came down to greet me, looking a
little aggrieved. He figures he's my shadow and was until
Freda and I got together. With my wife vulnerable, I felt
more protective than usual. That's why I'd left Sam with
Fred when I went out. Fred? It's her own joking diminutive
of Freda. Not many women could carry off a name like

that without having cynics raise their eyebrows, but she's a charmer and the name fits her like the men's hats some girls wear.

She patted me on the shoulder. 'Right now a shower is a pretty high priority, old sport. Go for it. I'll make us a salad with some of this abundance here.'

'I'm in danger of ending up healthy,' I said, 'if this marriage lasts,' and ducked as she turned the hose on me.

We were eating lunch when the phone rang. I wondered if it would be one of our storekeepers to report the boys were back in town but it was a citizen with another problem. There was a car in the lake on the far shore. He'd noticed it while he was fishing off a rock.

Fred said she was going to read for a while, so I left Sam on watch in case Kershaw intended keeping his promise. I figured his presence would be enough to keep her safe and she didn't have to know I was worried for her. She had enough on her mind anyway. Then I drove off over the bridge at the north lock and down the west shore of the waterway, our section of the Derwent River system although this stretch is really a narrow lake.

I saw a crowd on the rock the fisherman had told me about. They were staring down and when I joined them I saw the car's rear end, a couple of feet underwater.

I asked, 'Is Tom Fielding here?'

A lean young guy with an expensive graphite fishing-rod said, 'I'm Fielding.'

'Thank you for calling in. When did you see the car?'

'About half an hour before I called you. I ran back home and telephoned. Is it stolen.'

'Can't say without seeing the licence plate, but it shouldn't be in there, that's certain. There's a car missing from Parry Sound.' I looked around at the crowd. Most of them would have been in bed before the car was even stolen, I figured, we get only a couple of TV channels locally. There's not much to do after dark but slap mosquitoes.

'Does any of you live close by?'

A woman nodded, she was about my age, late thirties. A looker but not working at it, lean, self-possessed, a cool, managerial type, I knew her by sight. 'That's my place over there.' She pointed to a white-painted cottage on the far side of the road.

'You're Ms Tracy, right?'

'Right.'

'Did you hear anything last night, Ms Tracy?'

She shook her head. 'No, but I was out until around twelve-thirty.'

As we spoke I was weighing up the terrain. The rock we were on sloped towards the water. One man could have pushed it into the lake unassisted. The splash would have been loud, but splashes aren't uncommon. My radio squawked and I held up one finger, 'Excuse me a minute, please.' I went back to the car and picked up the mike. 'Police chief.'

It was Gilles Perrault, the guy who runs the bait store on Main Street, reaching me through the phone line which kicks into my radio link. 'Reid. Gilles Perrault. Come quick. Kids been in, pushed the tank over, stole all kinds of stuff.'

'Be right there.' I took a moment to tell the crowd I'd be back with a tow truck. Then I told Ms Tracy, 'I have an emergency to attend to, could I come and talk to you later, please?'

'Of course. I'll be around until six.' She wanted to say more and I gave her a half-second before she blurted, 'I heard the radio. A swarming? Does that mean there are teen gangs in town?'

'I'm about to find out.' I inclined my head to her and left. On the way I called Fred and had her patch me through to Kinski's Garage. When they answered I told Paul about the submerged car and asked him to bring his tow truck up and start hauling it out. He swore when he heard it was under water, then grunted, so I guessed he'd find some way to get a chain on it. Then I put my foot down and picked up speed to Main Street.

The gang had really done a job on Perrault's store. His floor was awash with water and minnows wriggling every which way and muddy with a mixture of worms and moss. Gilles and an elderly customer were struggling to set the fish tank back on its base. It was a galvanized cattle trough but lined with bricks on the bottom and heavy.

He was swearing rapidly in French as he worked and he didn't stop until we had the tank back in place and he had run a hose into it. Then he thanked us and set about scooping up his stock. I hooked a pail off the wall and helped him. Sightseers crowded around the doorway, but none came in to help, they stood there drinking up the sight. It's the same at every kind of calamity. Some help, most watch.

It took us about five minutes to get most of the shiners back in the tank which was filling slowly. While Gilles hunted down the last of his minnows off the floor I asked him what had happened.

'Was kids. Couple big, maybe seventeen, eighteen. The rest younger. They came in, one came up to the counter an' then the rest ran wild, grabbin' stuff, tippin' the tank. I try to stop dem an' one big one push me over. Two, t'ree others was throwin' worms out of the fridge.'

'Did you see the bunch I had the heyrube with earlier?'

'No. I was busy an' it was over quick. Some customer tol' me. Said they was gonna kill a dog. But I never seen these kids before.' He found a dustpan and started sweeping up the worms, swearing again in his guttural Québecois French.

It sounded like the return of the dog-bashers, looking to pay me back for chasing them off earlier, but I dug for details. 'Were they wearing any kind of uniform? The same baseball caps maybe or a handkerchief hanging out of their pockets, anything?'

'I never seen nothin',' Gilles said miserably. 'They took lures, couple rods, anythin' they could grab.'

I asked the customer, 'Were you in here, sir, when this happened?'

'No. I got here as they were running out of the place. About knocked me over.'

I washed my fishy hands, took the customer's name and address and told Gilles to make a list of what had been stolen while I tried to trace the kids, then I went outside, leaving the customer beating Gilles down on his bait purchase, claiming that the minnows were shocked and would go belly up in no time.

A couple of people claimed to have seen the kids leaving but no two of their descriptions jibed so I had nothing to go on. I gave up, going into each of the stores and telling each of the clerks to phone the moment they recognized any of the kids or if a bunch of youths came in at once, not to wait until they swarmed the place. Then I saw Kinski's tow truck heading north up the other side of the lake and I got back in the car and followed it up.

It turned off the roadway and backed down the rock through the crowd which had swelled since I left. When it stopped, just as I arrived. I saw it was Kinski himself, one of the hard-working Poles who got out of their country a year or two ago when Solidarity was making waves, and he had his son with him, a lean blond boy in jeans and a T-shirt which he shucked as soon as he got out of the car, revealing a swimsuit.

Paul waited for me to walk over, then said, 'Peter swims good. He come with me to put on the chain.'

'Good thinking. Don't try anything tricky, Peter, like getting yourself underneath the car, duck down and reach under, that's all.'

'No worries.' He grinned cheerfully while his father unhitched the hook and loosened the tow cable.

As we waited I asked him, 'Tell me, Pete, have you heard anything about any gangs around here?'

'Gangs?' I could tell he hadn't.

'Yeah, any bunch of losers hanging around together, maybe wearing something the same, same belt, same cap, same coloured shoe-laces, anything like that?'

He shrugged. 'I been workin' with Dad all summer, running the pumps an' that.'

'OK, thanks. If you hear anything, see a bunch of kids in a car together, make a note of the number, would you, and call me.'

'No worries,' he said again, then took the hook from his father and snapped on a scuba mask. He clambered down the rock and dropped neatly into the water, holding his mask on. His father let the hook loose and let it run down to water level where Peter took it. Then he took a couple of deep breaths and sank under the water. He came up once for more air, then the second time he gave us a thumbs-up.

'Out the way,' Paul called, and put the crane in gear. The truck lurched once, then locked, and the car came backwards out of the water with Peter treading water, clear of it. I saw that the driver's window was open. That was good. It probably meant the driver hadn't drowned. But I went to the left side of the car and checked anyway as the car cleared the water's edge. I'd already noted that it was the Honda that had been stolen from Parry Sound, a town half an hour north of here up the highway.

The crowd swarmed around it as it came out of the water and I had to tell them to back off, missing Sam; one hiss from me and he would have kept them back with no trouble.

When Paul had it up on the rock I took a better look inside. It was empty and the radio was missing and the seats had been slashed with a knife. Another act of gang mischief. Three in one day. If there was any truth to the old superstition, that was our quota for a while.

I opened the door to let the water out. The key was in

the ignition, I noticed, a single key, not ring. Odd. Just
about everybody keeps their keys together on a ring. Having
it separated out like that looked deliberate.

Paul got down from the cab of his truck and came to tie
off the wheel. He saw the slashed unholstery and spat
angrily. 'Punks. Big tough guys with a knife, yeah?'

'Gutless,' I said automatically. 'Can you take it to your
yard? I'd like to look it over before the owner has it picked
up.'

He agreed and waited for Peter, who was towelling himself off and slipping his T-shirt back on, then drove off with
the Honda trailing.

I took ten minutes to check with the neighbours, making
sure nobody had heard anything. Nobody had. The only
help I got was that there had been a ballgame on TV until
close to eleven, after that all the residents had been asleep,
except for Ms Tracy who had not got home until after
twelve and had read for an hour or so before turning off the
lights.

'You're sure you heard nothing?' I was a bit surprised
that the noise hadn't woken her up. The splash would have
been loud enough to have startled people. And if kids had
done this, there could have been some yelling going on.

'I have an air-conditioner in the bedroom window,' she
explained. 'It's pretty noisy.' Then, surprisingly, she added,
'Come and see for yourself.'

'OK.' I walked with her, weighing up the facts. Allowing
that the noise might have reached her before she went to
sleep, there were two windows of time in which someone
could have driven the car into the lake, just around midnight or after two in the morning. The only snag was that
if everyone within a couple of hundred yards had air-
conditioning they would all have been deaf to the noise. Ah
well, no big deal, the car was intact, more or less, my job
was over when I'd reported it found.

I had an odd feeling about Ms Tracy. She was cool to

the point of rudeness and I wondered why. She had never crossed my path before and had no cause for resentment. Maybe she had some old militant attitude towards the police. A lot of people got that way in the 'sixties. All I knew was that she owned the cottage and came up here on and off all summer. There didn't seem to be any men, or women for that matter, in her life. She seemed to be one of those people who pass through life without touching the sides.

Today she was wearing blue jeans and a cotton top knotted around her waist offering the occasional flash of firm brown belly. Not exactly erotic but attractive. And she wanted to help me. A minor mystery.

I followed her to the back of her cottage, the kind of winterized place that a lot of our long-time visitors build with plans for retiring here. Most don't. They stay in Toronto where the stores and their grandchildren make the winters more congenial.

The only concession to country living was a big screened verandah with comfortable chairs and a radio tuned to a classical music station. She opened the door and ushered me in. I stepped up on the porch and waited while she opened the main door of the house and said, 'Come on in, see for yourself.'

That was when my cop's instincts began to tickle. This was above and beyond the call of good citizenship. But I followed, keeping my hat on to show this wasn't a social call.

Her bedroom was comfortable, a queen-sized bed and a good shelf of books. There was a pile of bound typescripts on the side table. I'd seen my wife studying books like them. She's an actress.

The air-conditioner was running and it was as loud as she had suggested. She raised her voice slightly. 'See what I mean? I couldn't have heard a head-on crash.'

'True enough. Thank you.' I turned immediately and

went back through to the porch. She followed. 'I love this heat, don't you?'

'It helps to make up for the winters.' I paused and she leaned on the doorjamb, on one foot, the other raised on tiptoe behind her, a dated pin-up shot. 'Would you like some iced tea?'

'No, thank you. I have to look in at home. My wife's expecting a baby just about any minute.' I smiled to show I wasn't being standoffish. 'Thanks anyway. The reason I came with you is that I thought you might have something you wanted to tell me without the neighbours hearing.'

'Oh?' she cocked her head. 'Like what, for instance?' She looked the way she might have done in her office in town, exercising good control of some subordinate.

I raised my hands. 'No idea. But people have funny ideas about the police. It's unfashionable to be any more helpful than is absolutely necessary.'

'And you have me pegged for a feminist, lesbian maybe, because I'm Ms Tracy, not Mrs.'

'I've been a policeman too long to generalize about anybody.'

'This place is my hideaway.' she said softly. 'In Toronto I work like a dog. I'm a feature film producer and I deal with every variety of bastard. Rich creeps who want to put money into movies so they can get next to the actresses, actors with egos the size of Czechoslovakia, unions, bitchy gay beauticians, every kind of headache you can imagine. But here I can be alone, be myself.'

It was more impassioned than I needed and I wondered why she was telling me. 'Well, thanks for the help. Enjoy your stay. When are you going back to town?'

'Next week sometime. When's the baby due?' Tit for tat. If I'd been exploring the possibility of a little dalliance she was carrying the ball.

'Any moment.'

'*Mazel tov*,' she said and smiled as if she meant it. 'Let

me know when it happens. I don't always drink tea. We'll wet the baby's head.'

I didn't answer, just smiled and left, with the ripe summer warmth on my bare arms, feeling aroused. Chill out, I told myself. She was playing games.

I called in on Fred who was sitting on a chaise-longue by the back door, knitting. She got up when I arrived. 'Hi, honey. Like some iced tea?'

'You should be resting.' I wagged a finger at her. 'All this energy is getting me nervous. Sit still. I'll make it.'

'I phoned my mother this morning. She tells me the energy means today's the day,' she said cheerfully. 'Can't be soon enough for me, I'm tired of looking like the side of a house.'

'It's still the nicest-looking house in the neighbourhood, even with the bay window,' I said. She threw a cushion at me.

She likes an instant tea mix, so I chopped up a lemon and threw in the ice cubes and had the whole thing ready in a couple of minutes. She put her knitting down when I carried the tray out to the back yard and poured. She laid the cold glass against her cheek. 'Mmmm,' she said happily.

'Just had a lady make a veiled pass at me,' I said.

'Not surprising. You're almost attractive in a roughcast sort of way.' She sipped her tea. 'Who was it?'

'Woman called Tracy. Don't know her first name. She lives, summers anyway, across the lake, about half a mile south of the bridge. Says she's in the film business in Toronto.'

Fred frowned. 'Not an actress?'

'Production, she said. Was telling me this place is her hideaway, away from terrible people like actresses and people wishing to have their wicked way with them.'

Fred wrinkled her nose at me. 'Look where it gets us.' She patted her stomach. 'Would it be Marcia Tracy, I wonder? She's head honcho at Northland Productions in Toronto.'

'Thirty-fiveish, trim, not much make-up, blonde.'

'Did she have a mole on her left buttock?'

'Right,' I said and Fred laughed.

'She's a ballbreaker. Two ex-husbands and a string of hopeful young studs behind her.'

'Fear not. I retreated with my honour intact.'

'Good for you, dear,' she said. 'Not much longer and we can make the bedsprings sing their old sweet song.'

'You're having a private room at the hospital?'

'You're a terrible man, Bennett,' she said.

I finished my tea and kissed her before heading down to Kinski's to look at the car. We've got a good thing going and I guess I'm one of nature's monogamists. It's my second marriage. My first was a girl I met in college. I dropped out but she got a degree in math, which has led her into computer sales. I was probably grating on her from the time I joined the Toronto Police Department and it fell apart completely when I cancelled a couple of bikers who were raping a variety store clerk. I was arrested for manslaughter and even though the case was dropped, Amy was long gone. There had been other women before Fred but not since she came into my life a year ago. I guess I'm terminally married.

Paul Kinski had the Honda in his pound. He does the tow work for the Ontario Provincial Police in this area and his yard is half filled with wrecks he's scraped off the rocks and roadways for fifty miles each way, rusting gently while the insurance companies and the courts dispense their decisions. The Honda looked almost new among them.

I called the Parry Sound detachment and reported the car recovered. The dispatcher read me off the name and address of the owner, then stopped. 'Hey, here's a thing. He's from your neck of the woods, Reid. Says he's staying at Pickerel Point Lodge, Murphy's Harbour. Be there for a week.'

'Pickerel Point? I wonder why he reported it stolen to you guys? Did he come into the office or call in?'

'No idea. No sweat anyways, cross it off your worry list.'

I hung up and called Pickerel Point Lodge. The manager put me on hold while she went out to the tennis court and dragged the owner in. His name was John Waites and he sounded like a yuppie.

'Mrs James said this was important.'

'Police chief here. We've recovered your car. It's at Kinski's Garage, Petro-Canada station on Highway 69, half a mile south of the Harbour.'

'What kind of condition is it in?' An unusual reaction.

'Well, it wasn't cracked up but it's been in the lake and somebody has ripped off the radio and slashed the seats.'

'Slashed the seats?' There was a flutter of sound as if he had changed hands on the receiver. 'Well, goddamn it,' he said. 'When did that happen? After it was pulled out?'

I didn't like him, I decided. 'It was done when the car was recovered from the lake.'

'Very well. I'll come down and look. Stay there.' He hung up before I could tell him it wasn't driveable. Serve him right, I thought, he sounded like a creep.

There was nothing else going on, so I accepted Paul's offer of a cup of coffee and went into his little diner to enjoy it. He makes good coffee and I was OD'd on iced tea. I sat and savoured it until a Mercedes pulled into the lot, avoiding the pumps, and a young guy got out of the passenger side. He was wearing tennis gear that revealed he had a good build and a tan. He was around five-nine and had neat, yuppie hair, dark and a little long but immaculately sculpted over his round head.

He came to the door and I checked behind him, trying to recognize the driver of the car, a woman who left without looking back.

He spoke to Peter at the pumps and followed the boy's finger to the coffee shop. I sat and waited for the grand entrance. He came up to me. 'John Waites. You called me about my wife's car.'

'The blue Honda, licence MW?'

'Right. Where is it?'

I got up and led him out to the car. I saw Paul shaking his head. He has European manners and hates impoliteness. Waites wrenched the door open and swore. 'Look at that. Vandalism.'

I said nothing until he got in and turned the key. Nothing happened. 'You would have been smarter to hold your ride for a while,' I said.

He swore again and banged the wheel with his hand. It all seemed a little too keyed up. Most people who get their cars back are sullen but they don't explode. 'Was that your wife in the Mercedes?' I asked.

He glared at me. 'No, it wasn't. If it's any of your damn business my dear Moira walked out yesterday, taking this car with her.'

'And then she called you from Parry Sound and told you it was stolen?'

'No. I did that.' He got out of the car and slammed the door. 'I was mad at her and I knew she was going up there. She has a friend there, some other dippy painter. The car is in my name and I was so angry when she left I reported it stolen, just to embarrass her.'

'That constitutes public mischief,' I said. 'You could be summonsed.' I was stretching it but only slightly, he had certainly bent the law although nothing would be done about it.

'I wonder what else they took,' he said. 'I had my golf clubs in the back.'

'You didn't take them out when she packed the car and left?'

'She did it while I was out. Left me a note.' He took the

key out of the ignition and undid the trunk. I looked over
his shoulder as he did it and then shoved him aside before
he could reach in. A woman's body was coiled in the trunk,
her fair hair pasted over her face with the water that had
drowned her.

CHAPTER 2

Waites reeled back, covering his face with both hands. I
held him by the elbow until I was sure he wouldn't collapse
and he stood rocking up and down from the waist. When I
was sure he wouldn't keel over I turned my attention to the
dead woman, going by the book, checking for a pulse. There
was none of course, and she had a slight froth around her
mouth. She had drowned.

Waites came back to the car. There were tears in his eyes
and he made as if to lean on the rim of the trunk but I
didn't let him touch it, putting my hand on his shoulder,
propping him. 'I'm sorry, Mr Waites. Your wife is gone.
Come inside.'

He shambled beside me to the diner. Paul Kinski looked
up in surprise. I raised one finger to him and he bit down
his questions and waited while I sat Waites in a booth. 'Do
you have any liquor, Paul? Vodka, something?'

'Rye I got.' He raised an eyebrow at me and I held up
one hand where Waites couldn't see it.

'Rye'd be good, can you get a shot for Mr Waites, please.
This is an emergency.'

He went back into the house and came out with a bottle
of Black Velvet. I took it off him and sloshed an ounce or
so in a coffee cup and took it over to Waites. 'She was alive
yesterday,' he said in a puzzled tone. 'Then we had a fight.
Over nothing at all, really. She wanted to paint, I wanted
her to play golf. Stupid. And it got kind of nasty and I went

out for a walk and she left. And now she's never coming back.'

Paul Kinski was trying hard to overhear. I looked across at him. 'Can you get Mr Waites a cup of coffee, please? And can I use your phone?'

'Sure, come in back.' He walked out from behind the counter and drew back the curtain that led to the private section of the house. I went through and he followed me, his Polish accent coming out in his anxiety. 'What's happening, Chief? He's upset about the seats so much?'

'His wife's body is in the trunk. Make sure nobody gets into your yard. I've got to call the doctor.'

We went into the kitchen, where Paul's wife was stirring something on the stove. She hasn't learned much English yet but young Peter has taught me a couple of words of Polish so I smiled and said '*Djen dobrie*' and she smiled back, showing a European gold tooth.

I took the phone and called Dr McQuaig. Fortunately he was in and promised to come right over. Next I called Carl Simmonds, the local photographer. He was just heading out on a wedding shoot but he said he'd come to the garage first. Finally I called McKenney's funeral parlour and asked them to send a hearse.

Then I went back out to the front and sat down across from Waites in the booth. 'What are you going to do?' he asked in a dull voice.

'There's going to be a full investigation. I have the doctor coming and the photographer. I'm going to fingerprint the car and the doctor will do what he has to.'

'You mean he'll see if she's been raped. Why don't you talk straight?' He was angry. There were no tears in his eyes.

'We'll want to talk to this person she was going to see. Do you have a name?'

'Carolyn Jeffries and her husband, of course. They run a

framing gallery, sell paints and frames and crap in Parry Sound.'

'Did your wife tell you she was going to see them?'

'She goes there all the time. She and the woman were in Art College together. I think Moira has— He stopped and corrected himself. 'I think she had a soft spot for the husband. He's an American hippy, bearded pinko type.'

'You don't like these people?'

'What's that got to do with anything? They weren't my friends, were they? Anyway, what's not to like? Granola and sandals and all that 'sixties garbage.' His bereavement hadn't made him any more charitable.

'When did your wife leave? What time?'

'Four o'clock was the tee-off time.' He fixed me suddenly with a bleak stare. 'You can check that if you want to. At the Pines.'

'And you had a fight and she left. What time was that, do you remember exactly?'

'It went on,' he said vaguely. 'I'm not sure when it finished except that it was too late for golf and anyway, by the time I came back she was gone and my clubs were missing.' He was wearing a Rolex and looked like the kind of guy who measured out his day in fifteen-second intervals, Why was he being vague.

'Sorry for asking but did you and your wife argue a lot?'

He snorted mirthlessly. 'The reason we came up here was we were trying to get something going again. Things have been rough. This holiday was kind of one last try before she went home and called her lawyer.'

'It was that bad?'

'I don't know why we ever got married except maybe she needed a meal ticket. All she cared about was painting and I was dumb enough to let her sit home doing it while I worked.'

'But it didn't work out?'

'No.' He pursed his lips. 'It didn't work out. I got tired

of coming home at nine, ten o'clock at night and finding
the breakfast dishes in the sink while she sat in front of one
of her stupid bloody paintings with no thought of time in
her head. No dinner ready, not even dressed tidily enough
that we could eat out anywhere reasonable. She was a slob.'

'The clothes she's wearing now look tidy.'

He looked at me with something like a sneer. 'Up here
she'd've fit in like feet into shoes. That was the best she
ever dressed.'

'You say she left a note. Do you still have it?'

'No. I flushed it down the john. I was angry.' Dis-
appointing but in character.

Dr McQuaig's station wagon pulled into the lot and I
stood up. 'The doctor just got here. Excuse me a minute.
If you need more coffee, another drink, Paul will bring it
to you.' He shook his head. I could see he had barely tasted
his rye.

McQuaig is a tall old Scot and he was wearing paint-
stained grey slacks and a check shirt. He had a beat-up hat
on with a small Mepps spinner hanging on the band.

'Hi, Reid. An odd place for a drowning? Did Mrs Kinski
slip in the shower?'

'No, this one's a homicide, Doc. Found a woman's body
in the trunk of a car that spent the night in the lake.'

'Well I'm damned.' He came with me and bent over the
body to check the throat with his forefinger. 'No doubt
about it.' He peered at the foam around the mouth. 'This
is classic drowning, Reid. She was alive when she went into
the water, although she wasna kicking.'

'That's what I thought. If she'd been concious at the time
she would have been scrabbling at the catch or pressing at
the lid, or something. But she just lay there and died.'

He tilted his hat back and scratched his head thoughtfully. 'Ay, that's how it looks. I'll know better when I've
examined her.'

'I've got McKenney coming for the body shortly. First I want Carl to photograph everything.'

'Right. I'll be at McKenney's in an hour. First I'll try a few more casts at that bass beside my dock.'

'Try a Fireplug if you've got one,' I said and he sighed.

'I think you've shares in the company, Reid. You never recommend anything else these days.'

As he left Carl Simmonds pulled in. He's the only chronic bachelor in Murphy's Harbour, a sweet guy but with a toughness to him that has been a big help to me on a lot of cases. Today he was wearing his working gear, a safari jacket, pockets crammed with gadgets and spare film, and he was carrying his Leica.

We shook hands and he said, 'A drowning you said, Reid?'

'Yeah, Carl, a homicide. Woman was shut in the trunk of a car and the car was driven into the lake, just south of the lock on the west side.'

'Hmmm.' He took out his light-meter and thrust it close to the face of the dead woman. 'Pleasant-looking girl,' he said. 'Madly Woodstock.'

'That's what the grieving husband says. Only he's more mad than grieving.'

'Sounds suspicious.' Carl's voice had a playful yodel.

'We'll see. Meantime, if you could get all the angles, please. And then take a few shots of the interior. The seats have been slashed pretty badly.'

He looked up from his viewfinder. 'Sounds like teenagers. I guess you heard about downtown this morning? Two incidents.'

'I was there for one of them. This could tie in.'

He took half a reel of film, including close-ups of the foam at the mouth and of the dead woman's limp left hand lying across her body. Then McKenney and his ghoul-in-training arrived and I let them remove the body. It had not stiffened much and they laid it on their gurney and we got our first look at her face. Pleasant, I thought. Carl had picked the right word. No make-up, a fresh-faced, natural-seeming blonde in her late twenties. She was wearing a pale blue cotton blouse and a printed peasant type skirt and sandals. Her clothes were still wet and I could see that she wasn't wearing a brassiere, nor in much need of one.

For once McKenney worked without questions. He's a pale man in his fifties with a set of false teeth that look like a row of Chiclets. He's also the world's worst gossip and I knew he wanted facts to go on, but I gave him only one. 'The husband's in the diner. I'll bring him in later on to tell you about the arrangements. I'd guess she'll have to go to Toronto. Meantime the doctor will be there in an hour, if you could be ready, please.'

'Of course, Chief.' He nodded slowly. 'Whatever you say.'

'Thanks, Les. I'd be sunk without you.' Manners cost nothing, my dad always said.

They drove off and Carl took a few more shots of the interior of the trunk, then said, 'Got to go. It's only half an hour to the wedding and the family will be screaming for blood.'

'Thanks, Carl, can you call me when you've printed these up.?'

'For sure.' He drove away and I closed the lid and went back into the coffee shop. Waites was sitting with his shoulders slumped, gazing into his coffee cup. A couple of other customers had come in and were looking at him curiously.

'We can go now, Mr Waites. I'll drive you back to the lodge. Later I'll ask you to come down to the funeral parlour and make arrangements for your wife. And just for my report, I'll have to ask you to identify her, formally.'

'You thrive on this, don't you?' he said angrily.

'It's my job, that's all. I wish it wasn't distressing but sometimes it is.'

I led him to the cruiser, dropping five bucks on the coun-

ter for Paul, who protested until I waved him off. Rye isn't
cheap and he had been invaluable, keeping Waites there
while I worked.

As I drove Waites back to his hotel I went over the case.
Waites himself was the most likely suspect. There was only
his word for it that his wife had driven away. A more prob-
able suggestion was that he had driven off with her himself,
bumped her on the head maybe, then slashed the seats of
his car to make it look like vandalism and driven it into the
lake. His hotel was only half a mile from the place the car
had been found.

Against that was his claim that his golf clubs had been
in the car. If they turned up in his possession I would know
he had been lying to me although that still would not prove
him guilty.

The only confusing fact was the time he had reported
the car stolen. Six-thirty p.m., daylight. He wouldn't have
reported it missing and then run the risk of being found
driving it, with his wife's body in the trunk.

At the hotel I went up to his room with him and checked
the closet, not telling him why. I wanted to see that his golf
clubs weren't there and none of his wife's things. Then I
went in for a word with Mrs James who runs the place. She
was brisk but friendly. It turned out she had been doing
her books the day before and had barely left the office.
But she called in the waitress who had been on duty at
dinner-time and the girl reported that Waites had been
there from the time she came on duty. He had sat at the
bar all evening, with a break for dinner, then back to the
bar. 'You know, like a movie, like drowning his sorrows.
Didn't talk, didn't do anything. Just sat and drank.'

'Was he on his own?'

'Yes. Usually his wife's with him but not last night.'

'You're sure of that? You know the guy I mean?'

'Positive. 'Scuse me, Mrs James, but like he's picky, eh.
His wife's nice but he's always finding fault, sent his steak

back one night, complained that the coffee was cold. You
know.'

'You know his wife, do you?' She nodded and I asked,
'Did you see her drive away yesterday afternoon, around
four, five o'clock?'

'I'm in the dining-room from four on,' she explained,
'Sorry.'

'Thanks anyway. There's one other thing. He says his
golf clubs are missing. Have you seen them around
anywhere?'

'Haven't seen any layin' around. I could ask Chuck.'

'Chuck's our handyman. He's here all day.' Mrs James
explained.

'Good, could you talk to him, please?'

She left and Mrs James asked, 'What's going on, Chief?
There's more to this than a set of golf clubs missing.'

'His wife has drowned in his car. He says she took off in
it yesterday. I want to know if that's true.'

She puffed out her cheeks in a little gasp of surprise.
'Lord, that's terrible. I'll ask around, see if anybody heard
anything.'

''Preciate that. Try not to say too much, please.'

She said, 'Count on it,' and picked up the phone. I left
after talking to Chuck, who had been away from the lodge
from five until six, taking garbage to the town dump. No
help there.

Dr McQuaig arrived at the funeral parlour as I did and
we walked in together. 'You're quick,' I told him. 'Thought
you'd still be fighting that bass.'

'Three pound, smallmouth,' he said happily. 'Damn if
you weren't right with the Fireplug. He came from under
a lily-pad and nearly tore my arm off.'

'I'll make a fisherman of you yet.'

McKenney had the body waiting for us in his preparation
room, a grim place with a stainless steel table with draining
grooves on it. He wheeled the gurney out and stood back,

hands folded in front of him, waiting for the revels to begin.

'I'd like to keep this in the family, Les,' McQuaig said, 'If you don't mind, please. This is Chief Bennett's investigation.'

McKenney nodded without speaking and left and the doctor pulled the sheet off the young woman's body and pulled up her eyelids to look at her eyes. 'Her pupils are different sizes. I think the wee thing had a concussion.'

He rolled the body over, gently and felt in her hair. 'Ah-ah.'

'What is it?'

'She's been hit on the temple.' He fingered the spot, stooping to peer at it. 'It was one hell of a smash, the wound itself is depressed, although there's some swelling around it.'

'Any guesses about the weapon, or the guy who did it?'

'It's a small wound, must have been done with something small but heavy, a small rock held in one hand maybe.'

'Could it have been done with a golf club?'

He looked up in surprise. 'Ay, it could. A driver maybe. All that power concentrated in one spot. What makes you ask?'

I told him and he gave me the measurement of the wound and I made notes. Then he undressed the body and examined it thoroughly. Waites was right, I realized. She had been wearing the kind of simple clothing that had been popular in the hippy culture. Even her panties were plain white cotton, worn for comfort, not for any excitement they might generate, some kind of statement on a woman this young and attractive.

'You want me to check if she was sexually assaulted?'

'Yeah, please,' I said and looked out of the window while he made his examination. There are some things about police work that I don't want to learn. Then he cleared his throat and I turned back. 'I'd say she wasna touched sexually,' he decided. 'But I'll take some swabs to be sure.'

He did so and I stored each one separately in its own plastic bag for shipment to the forensics centre in Toronto. 'I've a refrigerated flask in the car you can use to ship that,' he said. 'I'll bring it in while you finish.'

'One last thing. Any idea what time she died? It would help me know when the car went into the lake.'

He put one hand on his chin and thought about it. 'I dinna think anybody, even an experienced pathologist could help you much, Reid. The water temperature has retarded the rigor mortis. The best opinion you could get would be no better than mine.'

'Which is what?'

'Something between twelve and sixteen hours back, I'd say.'

'Thanks.' It was no real help, encompassing both of the windows of opportunity when nobody within earshot would have been awake. My best hope was to make a house to house canvass along both sides of the lake within half a mile of the site. The sound of the car going into the lake could have travelled across the water and been heard on my side almost as loud as it was at the scene.

'Thanks, Doc. You've been very helpful. If you could get that flask I'd appreciate it.' He left and I wrote up my notes and then the door opened on McKenney. 'Chief, the bereaved is here.'

'Thanks, Les, hold him a second while I cover her up, then I'll come out for him.'

He went back out and I folded the dead woman's wet clothes and put them at her feet, then covered the body with the sheet and went out to the reception room with its purple drapes and piped organ music. Waites was sitting there, grey-faced. He was fully dressed now in expensive casual wear with a monogrammed JS on the shirt pocket. He looked up bleakly.

'Thank you for coming in, Mr Waites. Could I ask you to come with me, please?'

He didn't speak but I could see he was holding himself together very hard. I went ahead of him into the preparation room, sensing his revulsion at the surroundings. He walked slowly up to the gurney and stood, hands at his side, fists clenched.

I was next to him, in case he fainted. It happens sometimes to even the toughest men. 'Mr Waites. I'm going to expose the face and I want you to identify her for me. She doesn't look dreadful, I promise you.'

He nodded and I rolled the sheet down, studying his face as I did so. He was the prime suspect and I wanted to catch his reaction completely.

It startled me. He gasped and said. 'There must be some mistake. That's not Moira. That's her friend, Carolyn Jeffries.'

CHAPTER 3

He turned away from the gurney and bent from the waist as if he'd been punched in the gut. 'Sit down,' I commanded, and pulled a chair over for him. He collapsed on to it, and sat with his shoulders hunched, face in his hands. Relieved? Horrified? It was impossible to tell. At last he whispered, 'That's not Moira. Moira's still alive.'

'You're absolutely sure this is Mrs Jeffries?' I was floundering. The neat little case I'd been building was in ruins.

'They look like sisters,' he said. 'In fact, that was their cutesy name for one another. They'd call one another "Sis".' He hissed the word and I realized he was angry at the memory.

'How close were they?'

He looked up at me, focusing slowly on my face. There were no tears in his eyes. 'Are you asking if my wife was straight?'

'I'm asking how close they were? Did they talk to each other every day, every week? How often did they get together?'

'Every couple of weeks they'd visit, either way. And they spoke to each other every day or two.' He shook his head impatiently. 'How should I know? I work every day just about.'

'Work at what?'

He stood up angrily. 'What difference does that make?'

'Look, Mr Waites, I've got a dead woman on my hands. You're one of the few people who can tell me how she fits into the world. Indulge me, could you, please?'

He reached into his back pocket and pulled out his billfold. He had a sheaf of business cards in there and he handed me one. I read it: John Waites, LL.B. of Donnely, Waites, Egan.

'Thank you. Just a couple more questions. First, what's the name of this woman's husband?'

'Stu. Stu Jeffries. He's a failed MBA type.' He threw in the second sentence with an angry sneer.

'I'm not sure what that means.' MBA I understood but what did this man mean by failed? That could be important.

'Oh, he got the degree, Harvard no less. But he couldn't cut it in business, not in the real world.' Waites was almost hissing again and now I could read his jealousy of the husband and impatience with a lifestyle he could not understand. 'So he and, her—' he paused and waved vaguely at the dead woman—'they copped out. They came up here and opened up their starving artist hideaway.'

'Did they make a living at it?'

'Sure, enough to live on if you're into rolled oats and alfalfa sprouts and making your own clothes out of spiderwebs, you know the routine.'

'You said your wife was kind of taken with this Stu. Why did you think that?'

'He knows all the words to "The Red Flag", maybe.' Waites turned away from me towards the door. 'How in Hell would I know what she saw in him, goddamn loser.'

'Where are you going now?'

'Home.' He paused with one hand on the doorknob. 'To the lodge. I'm not going to let her ruin my vacation, I've worked too hard to run back to Toronto and say, "There there, poor thing."' He pursed his lips angrily and left the room before I could say anything.

I did the necessary policework. There was a telephone in the corner of the room and I rang Parry Sound police detatchment and spoke to the inspector on duty. 'We have a homicide here, Inspector. The deceased is a Parry Sound resident. A Carolyn Jeffries, around thirty, slim, blonde, no make-up. Apparently she and her husband Stuart run some kind of art supply shop in town.'

I was lucky. They have two inspectors and I'd struck the one of them who had experience in detective work. He asked the right questions and I was able to fill him in within a couple of minutes. He said he would send a car to the store and break the news to the husband, as well as checking to see if Moira Waites had arrived. He would keep me posted on developments, and send his own crime team down to examine the car and take over the investigation.

Dr McQuaig came back with his flask and I put the plastic evidence bags into it and had McKenney fill it with ice. It could go to the Parry Sound detectives when they arrived, one less headache for me. Then I headed out to make a house to house canvass around the lake to try and uncover any witnesses to the car's going into the water.

I started around the corner from the funeral home, in the town itself. Town is overstating it a little. Officially we're an incorporated village, the lowest form of urban life. We have a Main Street with the bank, bait store, grocery, liquor/beer store, a Chinese restaurant specializing in hamburgers and a cluster of houses, most of them taking in summer guests, and a couple of side-streets of houses which also rent rooms to tourists. The rest of the village is straggled around the shoreline of the lake, every fifty yards or so.

Main Street is wide with the Lakeside Hotel and Marina on the water and a bridge over the lock. It's an unmade street, dusty in summer and lined with parked cars and with a knot of kids listening to music and giggling together. Remembering the two hassles from the morning, I stopped to talk to the kids. This was the early teen crowd, at the age when self-confidence only comes with numbers, before they get to the pairing-off stage. The girls were more forthcoming than the boys who all acted supercool. A couple of them had seen the swarming at the bait store but they didn't know any of the kids involved in it.

'They're not from around here, Chief,' Debby Vanderheyden told me. 'Like, we wouldn't do something like that.'

Her friends all giggled and said 'Oh no' with mocking innocence, all a joke. They wouldn't need to swarm a store, I thought, all of them already knew who they were. Gangs are made up of losers looking for a sense of belonging.

One of the bolder girls asked how my wife was and they all giggled again. It was hard for them to imagine how an old guy like me had caused a pregnancy.

I asked them to call the station if they saw any gangs of kids in town. It was good insurance, they would rather watch me tackling the situation than see another store ripped off. It wasn't that they were so very law-abiding, they just weren't sure what the cool reaction was when a gang came to town.

Gilles Perault was busy and I lingered with him until he had time to talk. He wanted to discuss his swarming but I slowly got him around to asking if he knew if anyone had been out fishing the night before. The occasional dedicated man will go out after dark for pickerel and there was a chance one of them might have seen the car go into the lake. Gilles told me he'd check and I left town to drive up the east shore, knocking on doors.

It was sleepy mid-afternoon time. The trees were buzzing with cicadas and the heat was enough to soften the bones, sending most vacationing adults for a siesta.

I called at a dozen or so houses, talking to the occasional group of swimming children but getting no help and causing a little embarrassment at some places where guys came to the door yawning hugely and explaining that their wives were lying down at the moment. Nobody had heard anything the night before.

Sam was on the verandah at my place and he bounded down to the car to greet me, wagging his tail and keening low in his throat. I took a moment to fuss him, then went in. Freda met me at the door.

'Time to go, old sport,' she said. 'My water broke about an hour ago. I called the doctor and he said I should head up to the hospital.' Her face was a little pale but she seemed confident and I put my arm around her.

'I'll get your bag.'

'It's in the kitchen, behind the door, ready for a flying start.' She sounded as cheerful as ever, but she doesn't panic easily so I didn't waste any time. I just grabbed her bag and led her out to the police car.

'Really? You're taking me in that?' she laughed. 'The nurses'll think I'm a charity case.'

'Not a chance.' I didn't feel much like joking. All I had to do was stand around while she did the work. 'This thing's got a siren. If the stork picks up speed, I can still get you there on time.'

I tossed her bag in the rear seat and put her in front, handing her the seat-belt which she put on carefully. Then I told Sam 'Keep' and left him in charge.

The same bunch of kids on Main Street saw us together and instantly worked out what was happening. Some of the noisier girls called out good wishes and Fred waved. Now we were on our way I asked her about the pains and she told me there weren't any. 'But my water's broken. That's why he wants me up there.'

'Is that normal?' I had been to Lamaze classes with her through the winter but I was too close to this birth to be objective.

'Later is better but it's no cause for alarm.'

She sounded relaxed and I reached out my hand to squeeze hers. 'Hang in there, have you there in half an hour. Just keep me posted on the pains.'

'It's a bit like your tooth stopping aching when you head for the dentist. Nothing's happening.'

'That's a comfort. I like leaving tricky jobs to the experts.'

She didn't say much and I concentrated on my driving, pushing the speed to the limits of safety, overtaking everything in front of me. One doddery old guy didn't look in his mirror to check my flashing lights behind him and I gave him a quick squirt of the siren which scared him out of his coma. He pulled right on to the shoulder in a cloud of dust and sat there while I accelerated over the top of the hill in front and lost him.

We came into Parry Sound twenty minutes later and I eased into the last space in front of the Emergency door at the hospital. Fred wouldn't let me get a wheelchair and we walked in arm in arm. The nurse on duty glanced at us oddly, wondering if a mercy call had turned into a romance. 'My wife's water has broken, Dr Rosen is her doctor, he said to come in.'

She pushed a form at me. 'Fill this out, please.'

'Not until she's taken care of,' I said and the nurse shook her head pityingly and said, 'Fathers,' but she got a wheelchair and whisked Fred away. 'Your husband can come and see you when he's been a good boy and filled out the form.'

I squeezed Fred's shoulder and waited until the nurse

came back, then filled in the form, thanking my stars that
I'd moved back to Ontario after my service in the US
Marines. I love the States but hospitals there cost an arm
and leg. Here it's all paid for.

Twenty minutes later I was up in an examination room
with Fred, waiting for her doctor to get in from the golf
course, it was Wednesday after all, his half day. He had
spoken to her from the clubhouse, Fred told me, where he'd
come in from the first tee to answer his pager. I guessed
he'd lingered to hit a few balls but he was there in ten
minutes, a small, young guy with round glasses and not
much of a tan.

He whisked me out of the room to examine her, then
came out to report. 'It may be some time,' he said and
immediately went over my head with details of dilation.
'Are you attending the birth?'

'I've taken the classes but honestly the idea scares the
hell out of me. I don't want to be in the way.'

'Thank God,' he said earnestly. 'Some of the fathers are
a royal pain in the ass.' He gave an apologetic half-smile
and went on, 'You won't be needed for a couple of hours
anyway. Why don't you talk it over with your wife? Then,
if you've got anything else to do come back at—'he checked
his watch—'let's say six o'clock.'

'Thank you, Doctor.' I went back in to see Fred who was
being moved out to a pre-natal room. I walked with her as
far as the door. The nurse left us there for a moment to
talk, tactfully heading off somewhere else.

'Look, Reid, you don't have to be here, you know,' Fred
said.

I stopped and gave her a quick kiss. 'I'm all trained up
to help, wouldn't want to waste all that knowledge.'

'Yes, you would,' she said firmly. 'Why don't you head
out for an hour or two anyway? If you come in with me
now you'll have to gown up and you're stuck here for the
rest of the time.'

I weakened, very easily. 'Well, I have to check with the local people. I didn't tell you before but a Parry Sound woman has drowned at the Harbour. I should talk to the police here.'

'*Vaya con Dios*,' she said and waved me away.

The nurse must have been hovering. She was back in a moment, all brisk. 'You can come inside but you'll have to change.'

'I'm coming back later.' Fred was with me on the decision, so why did I feel like I was retreating under fire?

The OPP constable on duty at the Parry Sound desk was a fishing buddy of mine and he stuck out his hand and asked after Fred. 'In the hospital, the doctor says to come back at supper-time. Figured I'd check on the Carolyn Jeffries investigation.'

'The inspector's in his office. Come on through.' He flipped up the hinged section of the desk and opened the gate.

'Thanks, Mike.' I went through and tapped on Inspector Dunn's door. It was open and he was on the phone. He waved me in. 'Chief Bennet just walked in, I'll put him on,' he said. He handed me the phone. 'S'arnt Holland, he's at the Jeffries' store.'

'Thank you.' I took the phone. 'Hi, Bill, Reid Bennett. What did you find out?'

'Hi, Reid.' Bill Holland is a good detective although he hasn't had much homicide experience. 'I was just in the store. There's a kid working there, says she hasn't seen hide nor hair of the Jeffries since yesterday. She came in and opened up like always, nobody there. First time ever.'

'Do they live over the store?'

'No. Got a place on the water on the edge of town. The girl, her name's Peggy Lindhoff, says she's rung the house, no answer. First time she's ever had to open up on her own. She figures something's wrong.'

'Let me explain. The owner of the stolen car says his wife

had big eyes for this Stu Jeffries guy. She was a good friend
of the wife but her husband led me to believe that she liked
the husband a lot.'

'You sayin' they might have killed the wife so they could
be together?'

'It's possible, but according to the husband, who's a
lawyer, his wife and the Jeffries couple were all kind of
hippy. They'd have shacked up together or something like
that if they had hankerings. Not the types for a crime of
passion.'

'Well, it's strange. This clerk says the Jeffries were always
there ahead of her. She's not a partner or anything, only
helps out in the summer, says they're nice people.'

'I don't know much about them, except that the other
woman's husband doesn't like any of them, including his
wife.'

There was a pause and Holland said, 'Guess I should
drive down to their house, see if there's any sign of life or
if the car's still there. No matter what anybody thinks, this
Jeffries guy and the Waites woman could've offed the wife
and left for parts unknown.'

'I'll come down there and meet you. Where is it?' He
told me and gave directions and I hung up and spoke to
the inspector. 'I'll go over there. I'll need the husband to
identify his wife's body. It's at the funeral parlour in Murphy's Harbour.'

'OK.' Dunn stood up. 'On the face of it, it sounds like a
triangle. Even hippies get jealous, least these days they do.'

The Jeffries house made Waites' description of their lifestyle seem appropriate. It was small and neat with artfully
contrasting blue shutters and a big well-kept garden. There
was a bright yellow VW beetle in the driveway.

Holland was waiting for me, in his car. He's a typical
old-time copper, big, running to fat, wearing a neat suit
that looked like it came with two pairs of pants. He got out
and shook hands. 'Hi, Reid, how's the wife?'

I told him and we opened the gate and walked up to the gingerbread porch. There were potted geraniums all along the sill and a set of oriental windchimes hanging silent in the stillness.

The door had an old-fashioned ratchet bell and Holland cranked the handle on it a few time. Nobody answered. There was no sound from inside. A woman in a big sunhat was watering her flowers in the next yard and Holland sauntered over to talk to her. No, she hadn't seen the Jeffries that day. 'Are they in trouble?' she wanted to know.

'No, ma'am. This is a social call,' Holland lied easily. He came back to the verandah. 'This is a pain,' he said.

'There's a cagebird singing in the house,' I said. 'People like this would've set it out here this morning if they'd gone to their store.'

'Y'reckon?' He looked at me thoughtfully. 'Guess you're right. An' if they're not, they could be long gone while we're waiting around here for them to come back.'

I bent and flipped the doormat over. A key lay under it. 'How convenient,' Holland said. 'Lemme see that a minute.'

He took the key and tried the door. It opened and he stepped inside and called 'Hello, Mr Jeffries. Anybody home?'

The cagebird fell silent and I stepped in after him. The house was tiny inside but beautifully furnished, not expensively but with real style, antique Ontario pine everywhere, contrasting with bold modern paintings and good prints. We glanced into the two rooms off the centre hall. One was a dining-room, the other a sitting-room with a big bookshelf and an expensive music system. The birdcage was hanging in the window and I could see from the door that the water container was empty. That seemed out of character with the rest of the house and I followed Holland through to the kitchen. There were unwashed dishes in the sink, dinner dishes, and a glass baking pan with some dried-out greenish

stuff still in it. Holland looked at the mess. 'Two plates.
They didn't all eat together.'

'Let's check upstairs.' I led now, up the polished stairs
to the bedrooms. Both were empty and were neatly made.
There was nobody there, even in the closets or the
bathroom.

'Looks like they've been away all night,' Holland said.
He scratched under his chin thoughtfully. 'But their car's
still in the driveway.'

'The wife's body was in the Accord.' I thought out loud.
'And that bug of theirs stands out like a burning bush. If
the other two were taking off somewhere maybe they rented
another car.'

'I'll check that out,' Holland said. He was opening the
drawers in the chest of the bigger bedroom. It was full of
neatly folded men's socks and underclothes. 'If the husband
was takin' off he was travellin' light. Did this Waites woman
have a whole bunch of money maybe?'

'Didn't sound like it, to hear her husband talk. He said
she married him because she needed a meal ticket.'

'Yeah, but maybe she's got a satchelful of his credit
cards.' Holland was rolling the thoughts around in his
mind.

'Could be. But she was a painter, not into shopping,
according to the husband.'

'I'd like to talk to that sonofabitch,' Holland said. ''S he
still at the Harbour?'

'Says he's leaving for Toronto when he can get a car. I've
got his home address and phone if you want to call him.'

'Thanks.' Holland copied the information into his book,
then closed it firmly. 'Come on, we're through here.'

We went downstairs and I unhooked the birdcage and
took it with me as we left. 'Where you takin' that?' Holland
asked.

'Leave it next door, give us a chance to talk to the
neighbour.'

He grunted but we walked over to the fence and spoke to the woman who was still standing in the same place, obviously curious about us. 'The Jeffries have been called away,' Holland said. 'If you see anybody in there, could you give me a call, please, Sergeant Holland. Don't go over there, please, just call. And could you take care of their bird for them?'

'Of course, Sergeant.' She took the cage happily, a mystery of her very own, right next door.

She wanted to talk at length but Holland just nodded and beamed and we walked back to our cars. I took a minute to talk to him about the dead woman, mentioning the wound on the temple.

'Golf clubs?' he said. 'Likely ended up in the lake somewhere but I'll flag it at the station, see if anybody comes in with a set they've found somewhere.'

'Good idea. What's next?'

He yawned. 'Guess I should print the car you got out of the lake. Where's it at?' I told him and he said, 'Better get it up here in our pound where it's secure, be easier to get at anyway.'

He slumped into his car. 'Thanks for the help. I'll call if I hear anything.'

'Fine. I'll head back to the hospital, see if anything's happening.'

'Yeah. Good luck, hope everything goes OK.' He waved and left and I got into my own car and drove back into the heart of town. It was only five o'clock so I pulled in at a diner and ordered a burger and coffee. I wasn't hungry but remembered what they'd told us at the Lamaze classes: eat normally or you'll pass out in the delivery room. This was a duty.

The place was half full but I got a seat by the window and sat there looking out as I waited. The place next door was one of the better eating spots in town and I watched the first of the evening's customers drifting in. Most were holiday-makers, young groups of men and women laughing together, but as I was eating I saw a Mercedes pull into the lot. It jangled my memory and I realized it was the same model and colour as the one that had dropped Waites at the gas station. I would check the licence when I left, I decided, to see if I was right. I watched it and as its doors opened I saw that Ms Tracy was driving. She had a young guy with her and when he turned to speak to her I realized he was the leader of the gang I'd chased out of Murphy's Harbour earlier.

He was talking animatedly, giving the impression that he was very much in control of himself, sophisticated even, not like the angry gang member he had been that morning. He seemed older, more mature and, most important of all, he seemed to be courting Ms Tracy, acting with the eager agreeableness of a man trying to win over a new conquest.

I considered my options. My authority doesn't extend beyond the limits of my own bailiwick. If I went up to the kid here and asked him questions he could tell me to go to hell. Then he and Ms Tracy would leave before I could get a local guy to do the asking for me. I had to get something on him without his knowing.

I paid and tipped the waitress and went out to the parking lot. First I checked the licence plate of the Mercedes. It was the same one that Waites had ridden in, so he and Ms Tracy were friends at least. With that done, I went through the back door of the hotel. The kitchen was busy but one of the cooks waved and made a drinking motion with his hands. Did I want a coffee, beer, something? 'I'd like to talk to the manager or one of the waiters, can you call them for me, please?'

He went to the door with its glass panel and waved through it. A moment later a trim young woman in a smart blouse and skirt came through the door. The cook pointed at me and she spoke, smiling formally. 'Yes, what's up?'

'I'm here to ask a favour, please. Can you help me?'

'Depends what it is.' She was intrigued.

'There's a couple who came in three or four minutes ago, a woman around thirty-five, wearing a green top and a gold chain. There's a man with her, a little younger.'

'They're at table fourteen.' She cocked her head. 'You want to talk to them?'

'No, but I'd very much like to get the young man's glass or bottle if he orders a drink. Is that possible, do you think, please?'

I never majored in charm but I applied all I had. She frowned. 'Is this going to make me liable in some court case?'

'Nobody else will ever know, I promise, it'll help me in an investigation I'm conducting.'

'Stay here,' she commanded and clacked out of the kitchen on her high heels, skirt swinging to stir a man's heartstrings. I waited four or five minutes before she returned, wearing a white glove on her right hand, carrying a highball glass. 'I put white gloves on the waiter. The only prints on this are your guy's right hand.'

'Thank you very much. I appreciate this.'

I held out my left hand, flat, but she said, 'Hold on, we have plastic bags somewhere.' One of the kitchen staff brought her one and she slipped the glass into it and handed it to me. 'There. Hope it helps. If it helps your case any, he drinks Glenfiddich.'

'Glad he can afford it.' I hefted the bag with my left hand and touched the peak of my cap with the right. 'You've saved me a lot of work.'

'Your name's Bennett, isn't it?' she said.

'That's right. I'm from Murphy's Harbour.'

'I was down there visiting one time and my friend told me you were a tough cop, lived alone with a big dog.'

'That's Sam, my German shepherd. He's off duty tonight.'

'And you're working on a case?'

'Kind of. I'm also waiting for word from the hospital about my wife, she's having a baby.'

'Oh.' Her tone became brisker. 'Well, glad I could help.'

She tritch-tratched away and I left with my package, remembering how lonely it can be when you're single.

I debated whether to hand over the glass to Holland for comparison with the prints he found on Waites' car but decided against it. I would check them myself and let him have them later. Right now the fact that this kid had been a gang member might be completely irrelevant to the murder he was investigating. The only tie I could see was that both he and the husband knew the Tracy woman. I would call in on her later, I decided, and ask about the boy. Meantime I went back to the hospital, where I met Dr Rosen who shook his head at me. 'Your wife's fine. She hasn't started having contractions, but the baby's head is high so I'm keeping her in bed. If she's still hanging fire this evening I'll induce labour.'

'Is that normal?'

'I do it all the time,' he said. 'For now we've moved her to a ward. Why don't you go and see her?'

The hospital gift shop was open and they had a flowers for sale, locally grown roses, bundled by volunteers with more enthusiasm than skill. I bought a bunch anyway and went up to Fred's room.

She was sitting up in bed, reading a magazine. There was another woman in the bed next to her, sleeping.

Fred greeted me excitedly and repeated what the doctor had said. I went back to the nurse's station for a vase and put the flowers in water while we discussed what to do.

'You should go home and give Sam his supper,' Fred said firmly. 'I'm stuck in neutral right now. Nothing's going to happen tonight, they tell me. You can check around town like you do every night and call up at midnight.'

'I should be here,' I argued feebly.

'Sam is family too,' Fred said. 'You can't do anything here and he needs you.'

She was firm about it and relaxed. 'This is the most natural business in the world. And anyway, all I have to do overnight is sleep.'

'Well, I have to feed Sam, that's certain.'

'And check your properties,' she said with a smile. 'You know you always do, even on your day off.'

In the end that's what I did, thankful to be out of the hospital. My own stays have always been painful, both here and in Nam, recovering from wounds. I knew that Fred would be going through something just as hard, even though it was going to be great afterwards.

The light was fading and the kids had gone from Main Street and the village was settling down for a quiet night. There was music coming from the open windows of the Lakeside Hotel at the Marina and a crowd of cars filled the parking lot of the beer parlour below the bridge, where the blue collar drinking gets done, but there were no people on the street. They were home, eating supper and rubbing lotion on their sunburns.

Sam was off the verandah when I pulled in and he looked up and barked at me. He isn't excitable and I knew something had happened. I called him over and fussed him and then let him lead me back to where he had been standing. He took me to his find, a package in the red-brown coarse paper they use in butcher shops to wrap meat. This one had obviously hit the gravel of the drive and rolled a couple of times and I could see that it had been opened, the original brown tape torn, then refastened with scotch tape. I picked it up, feeling the squashiness that announced it had hamburg meat inside. There was barely enough light left to examine it so I clicked my tongue at Sam and went into the house with him, carrying the package with me. I laid it on the countertop and slit it open with my pocket-knife. There was hamburg inside right enough, but it had been laced with a coarse white powder.

I let it lie there while I bent down to pat Sam's head as he looked up at me. 'Good thing you remembered your training, old buddy. This stuff's been baited.'

CHAPTER 4

TV cops can identify poisons at a glance. I can't, I must have been away the day they covered it at the academy. But it figured to be nasty. If Sam had been less well trained it would have killed him. I wondered who had tried it on. The teen gang probably, getting even for their loss of face that morning. I saved the evidence in case I got the chance to prove anything, rewrapping the meat and marking it 'Evidence. Poison.' and drawing a skull and crossbones on the package. Then I bagged it and stuck it in the freezer to send to the forensics centre when I had a chance.

Sam watched me closely. Hovering over the meat until I came home had sharpened his appetite. But his training had stuck, and saved his life. So, as a special reward I defrosted a chunk of our own hamburger meat to give him with his chow.

When he'd finished I sat on the back porch and had a beer, trying to find a pattern to the day. So much had happened. A teen-gang had come to town, then the car in the lake, looking like it had been stolen by kids, vandalized. And most important, the dead woman in the trunk.

Was there a thread to it all? I couldn't see one, except for Marcia Tracy. She had turned up in both the puzzles. There was no reason why she shouldn't know both John Waites and the kid from the gang. It was just the timing of her involvement that intrigued me. I would have to talk to her, especially about the gang leader. He'd looked very different up in Parry Sound, dressed neatly, acting confidently, not like a rebel. How could he be two completely different people in the course of a single day? I needed to talk to him, not the way I would have had to on the street in Parry Sound, he could have brushed me off there, knowing I had no jurisdiction. No, it had to be a formal interrogation.

When I finished my beer I walked Sam around the property, telling him to Seek, his order to check for people hiding. He ran everywhere in the darkness, under the willows along the edge of the lake, out along the dock and into my boat, and into the woods on the far side of the road from the house. I was concerned about Kershaw on top of my other worries, but when Sam found nothing we drove back to the police station.

It was as I'd left it, except for a long roll of messages peeling off the teletype. I tore them off and skimmed them to see if Kershaw had been re-arrested. He hadn't been, but there had been a break-in overnight at a cottage in Orillia, about half the distance from Toronto to Murphy's Harbour. Not a startling event, but the perp had stolen some clothing, something a fugitive might have done, and the place was on the way to the Harbour.

The only other message that stopped me was a report of another gang swarming up at Pointe au Baril. It lies north of us, the other side of Parry Sound. A nondescript bunch of teens had hit the grocery, taking stuff but not really stealing it, tossing it away contemptuously as they drove out of town. Routine teen-gang behaviour but the report made me frown. Why would a gang, possible the same gang, hit two little resorts, fifty miles apart, and leave the big town in between untouched? Where did they come from? Gang problems are usually local. It's your own doctor's and lawyer's sons who band together and raise hell. It's their way of letting the neighbours know how little they care for their parents. Hitting on total strangers in two widely separated places was not normal gang practice and that was puzzling.

Nothing on the list called for action, so I locked up and drove up to Carl Simmonds' place. He was out on the lawn, on a swing seat, nursing a drink, but he got up and came to the gate to greet me. 'I hear you took Freda to the hospital. Is everything OK?'

'Fine, thanks, no action yet. I'm heading back at midnight.'

'Don't worry, Reid. I know she's going to be fine,' he said. 'How about a beer while I get you the pictures?'

We went inside and he cracked a beer for both of us and pulled out an envelope of eight by tens. Like all his work, they were excellent, crisp and clear. They didn't reveal anything I'd missed, but I thanked him.

He kibitzed a little bow. 'I hope the Andersons are as happy with their wedding shots. It was very difficult to hide the bride's big tummy.'

We went back outside and sat, with Sam lying beside me on the grass while we drank our beer. My mind was still running around the events of the day and I needed to talk. For a year now I've had Fred to discuss things with, getting the benefit of a non-police point of view. It prompted me to open up a little to Carl. I knew he wasn't a gossip, my information was safe.

'Do you know anything about a woman called Tracy? She has a place on the other side of the lake, where that car went into the water last night?'

'That would be Marcia Tracy, the movie producer from Toronto,' he said at once. 'A friend of mine in Toronto works as a hairdresser in her studio. Tough lady, he says.'

'She seems to have a strange mixture of friends.'

'Maybe not friends, according to Claude, But she'd have lots of courtiers. She's important in the film business in Toronto.'

I thought about it a moment and then said, 'Well, I saw

her today with the owner of that Honda. She drove him to Kinski's.'

'The poor man whose wife was in the trunk?'

'It turned out it wasn't his wife, but that's a different story.'

Another man might have cut in, pressing for details but Carl didn't. He asked, 'And?'

'And I saw her up in Parry Sound with the kid who was running that gang this morning.'

'On the street? It might just have been a casual contact of some kind?'

'No, they were having dinner at Pietro's.'

'You're sure it was the same kid?'

'Positive.'

Carl was excited now. 'Dinner at Pietro's. Very fancy. Was he trying to sweet-talk her, maybe?'

'A seduction? Could be, I guess. Fred says she's got a string of young guys behind her.'

'Actors, of course,' Carl said and suddenly I could see the connection.

'If this guy's an actor, maybe this gang thing is his way of auditioning.'

'With actors, anything's possible,' Carl said. 'If she was remaking *The Wild Bunch* he would have turned up on a big Harley. Perhaps she's doing something about youth gangs.'

'That makes sense.' I drained my beer and stood up, picking up the envelope of photographs. 'Thanks for the beer and the wisdom, Carl. You'll send your bill for these to the station, will you?'

'Plus sales tax,' he said happily. 'Glad to have helped. Give my love to Fred when you see her.'

'I will. But I've got a call to make first.'

Sam whisked into the car ahead of me and curled up on the passenger seat, then I drove off, around the lake to Ms Tracy's house. There were lights on and her car was in the driveway. I got out and went to the door. The radio was

playing soft rock, a song that had been big the year I joined
the Marines.

Marcia Tracy came out of the living-room looking surprised. She was wearing a cotton housecoat, practical
enough that I scratched the idea that she was entertaining
a young lover. She was wearing half-glasses on her nose
and carrying on of the typescripts I'd seen in her bedroom.

When she recognized me she took off her glasses and
opened the door. 'Well, this is a surprise. Am I to congratu-
late you, Chief?'

'Nothing's happened yet, Ms Tracy. I wondered if I
might ask you a couple of questions, if you don't mind.'

Her tone didn't change. 'Just like Peter Falk,' she said.
'Come in.'

She opened the door and I came in and stood on the
porch, keeping my hat on.

'I was having a scotch. Could I get you something?'

'No, thank you. I won't keep you long.'

'Too bad,' she teased. She smelt of some light fragrance,
outdoorsy but provocative. When I didn't speak she said,
'Well?'

'What's the name of your new picture? The one you're
planning right now?'

'What an odd question from an officer of the law. Are
you trying to get your wife a part? I understand she's very
good.'

'She's hung up her skates,' I said, smiling to ease the
tension I could fell building up in me. 'No, I wondered if
you were doing a picture about teen-gangs?'

She was just as light but her eyes narrowed a fraction.
'Why do you ask that?'

'Well, I had a run-in with a gang this morning, in town.
I was off duty at the time and the only way I could resolve
it was to neutralize the leader, boy about twenty maybe,
six-foot, dark hair, useful-looking build.'

'Sounds yummy.'

'I wondered if you'd tell me his name, please?'

'Me?' She must have done some acting herself, she was almost convincing.

'Yes. You had dinner with him in Parry Sound. I'd like to talk to him.'

'That boy's an actor. He drove up from Toronto to see me.'

'In an old Ford Fairlane with four other kids.'

'I don't know how he travelled.' She shrugged and I could see she was enjoying herself, playing the tycoon, keeping me at bay.

'I'd really like to talk to him. Could I ask you for his name, please?'

'Is he in some kind of trouble?'

'Not at all.' I shook my head, all hearty and friendly. 'But he might be able to help me, that's all.'

'Sit down,' she said. 'This is very interesting.'

There was no reason not to, so I did, taking off my hat. She sat opposite, letting a flash of leg show, then adjusting her housecoat. 'You really think it's the same boy?'

She was playing games with me so I took another track.

'You have a lot of friends, Ms Tracy.'

'One does tend to, in my circle.' She reached out to the coffee table and set down her script. 'I don't see how it can interest a policeman.'

'At around one o'clock today you drove John Waites down to the gas station on the highway where his car had been recovered. Have you spoken to him since?'

'No, why?' She had hazel eyes and there were tiny flecks of gold in the pupils, she was almost beautiful, I realized, but too square in the face, too strong to be appealing to most men.

'Because there was a woman's body in the trunk.' I watched her and she gasped and almost dropped her glass. It looked genuine. She stared at me for a long moment, then took a quick gulp of her drink.

'She drowned when his car went into the lake. Waites thought it was his wife at first.'

'It wasn't?'

'No. It was another woman, similar in appearance. He identified her later as a friend of his wife's, a Carolyn Jeffries.'

Now her composure had gone. She set down her drink and stood up, hugging her arms around her. I sat and said nothing until she turned to speak to me. 'What are you trying to tell me?'

'Nothing that isn't public knowledge,' I said. 'It's just that I lead a quiet life here. Then, in one day there are two teen-gang incidents and a homicide. The car with the body in it had been roughed up the way kids might have done it. That's all I have, but I see you in touch with all the players and I wondered if there was anything you wanted to tell me.'

'Like what?' There was a cigarette box on the coffee table and she opened it and took one out. She looked around for matches but couldn't see any. I stood up and took out a pack of Lakeside Tavern matches and lit for her. She cupped my hand as she took the light and I could feel that she was trembling.

'Like, is there some connection that I'm not seeing? Between Waites and this actor whose name you haven't told me yet.'

'I know them both,' she said softly. 'John Waites is my lawyer. Eric Hanson is an actor. I know both of them, professionally.'

'I'd like to talk to Hanson. Do you know where he is?'

'No.' She said it quickly, then took a quick drag on her cigarette and said, 'No, I'm sorry, I don't know. If you call my office in the morning they'll put you in touch with his agent. He'll tell you.'

'That would be helpful, Ms Tracy, and I'd appreciate it, but it would be even better if I could talk to him tonight.

If you could tell me, for instance, whether he's here now. Then I could talk to him and get out of your life.'

'He's not. And I don't like your tone.' She was suddenly all angles, lean and rigid as she stubbed the cigarette and tugged her housecoat closer at the throat. 'Please leave.'

I stood up. 'Thank you for the help, Ms Tracy.' I was going by the book now, lots of formality, no rudeness, leaving right away. She would have no cause to complain about me to the village council or the Police Commission.

She said nothing and I put on my cap and left, clicking my tongue for Sam who had been waiting outside.

I drove slowly down the road around the lake, past Pickerel Point Lodge. It isn't big, by city standards, a couple of dozen rooms, two tennis courts and a beach and private dock with a row of good-sized cruisers tied up. By night it looks its best, the floodlights and the light at the end of the dock magnifying the importance of everything. I could see a fisherman on the dock, using a surface lure by the look of it, retrieving in slow stages, hoping to prod a pickerel into action.

I debated going in to see if Waites had gone back to Toronto but decided against it. I had nothing specific to ask him and he was a lawyer, he'd brush me off like a fly and it might screw up Holland's investigation, whenever that happened. So I took one last spin through town, checking the locks on all the properties that were closed for the night, then headed up the highway. But I was still restless and I slowed as I passed each motel, checking the parking lot for the Ford that Eric Hanson had been driving. I wanted to know more about him, specifically if stealing the Accord had been part of the game he was playing with Marcia Tracy.

I recognized Hanson's Fairlane, ten miles north of the Harbour parked at the Northont Motel. It's a cheap place, individual cabins about fifteen feet square, white paint peeling off them. A new guy took it over last spring but he's going quietly broke. Now, in peak season, there were cars outside only three of the places.

I went to the office and stepped into a museum of despair. Everything needed paint and there was dust on the furniture and drapes and tired old folders and the few tatty souvenirs of the area. The owner, a sour man in a T-shirt, came through a bead curtain behind the office and nodded. 'Need a room, Officer?'

'Not tonight, thanks. But I'm interested in the people whose car is outside unit three. Could I see who it's registered to?'

'You gotta warrant?'

'I don't need one. Haven't you read the Inn-keepers' Act?' I wasn't sure myself what it said but it figured he hadn't read it.

'I'm too goddamn busy to read everything I'm s'posed to,' he said and pulled out a box of cards. 'What unit was that?'

'Three. The car's a Ford.'

'Three. Yeah, Sidney Greenstreet, Niagara Falls.'

I didn't laugh but it looked like I'd found my actor. 'Thanks.'

He mumbled something but slapped the box shut and went back through the curtain. I paused outside to whistle Sam to my side, then walked over the unit. The light was on inside and rap music was jabbering away, loud, with lots of bass to it. Teen-gang opera.

I knocked but nobody answered so I used the heel of my hand, thumping even louder than the bass on the ghetto-blaster. Nobody came and I tried the door handle. The door swung open away from me and then a man hurled himself at me, screaming something.

Instinctively I stuck my left hand out, palm towards him catching him flat in the chest. He stumbled but recovered in a moment and came at me again, flailing and kicking, his face contorted with fury. I tried to hold him but he was too strong, too quick, and I knew he was zonked on something dangerous. I told Sam 'Fight' and he snarled and grabbed at the man's arm but the guy was too far gone to take any notice. He lashed out with his other hand and his feet, screaming non-stop. He landed a good clunk on the side of my head and I staggered, then drew my stick and hit him hard on the collar-bone of his free arm. It connected and his arm fell limp but he kept on closing on me and kicking, totally ignoring Sam. I knew I had to do put him down.

I slid my hand down the shaft of the stick until only four inches projected out of my fist and stabbed him in the gut. It would have stopped any normal man but he didn't pause and I had to do it again before the wind went out of him and he collapsed, still trying to kick, his legs moving feebly as he fought for breath.

'Easy,' I said and Sam released his arm and stood back, hovering over him as I rolled him on his face and cuffed his right wrist through his belt to his left ankle, bending him in half backwards.

'Keep,' I ordered and Sam stood, growling into the man's face as he struggled to breathe. I took a quick look around the cabin. There was nobody else there and from the single six-pack of Kronenbourg beer I figured he was alone. There was a plastic bag on the chest of drawers containing about three ounces of white powder. Angel dust, I figured, from the way he'd acted and I wondered if that was what he'd used to bait Sam, hoping he would turn on me and I'd have to shoot him.

In any case he was o.d.'d on something, and needed a hospital. It would take too long for an ambulance to reach us. I had to take him to Parry Sound.

I ran back to the office and reached over the desk to pick up the phone. The owner came blustering out of the back but I pulled out a dollar coin and tossed it to him. 'Police business.' I reached the Parry Sound police and told then what had happened. They were on the bit, they promised to have a man at the hospital by the time I got there and to send a narcotics guy to check the motel room.

'What's all this about?' The owner stretched up to his full five-foot-six and snarled at me. 'You can't come into my motel and start laying down the law. This is a free country.'

'You've got a kid in unit three who's o.d.'d. The OPP are sending a man. Don't disturb anything in there, please, or you're in deep trouble. I'm taking him to hospital.'

He had more to say but I didn't listen. I drove over to the unit and opened the rear door of the car.

The kid was fighting fit again but almost helpless. He still tried punching up at me with his free hand, aiming for my groin but I got hold of his arm and levered him on to his free leg and hopped him out to the car. It was a tussle getting him into the seat and he lay there smashing at the door with his free foot as I locked him in. Sam jumped into the front seat and I pulled off the lot and out to the highway, laying rubber up to the hospital.

A doctor and a couple of uniformed policemen were waiting for me and we got the kid out and laid him on a gurney while the doctor checked his eyes and then sponged his neck and gave him a shot.

It didn't take at once but by the time we reached the treatment room he was drowsy.

'What's he taken?' the doctor demanded.

'PCP, judging by the way he's acting. This was in his room.' I took the plastic bag out of my shirt pocket and gave it to him. He glanced at it, narrowing his eyes.

'Hard to say but you could be right. I'll need at least one man to stay with him. There's no knowing when he'll start fighting again.'

'We'll stay.' One of the Parry Sound men unlocked my handcuffs and gave them back to me. 'Pretty neat,' he said approvingly. 'Hand and foot together through the belt. Never seen that done.'

The doctor was sounding the boy's chest with a stethoscope. 'His heart's going like sixty.' He unclipped the earpieces and looked at me. 'How did you stop him?'

'I hit him in the solar plexus with the butt of my stick. I hope I haven't ruptured anything.'

'I hope so too,' the doctor said. 'I'll run some tests. Who is he anyway?'

'Goes by the name Eric Hanson. I want to talk to him when he comes down. Would that be possible?'

'Six hours at least, I'd say.' The doctor picked up the phone. 'Doctor Syme, Treatment Room Two. Can I have a restraint trolley here, please.' He hung up and looked at me levelly. 'What can you tell me about him that might help?'

'He was in a motel room. Looked like he'd eaten fried chicken and been drinking beer. He was alone when I found him, listening to loud rap music. He came to the door and went berserk.'

The doctor nodded. 'OK. Is he under arrest for anything?'

'Yes, assault police, namely me. And possession of drugs, namely that white powder I showed you. On top of which I want to talk to him about a homicide that occurred at Murphy's Harbour.'

The doctor whistled. 'He's been a busy boy. OK. I'll check him out, see what he's taken, see if you injured him. Then I'll sedate him. Are you staying here?'

'My wife's upstairs waiting to deliver a baby. I'll be up with her until that happens.' He nodded at me and I finished up the story. 'I don't have jurisdiction in Parry Sound but these officers will handle the arrest for me.'

'Fine.' He nodded briskly. 'I'll know where to find you if anything happens.'

I thanked him and went outside to make sure Sam was

comfortable, letting him out of the car to mark out a territory for him so he could get out of the car window as he wanted. Then I patted him on the head and said, 'Wish us luck,' and went upstairs to Fred's floor.

I was just in time. The nurse told me that she had been put on a Pit drip, which I knew meant they were inducing labour. 'She'll be fine,' she said cheerfully. 'Are you one of the Lamaze fathers?'

I confessed and she said, 'When did you eat last?'

'What's that got to do with anything?'

She shook her head and reached under the counter for a lunch bag. 'Here. I've got a sandwich. Eat it now, I don't want you passing out on me.'

Well, the instructor had warned me, so I thanked her and ate, gratefully. Then I washed up and changed into a hospital gown. They provided a locker so my gun was safe, but I took the bullets out anyway and put them in my left pocket. They were uncomfortable but a lot less so than they might have been fired into somebody from my Smith and Wesson.

Fred was in the delivery room, lying back, her face beaded up with sweat. I kissed her and made nice noises, as per instructions, then wiped her face with a damp cloth and fed her an ice chip to moisten her mouth.

The contractions were coming thick and fast and I wasn't able to do as much as I'd have liked because she had a pair of monitors attached to her abdomen but I did manage to turn her on her side and give her a back rub, which made me feel useful at least.

Every few minutes the nurse came in to check her drip and the monitors. After a while she started tuning in the baby's heartbeat on the Dopptone and we listened to the galloping noises that told us everything was all right so far.

About three o'clock the doctor turned up and things got hectic for Fred. She's got a lot of guts and she didn't make much fuss but it hurt me to see her in such distress. And then, at three-thirty, the miracle happened.

'A fine big girl,' Dr Rosen said happily. He turned the baby upside down and slapped her back gently and she cried. She wasn't alone in that.

Fred squeezed my hand very hard and I bent to hug her, and the room started to swim. The nurse grabbed me and steered me to a stool. 'Caught you,' she said brightly. 'Why is it always the big tough guys who fall apart.'

After a moment I felt better and moved the stool over beside the bed and took Fred's hand. 'Sorry about that.'

She squeezed my hand. Already she had her strength back, and her control. She pulled on my arm and I leant over and kissed her.

'You big suck,' she said gently. 'She's perfect. We did it.'

'You did,' I told her and sat there until she judged I was fit to hold the baby. She was red and wrinkled but I said, 'She reminds me of my kid sister.'

'We'll call her Louise. And Ann, for my mother.' Fred said.

After a while I was shooed away and I went and showered and got back into uniform and reloaded my gun again.

The same nurse was at her desk and she got me a cup of coffee, insisting on sugaring it but leaving it black. She found out which floor Hanson was on and I thanked her for everything and left.

My world had changed. Fred was well, and at thirty-eight I was a father for the first time. The nagging anxieties of the last few months were gone and I felt whole again. It was like coming back to the world from 'Nam.

One of the Parry Sound men was on duty at Hanson's bedside. Hanson was awake, his eyes wide. I saw the strap over his chest, buckled low to one side where he couldn't reach it. The cop yawned. 'How'd it go? Your wife OK?'

'Yeah, fine, thanks. Had a little girl.'

He shook my hand and congratulated me. 'They reckon

the baby's the same sex as the bossiest parent,' he said. 'Look at me, I got three girls.'

In my euphoria I laughed with him and said, 'Why don't you take a break? I'll sit with this guy a few minutes.'

'Wouldn't mind,' he said. 'He's been quiet. The doctor says he's not damaged any.'

He left and I stood at the foot of the bed looking at Hanson. 'Hi, how're you feeling?'

'Sore,' he said. 'My gut hurts.' His voice was different from what I remembered. He had dropped the roughness of his accent and he was a quiet, well-spoken kid again. Well, maybe not a kid, in his twenties, perhaps close to thirty. Had he been wearing make-up that morning? I wasn't sure.

'Feel like talking?' I wasn't going to force him. After what had happened upstairs the milk of human kindness was overflowing in me.

'Why not? I'm wide awake.' He seemed in control of himself so I put the questions to him.

'What was that nonsense at Murphy's Harbour yesterday? You're not a gang member.'

'Didn't convince you, huh?'

'Not really. What were you doing?'

'Research.' He tried to smile.

'How much research did you do?'

'Look, are you charging me over that?'

'I don't have to.' A nice neutral answer.

'I'll compensate the Frenchman at the baitstore. I didn't mean them to make a mess like they did.'

So he had done the swarming. 'Compensation should end that problem,' I told him. 'But there are a couple of other things I want to know about?'

'Like what?' He was wary.

'Like who loaded you up with PCP?'

'I don't know.'

'You didn't recognize the guy? Or you didn't see him?'

'I don't know anything about it.' He was firm now. 'Drugs aren't my thing. The odd joint at a party but nothing else.'

'Right now you're charged with possession of around four ounces of angel dust that I found in your room. Are you aware of that?'

He nodded. 'Yes. The cop who was here before you told me. He read me a whole song and dance about rights.'

'Did he mention anything else to you?'

'Isn't that enough?' It sounded like he'd been rehearsing that line. It came out perfectly.

'Did you go and your gang do anything else in your research project? Now's the time to tell me.'

'We swarmed the grocery at Pointe au Baril.' His pronunciation was perfect although the natives usually say Point-oh-Barrel.

'I know about that. What about the car?'

He frowned fleetingly. 'Car? You mean the Ford? I borrowed that from a friend of mine in Toronto.'

'What about the Accord you borrowed from Parry Sound?'

He was puzzled, or acting convincingly puzzled. 'Parry Sound? I didn't get up to anything in Parry Sound. The other stuff was research for a part I'm after. If I'd have come into Parry Sound it might have gotten ugly. I didn't need that.'

'Well, where did you get the Accord?'

'What Accord?' He tried to sit up, raising his shoulders as high as he could with the belt around his chest. 'I don't know what in Hell you're talking about.'

'Tell me about these other kids who were with you.' I kept my voice conversational. A nurse who was passing the open door paused to look in and I acknowledged her with a little wave. She nodded and went on.

'I picked them up in Wasaga Beach. Saw them bumming around together and turned them into a gang.'

'Where are they now?'

He shrugged. 'I split hours ago.'

'Did any of the others get into the angel dust?'

It was hard to tell whether he was giving me a performance but he looked anguished and close to tears. 'I was
alone and I don't know anything about any drugs and that's
the truth.'

'OK then. I'll just ask you one more question. Answer
that and I'm through with you. Deal?'

I knew he was lying by his answer. 'I don't care how
many questions you ask. I don't know anything about any
drugs.'

It was all I was going to get out of him but I put my
question anyway. 'Who joined you, at the motel, when you
were kicking back, drinking your beer?'

'Nobody did. I was on my own.'

'One last thing, then. What are the names of the other
kids?'

He relaxed, lying back and giving a little sigh. 'Let me
see. The big one's name is Chuck. I don't know any last
names but the other guys were Fred and Glenn and Phil.'

I took my notebook out of my shirt pocket and copied
down all the names and the descriptions he gave me, then
thanked him as if he'd been a help and went out to the door
to wave the Parry Sound cop back in. 'Watch him. He's
acting innocent but he figures he's smarter than we are.
Don't let him out of your sight.'

The cop was young and handsome with a little mous-
tache. He didn't like my suggesting he might goof. He just
nodded and went back in to sit with the kid. I left, hoping
he would stay alert. Hanson was tricky.

Sam jumped out of the car window and bounded to greet
me, wagging his tail. He was none the worse for his virgil
but I fussed him and told him he was an uncle and then
put him in the car and drove down to the Parry Sound
police station.

There was only a lone uniformed man on duty in the station but he knew me and let me look at the arrest report they had drawn up on Hanson. He was charged with assaulting me and possession of a restricted substance. There was a space left on the page for the chemical name to be added once their forensic people had checked out the powder. I thanked him and was about to leave when I saw a golf bag leaning against the wall in the corner of the office.

'Going golfing when you get off work?'

He looked around. 'Not me. That was there when I came on at twelve. The detectives found 'em at the motel where you caught the Hanson kid.'

I hadn't seen any clubs in the motel room but then, I hadn't looked in the closet. But I checked them out anyway. A fine-looking set including three different putters. And the monogram on the bag was JW, the same one I had noticed on Waites' shirtfront at the funeral parlour.

CHAPTER 5

The constable said, 'Don't touch it, it's tied in with that homicide this morning.'

'I know. And I'd be happier if it was out of the way until the detectives can fingerprint it. Could you put it somewhere?'

'Sure.' He picked the bag up carefully, putting both hands on the soft sides where his prints wouldn't blur any that already existed, and carried it into the inspector's office.

I thanked him and went back to the car and headed down the highway. Daylight was beginning to seep into the sky. It was almost fully light when I reached the Harbour and drove through town, slowing down to check from the car that no windows had been broken in any of the Main

Street properties. Normally I did it on foot but I was tired
and I didn't stop, just went up to my house and let Sam
out to seek again around the property.

There was nobody around and I stopped on the dock for
a minute or two, watching the night mist dispersing on the
surfaces of the lake and listening to the redwing blackbirds
in the reeds. I was one lucky man, I figured.

But I was still alert, so I sent Sam into the house ahead
of me to check it was clear before I went through to the
kitchen and put some coffee on while I made the phone
calls I had planned.

I let the baby announcements wait until I'd called
George Horn in Toronto. He's a one of a kind guy, an
Ojibway from the local reserve. He saved my hide one time,
using skills a non-Indian doesn't have. Since then he has
out-performed a whole crowd of city-bred hopefuls by
graduating high in his law class. Now he was articling in
the Crown Attorney's office in Toronto, on a fast track to
a judgeship, I reckon. A lot of guys would get swelled-
headed to have done what he's done but there's not an
ounce of arrogance in him. He's stayed the same as he was
when he ran the gas pump as a kid at the marina. I reached
him at his apartment.

'Hi, George, Reid Bennett. How are you?'

'Hey, Reid, good to hear from you. How's Fred?'

I told him about the baby and he congratulated me.
Then I asked, 'Do you have any time to do me a favour?'

'I can make time. What's up?'

'Well, there's three people I'd like to know more about.
One of them is in custody for drug trafficking. Should be
simple to chase him up.'

'In custody where?' He doesn't waste words.

'Parry Sound. The detectives will be following up, I
guess, but it would be faster for you, he's a Toronto
resident.'

He wrote down Hanson's name and then I told him

about the other two. 'This is a bit more complicated. First, a guy called John Waites. He's a lawyer.'

'Why are you interested?'

'His car was stolen and recovered with a dead woman in the trunk. She's a Parry Sound resident so they're following up, but this guy identified her as his wife at first, and now the dead woman's husband and Waites' wife are missing.'

We talked it over and he made notes. 'I've seen his name around the courts,' he said thoughtfully. 'He's a criminal lawyer. He's good. You think he killed this woman?'

I explained about the golf club and the concussion and he was quiet a moment. 'This guy Hanson, he had the clubs, right?'

'In his room at the motel. Only the driver was missing and that could have been the murder weapon.'

George was thoughtful. 'You'd think he'd have enough moxie to get rid of them if he'd killed that woman.'

'That's the way I see it. The other thing is, he claims, naturally, that he doesn't know anything about the PCP in his room. There could be a case that whoever dosed him up with the stuff also left the clubs there to incriminate him.'

'That's what a good lawyer would claim. You'd never get a jury to convict on a case like that.'

'Yeah, well, that's why I want to know about Waites. If he's a criminal lawyer he knows his share of rounders, guys who might off his wife for him and stick the blame on this dumb kid.'

'But you said it was a woman from Parry Sound killed.'

'She and the dead woman are very much alike to look at. If my theory is right, a contract guy may have goofed.'

He digested that in a moment's silence, then asked, 'So where does this Marcia Tracy fit in?'

'She knows both men. No law against that. But she knows Waites well enough to drive him out to the highway when his car was recovered and she had dinner with the Hanson kid the same night.'

He was silent again, recalling his days at the marina, trying to recall Marcia Tracy. 'She the woman who owns the old Dalton place on the west side of the lake, half a mile down from the lock?'

'That's where she lives when she's here. I don't know anything about any Dalton.'

'Before you came to the Harbour, Reid. He was a banker. He was widowed and married again. He died in Toronto around ten years back. I remember it involved pills and there was some discussion about did he fall or was he pushed. I guess Marcia Tracy is his widow.'

'Different name,' I objected.

'She's a big F feminist, in case you hadn't noticed. Likely that's her maiden name.'

'Apparently she's big in the film business in Toronto. A producer. Fred says she's well known, a ballbreaker with a couple of husbands behind her.'

'What's the name of her company?'

'Northlands Productions, I don't have an address.'

'OK. I'll look into it. Some of it I can do myself but I'll get Bill Serrel to do any legwork. Remember him?'

'Hell, yes.' Serrel was a sixtyish ex-cop. On retirement he had gone to work for the Crown Attorney's office. He was a quiet, thorough man, inclined to spend too much of his lunch-hour in the beer parlour, but aside from that a sound guy. 'Tell him hi,' I said.

'Will do. I'm coming to the Harbour tonight. It's my mom's birthday tomorrow so I've begged a day off to add to the weekend. I'll bring what I can find out with me, unless I hit something vital. Then I'll call.'

'Thanks, George. I owe you one.'

'*De nada*. See you tonight, and give my best to Fred.'

I hung up and called my sister in Toronto. She was just heading out to her job as creative director at an advertising

agency but she cheered with delight at news of the baby and
put her husband on to say hello. He's a Toronto homicide
detective by the name of Elmer Svensen. I played Cupid
for them a couple of years ago when Elmer and I worked
on a case together in Toronto and he met Lou, who was
divorced. He made all the usual noises about the baby and
then I had a word of shop with him.

'Ever run into a lawyer name of John Waites?'

'Yeah. Tough sonofabitch in court. You've seen him
there.'

'Don't remember him. It's been three years, remember.'

'He's been around longer than that. I recall he was in on
a case of yours two, three years before then. Junior counsel
representing that bank robber you shot.'

'Kershaw?'

'Yeah, that's the guy. Took a woman hostage. You got
your picture in the papers over that one.'

'That's the guy who skipped his guard on a day pass
from the pen, right?'

'The same one. Crazy, eh? We lock the bastards up and
the parole board says they can go to ball games with some
dopey baby-sitter.'

'And Waites was his lawyer.'

Elmer picked up my tone. 'What's he been up to,
Waites?'

I filled him in on the homicide and he clicked his tongue.
'You know, from this end, it sounds to me like Waites
could've been paying somebody to off his wife only they got
the wrong girl.'

'That's what I'm thinking, too. Any chance you could do
a little checking for me, Elmer, See if she was rich or if he
had a big insurance policy on her.'

'I can do that. Although you've already got a motive. A
guy like Waites wouldn't want a divorce. Under Ontario
family law he'd have to give her half of everything if

they'd've split up. He's a high liver. He wouldn't want her cutting into that.'

'Well, he's not exactly living high, taking his vacation at Pickerel Point Lodge. It's pretty fancy by our standards up here but the Côte d'Azur it ain't.'

'I'll ask around,' Elmer said. 'Gotta go. Louise has got her hand on the doorknob.'

'Thanks, Elmer. 'Preciate it.'

The next call I made was to Fred's parents. They live in the interior of British Columbia, which is three hours behind us on the clock. But her mother answered, sleepily.

'Good morning, Ann. It's Reid. I wouldn't have woken you up at four-thirty but there's great news. You're the grandmother of a beautiful little girl.'

'Oh Reid, that's wonderful.' Her soft West of England accent still persists after forty years in Canada. 'How's Fred?'

I gave her all the details and she asked all the right questions. Then I asked the ugly one. 'How's Harry today?'

'Still asleep, He had a bad night, Reid. God forgive me, I sometimes wish for his sake that it was over.'

'Maybe the good news will give him fresh heart.'

'I hope so. Look, it's impossible to travel right now. But as soon as you can, I hope you'll come out and see us. He'd love that.'

'Week after next unless something unforeseen crops up. Take care of yourself.'

'Bless you, Reid. I'll send Fred some flowers as soon as the store opens.'

That reminded me what I had to do: order some flowers and put an announcement in the paper. But it was too early to do either for another hour so I took my coffee into the living-room and sat on the couch. An hour later I was waking up, the full cup still in front of me. I got another cup and showered again and changed, then called and ordered roses at the Parry Sound florist's. I also placed an announcement in the paper. After that I put Sam in the scout car and drove down to Main Street.

Things move slowly in a resort town. The bait shop was open, of course. Gilles gets there at first light to be on hand for the early fishermen, but the grocery was just opening and the bank and liquor store employees were arriving for their ten o'clock starts. I stopped in to chat to Gilles, telling him that Hanson wanted to compensate him.

'I lost four rods an' five reels is all. I'll make up a bill,' he said angrily. 'But y'know, Chief, that young guy, 'e should do community service, 'im. Make 'im clean up in some place messy.'

'It could come to that. He's up on a couple other charges.' I was going to leave but he remembered Fred and I shared the news with him, which was a faster way of getting it around town than taking an ad in the newspaper.

It worked that way. I had trouble getting out of the station where I went to check the teletype. There was nothing on it about Kershaw. He was still at large but the phone rang continually with well-wishers. I managed to call Fred, who sounded strong and happy. I told her I'd be in at two o'clock and when I'd hung up I put the phone on the answering box, asking people to ring Parry Sound OPP if they couldn't reach me. I didn't want the air filled with congratulations and I'd be in touch with Parry Sound myself to pick up anything worthwhile. Next I took a quick run to the Northont Motel to see if the owner remembered any visitors to Hanson's cabin. He didn't and seemed glad of the fact. The cabin was locked and sealed with an OPP sticker, which had angered the owner even further.

I went back to the station and called Parry Sound to talk to Sergeant Holland. 'He's headed down your way, Reid,' the constable told me. 'He's going to get a statement from this Waites guy whose car was stolen.'

'Waites is still here?'

'Guess he must be. That's where Bill's headed.'

'Thanks. I'll join him there.'

Pickerel Point Lodge was busy. Four couples were out playing tennis and other people were getting ready to take their boats out but they were all comfortable Mom and Pop types, not like Waites. A yuppie like him would have been as out of place here as an ocelot at a kid's pet show. Coming here had been a real concession on his part. Maybe he really had been trying to please his wife. And maybe she had been genuinely difficult to get along with. But had he set her up for a killing?

There was no police car outside, so I parked and got out, taking Sam with me. It was going to be Holland's investigation. I would just wait and work with him, making sure Waites didn't leave.

Mrs James was in the lobby and she told me that Waites hadn't been down for breakfast. There was a 'do not disturb' sign on his doorknob. I asked her to head him off and call me if he came down, then walked through the lounge and out to the back of the building. The lounge gave on to a broad deck with recliner chairs on it and a sandy beach in front. A couple of pleasant-looking young mothers were sitting on the deck watching their children play at the water's edge. To the right was the long wall of the building, cut off from the deck by a five-foot wooden fence. To fill time while I waited for Holland I went down the steps in front of the deck and walked around the building the long way. That was when I noticed the rope.

It was the primitive fire-escape from an upstairs room, a two-inch rope with knots every few feet. Normally it should have been coiled under the window of the room but in one case it was hanging down, reaching almost to the ground.

The bedroom window from which it hung was open wide. All the others were open part way with a fly screen in the open section. That meant that somebody had come down the rope. I guess I should have gone around to the front

desk and asked whose room it was but I didn't take the
time. Calling on old boot-camp skills, I grabbed the rope
and walked myself up the wall to the room above. At
window-sill level I paused, raising my head cautiously to
look inside. Nothing seemed out of place but the bed had
not been slept in. I grabbed the window-sill and heaved
myself inside.

From the window I could see that the closet door was
open and there was a man's suit was lying on the floor next
to it, the pockets inside out. I took out my gun and
advanced towards the door of the bathroom which was ajar.

The door opened at a push of my toe and I saw, in the
mirror facing me that there was nobody hiding behind it.
Still with the gun in my hand I moved into the bathroom,
looking down around the door to check nobody was
crouched there. Nobody was. But John Waites was lying
face down in the empty tub, still dressed in the clothes he
had worn to the funeral parlour. And spreading out beneath
him was the rusting stain of day-old blood.

I holstered my gun and felt his throat automatically for
a pulse. There was none and the body was already stiff.

The security chain was in place on the door so I
unhooked it, then, carefully not touching anything else, I
went back to the window and slipped back down the rope.
A couple of kids were walking by towards the beach and
one of them said, 'Hey. Neat-oh. I'm gonna do that.'

He headed towards me but I told him, 'Stay down,
please. That's dangerous.' And as a safeguard I told Sam
'Keep' and left him there while I ran back to the deck and
up into the lodge.

Holland had just arrived. He was talking to Mrs James
and he looked up in surprise. 'Hell, Reid. I figured you'd
still be in bed, you were up all night.'

'Waites is dead,' I said.

Mrs James gasped but Holland made to go out the way
I had entered. 'No, he's up in his room. Somebody got out

down the fire-escape rope. I climbed up to check and he's dead.'

'The key, please.' Holland held out his hand to Mrs James, who pulled a key from the pocket of her skirt.

'This is the master. What are you going to do?'

'We're going to check. Then I'll need to talk to your staff. Don't let any of them go anywhere before I've done that, please.' Holland was polite even in his urgency. 'Which room is it?'

'Two-oh-six. Come on.' I led the way and we ran upstairs and Holland unlocked the door.

'Did you take the chain off?'

'Yes. Whoever it was went down the rope.'

We went into the bathroom and looked at the body. Holland didn't even touch it. 'The blood's good and dry. I'd say he was killed last night sometime.'

'Looks right to me,' I said. 'How'd you want to handle this? There's a doctor in town but he's not a forensics expert. You want to call your own people?'

'This is your turf.' He was grinning. 'Like, fair's fair, huh? I wanted to talk to this guy but Murphy's Harbour isn't my jurisdiction.'

'Fair trade. You took the Jeffries woman off my hands yesterday. I'll take care of this one. But I could use some help.'

'OK. Compromise.' He straightened up and looked at me. 'I'll help you for a while, call our crime scene guy in, then you take over.'

I guess it was ironic, two cops more or less tossing a coin to see who investigated a homicide, but places like Murphy's Harbour fall between the cracks of the police system. I'm fine with most things but a homicide investigation takes a team and there was just Sam and me. If we were going to find whoever had killed Waites, I'd need support.

We started by calling for help, Holland phoned his office

to send the crime-scene team. They're a small detatchment and their team consisted of one man, a jack of all trades. He would take the photographs, then dust for prints and, if necessary, vacuum the room for samples of lint that might have come from the murderer's clothing, although that would be hard to prove in court. Hotel rooms have so many people through them that a good lawyer can usually sway a jury on peripheral evidence like that.

To fill in the time until he arrived, we interviewed the staff. Nobody had seen or heard anything unusual but we established that Waites had ordered room service, an unusual request in such a small establishment at Pickerel Point Lodge. That had been at nine-thirty. He had ordered a bottle of Scotch, asking for Glenfiddich, but had settled for their bar brand, J. & B. The dining-room waitress who had taken the bottle and ice up was off duty until noon but Mrs James called her house. She was out but would come in to work as soon as she returned.

The Scotch order made me think, on two counts. To start with, Glenfiddich was Hanson's drink. Second, there had been no bottle in sight in the room. Perhaps the murderer had taken it with him. That suggested Kershaw as the murderer. He was on the run, cautious about going into public places like a liquor store, even if he had money. He would have taken the whisky without thinking.

After we'd talked to the staff we canvassed the other guests. The guy who had the room on one side of Waites was out fishing but the man the other side had heard nothing. He had gone up to his room and hit the sack early, around ten. Maybe by that time Waites was already dead.

And that was as far as we could go on a first sweep. Mrs James said she would have the other man call me when he came in from fishing, and that was it.

We went back up to the room and looked around, without touching anything, while we waited for the crime-scene expert. Two glasses had been used but the bottle of Scotch was gone. 'Should be some prints on these glasses anyway,' Holland said with satisfaction. 'Might be able to name the guy right off.'

'It could be this Kershaw who skipped on his day pass in Toronto,' I said. 'I found out this morning that Waites was his lawyer when he was sent up.'

'Getting even for the lousy defence?' Holland laughed.

'It's not that simple. If he'd been looking for Waites he would have stayed in Toronto, not come here. And if someone in Toronto had told him where Waites had gone, how did he know which room? Yet nobody downstairs saw anybody strange in here last night.'

Holland frowned, creasing his solid, single eyebrow. He looked like a puzzled chimpanzee. 'I thought his wife might've gone back home. If she had, she could have told the killer, but I've got the Toronto police checking his address. She didn't come back overnight, I know that.'

We stood there, looking at one another blankly, trying to see if there was some connection we'd missed. My own early theory had died with Waites. I had seen a possibility that he had set up his wife to be murdered. The man had seemed angry enough for it. And then the man who did the job had gotten the wrong woman. The idea made sense right up until somebody knifed Waites. But there was a second possibility.

'How about this? Waites set somebody up to kill his wife. My guess is it's this Kershaw. As a lawyer, Waites could have known in advance when Kershaw would be getting a day pass. He arranged to set him up with a car parked somewhere close to the ballpark in Toronto. So Kershaw, or whoever it was, comes up here and kills the wrong woman. Then the guy turns up here to collect whatever Waites had promised to pay him. Waites gets angry and tells him he's killed the wrong woman and he's not going to pay. So the guy knifes him.'

Holland unfurled his eyebrow and nodded. 'Some kind

of sense in that. We'll know for sure when Dave Stinson gets down here and fingerprints those glasses.'

'Guy like Kershaw would know enough to wipe the glass,' I said and Holland shrugged. 'For now, I like your idea. I'm going to get it on the air, see if we can round the sonofabitch up. He oughta be inside anyway.'

'OK. I'll wait here while you go use the phone.' He left and I stood at the door, looking over the room. There was a dent on the neatly made bed, as if someone had sat there with his back to the headboard, and the only chair in the room was facing it. Aside from that the only thing out of place was the suit on the floor with the pockets inside out. That didn't make sense to me. A professional criminal, even a bank robber, wouldn't have turned the pockets inside out. You do that only if somebody is wearing the pants. With a suit on a hanger you could check the pockets by scrunching up the fabric in one hand.

I checked the closet, pushing the door open wider with the back of my fingernails to avoid putting extra prints on it. It was empty except for a pair of golf shoes with trees in them. Waites had obviously been a perfectionist.

The missing clothes made me wonder more about the suit. If the killer had taken everything else, why had he left this? Maybe he'd been rushed and had grabbed the bag and left, or maybe it was a red-herring, that he wanted to show us that he'd gone through the pockets. Or maybe the suit was intended to lead us off track some way.

I was standing there when Holland appeared at the doorway, he was out of breath. 'Listen, they told me on the radio. You've got a problem in town. Somebody called in. There's a bunch of kids swarming the grocery.'

CHAPTER 6

He offered to come with me but that would have meant a delay while he sealed the room. I didn't need him anyway, not with Sam. I ran down and out the front door, whistling for Sam who bounded around the corner of the building and leapt into the front seat.

I spun away towards the lock, knowing I'd be too late but that somebody would probably have got the number of the car they'd left in. After yesterday's incident the kids around Main Street would have their eyes wide open.

I was right. The kids had all gathered at the door of the store. I wheeled up alongside. 'Did anybody get the number of their car?'

Two of them had taken it, and a description. This one was different, a newer car, a Chrysler Magic Wagon. Mommy's car for one of the little darlings, I guessed. 'Which way did they go?'

They had headed out straight along the side road to the south entrance to the highway. It figured from that they would be heading south, back to the anonymity of their own communities. 'Phone the OPP in Parry Sound and give them the car number. OK?'

'Right.' One of the girls dug into her shoulder-bag for a quarter and I spurted away down the highway.

The Magic Wagon was gone. I pushed the police car to the limit but there was no sign of them. By the time I was ten miles south I knew they had pulled off down one of the little side roads that led to enclaves of cottages on the beach. They would park there and giggle, maybe smoke up a while, then come out later in the day when the heat was off and they could get home without being stopped. By that time the local police would have called on the owner of the car and been told what a good boy little Johnny was and that he couldn't possibly have been mixed up in a swarming. We would be too late to do anything about it. The kids would disperse and the owner's son would have an alibi that put him fifty miles from the Harbour at the time.

Discouraged, I turned and drove back to Murphy's Harbour. The crowd had started to break down into little groups and they watched me as I went into the grocery. Mrs Horn, George's mother, was sitting on a hard chair at the entrance. She's a handsome, dignified woman and she was composed as she always is, but quietly angry. Behind her, the store owner was working along the shelves, picking things up and putting them back in place. When he saw me and pointed to Mrs Horn, I touched my cap to her. 'Hello, Jean. Were you here when it happened?'

'They killed my dog,' she said quietly.

'Where is he?'

'Jack put him in the back of my truck. I was just coming out of the store with my bags and they got out of their van and walked over and one of them hit Muskie on the head with a baseball bat. I tried to grab the boy but he pushed me over and they ran in here. Before I could do anything they were out and gone.'

'Did you see which of them killed Muskie?'

'Yes. I'll know him next time.'

'Good. We have the licence number, we'll have him arrested.' It was fine for me, an open and shut case, but it was a tragedy for her. That old hound of theirs had been a fixture in her life.

'Why would they do that, Reid?' She looked up at me, calm but angry, the way a lot of Indians have been with a lot of white men for a long time.

'I'm sorry it happened,' I said. 'It's some kind of initiation stunt they pull. To get into the gang a kid has to do something illegal. A lot of the time they go for dogs. One of them tried to bait Sam last night.'

'You'll get him, Reid.' It wasn't a question.

I had two homicides and an escaped con to worry about but this one was personal. 'I'll get him,' I promised.

She stood up slowly. 'Thank you.'

'Can you describe the kid who did it?'

'He was about eighteen, I think, dark hair, a little rat tail at the back. 'Bout three inches taller than me.' Five-nine, I registered. It sounded like the kid I'd picked out the day before as the number two in the gang.

'What was he wearing?'

'A T-shirt and jeans. On his T-shirt it said "Hermann's Gym." It was spelt with two ens.'

'Thank you. Would you like a cup of tea at the restaurant before you go home.'

'No, thank you, Reid.' She picked up her purse. 'Oh, and George phoned me. Congratulations on the baby.'

I thanked her and we shook hands and I put her into her pickup. Then I went back in and got the details of the swarming. Nothing much had been stolen, but they had ripped down a couple of pyramids of cans and used one big pop bottle to smash a bunch of others. I made soothing noises and got the owner to make a list of his losses and damage. Then I went back out to talk to the kids outside. One of them had seen the dog being killed and they confirmed the description Mrs Horn had given me. Yesterday's events had turned them all into good witnesses. I thanked them and made a note of the girl's name in my book against the time the case came to court, then I went to the station and reset the telephone to cut directly into my radio if it wasn't picked up.

I stood there for a moment, thinking what to do next. There was nothing much I could do until I'd traced the registration of the van and a policeman had spoken to the owners. But before I called the registry I called George Horn's office in Toronto. He was in court, his secretary told me so I gave her the message that his mother's dog had been killed, not saying how, and suggesting that a new puppy might make a good birthday present.

Then I rang the licence bureau and gave them the name of the gang's Magic Wagon, 382 HHD. The operator was back within fifteen seconds. 'Yeah, it's registered to a company, called Painters' Nook, 331 Main Street, Parry Sound.'

'Thank you,' I said and hung up. The long arm of coincidence had overreached itself again. Painters' Nook was the store run by the Jeffries.

That information sent me back up to see Holland at Pickerel Point Lodge. He was standing outside Waites' room, smoking a cigarette. 'Tryin' to stop but it's impossible when you're working,' he apologized. 'How'd it go?'

'The gang was driving a wagon registered to Painter's Nook. That's the Jeffries' place, right?'

'Yeah.' He stubbed his cigarette on the sole of his shoe and put the butt in his pocket. 'How in hell did they get their hands on that thing?'

'Maybe they stole it. But if so, where from? It wasn't at the store yesterday when you were there, was it?'

'No. I checked with the girl at the store yesterday, after we wondered how Jeffries had got away without taking his VW or the Waites woman's Accord. I meant to mention it to you, but with this killing it slipped my mind. Didn't seem that important anyway.'

'Maybe it's not. It could be coincidence, like winning the lottery the same day you're struck by lightning,' I said. 'Think about it. The Waites' Accord is stolen by what looks like a gang. The Jeffries woman is dead in the trunk. Then a gang, the same gang we had in town yesterday, turns up in Jeffries' other car. It sounds to me like Jeffries is behind this whole thing.'

'I've already broadcast a description of him as a missing person,' Holland said. 'Him and Moira Waites. I'll have it reissued, with the note that we want to talk to them about two homicides.'

'Did you check if this Jeffries has a record?'

'Yeah, he's clean. He's an American, from Milwaukee.'

'From the description I got the Jeffries are a crunchy granola kind of couple but I'm starting to doubt it. This gang using his car is just too much of a coincidence. Maybe it was him who put his wife in that car trunk and let the gang kids drive it into the lake. Maybe he and Moira Waites are off somewhere now, playing Mom and Pop.'

Holland swore softly. 'Hold on here, please, Reid. I'll phone the office, put out a stolen car call on that Magic Wagon, and get Jeffries posted as a homicide suspect.'

He pattered off downstairs and I went into the bedroom where Stinson was putting his camera away. He's a thin, balding guy, in his early thirties, looking more like an accountant than a cop. He stopped to shake hands with me. 'I hear tell you're a mother, congratulations.'

'Thanks, Dave. Yeah. Fine big girl, three point six kilograms.'

'Which is what? Close to eight pounds? Your wife OK?'

'Fine, thanks. I'm going up to see her later.' I wanted to talk about the case but you can't rush courtesies and he was genuinely concerned for Fred, so I let him get back to business.

'Well, I'm through taking pretty pictures. We turned the guy over. He's been stabbed in the chest, and then his throat was cut. Whoever did it wasn't fooling. They wanted the guy dead.'

'You going to print the glasses?'

'Thought I'd take them with me. I'm going to print the surfaces in here and seal the room. I'll do the glasses back at the office, I prefer working there.'

'Before you go, I've got a present for you. It's a glass used by a guy called Hanson. I arrested him last night for possession of drugs so I guess they've printed him now, anyway. If you get some prints maybe you can compare them with these.'

'Thanks, I guess,' He said. 'Means more work but what the hell.'

'What'd you make of the suit?'

He scratched the dome of his head and frowned. 'Been thinking about that. Whoever killed him took everything else but his golf shoes and the suit. And those pockets being turned inside out. Why would somebody do that?'

'That's what I was thinking. The only thing I came up with was that they wanted to draw attention to the suit, which means away from something else. Only I don't have any idea what else that could be.'

'Nor me.' He bent and picked up the suit jacket. He squeezed it in his fingerprints. 'Feels like silk. Waites had money, that's for sure.' Then he frowned. 'You'd figure he'd take better care to keep it pressed.'

'It's rumpled all right.' I said, and fingered the fabric. 'Shouldn't have got in that shape just from being dropped on the floor.'

Stinson gave a little chuckle. 'Looks like he's been swimming in it.'

'That's it,' I said. 'That's what must have happened.'

He looked puzzled so I explained about the car in the lake, with the dead woman in the trunk. 'This could be the suit he was wearing when he drove off that rock.'

'Why would he do that?' Stinson looked at me disbelievingly.

'Maybe he was planning suicide but chickened out.'

Stinson cocked his head suspiciously and took the suit from me. 'Could be. Anyway, I don't know if the Forensic lab can prove that it's been in the lake, but I'll ask them to check.'

'Good. Put it in a bag right away. There might be weed or something on it. Will you get a sample of lake water to compare?'

'Sure. There's one chance in a zillion it'll help, but those guys are good. They're using the OPP lab as an example in textbooks in the States these days.' He sounded wistful and I guessed he was sick of working in the sticks and wanted to get to Microscope Central in Toronto, where the miracles were performed.

'The other thing he left was the golf shoes.'

'Overlooked them, is my bet.' Stinson picked them up. 'Dinky little feet for a guy Waites' height.'

'Are they too small to be his?'

'Naah.' He shook his head cheerfully. 'Typical yuppie lawyer. Small hands, small feet, neat. And fussy as well. Lookit, shoe trees in his golf shoes.'

He snapped the little triggers on the trees and pulled them out. Surprisingly, they weren't normal shape. Instead of being pointed as the interior of the shoe would have been, both were cut away at the ends. We looked at one another without speaking, and Stinson tilted the shoes and gave them a shake. Inside each one was a small bag of clear, very strong plastic. And inside each bag were two neatly folded bindles of the kind street dealers use to package cocaine.

'Well, well,' Stinson said happily. 'So the late lamented had a hungry nose.'

'You sure it's coke?' I was thinking of Hanson and his own stash of powder, together with the evidence of his behaviour. He hadn't been using coke.

'I can't tell.' Stinson opened one package carefully, not breaking the neatness of the folds. 'I'll have forensics take a look at it. Why'd you ask?'

'The kid I pulled in was high on angel dust.'

Stinson refolded the bindle and put it back in its plastic bag. 'Wouldn't expect a guy like this to be on that kind of crap. Coke, yeah, seems like half the guys in his bracket are.'

'I'd appreciate knowing, please, Dave. Right now I've got a call to make.'

'OK, I'll give you a ding when I find out, OK?'

'Thanks.' I went back to my car and got the bag containing Hanson's Scotch glass out of the glove box. A bunch of little kids had gathered around the car, trying to get Sam's attention. I let him out so they could pet him and they did, happily, while I went back into the lodge to find Holland. He was using the telephone in Mrs James's office and I waited until he'd finished, then gave him the glass, with the news of where I'd got it.

'OK, thanks.' He took it. 'Where're you headed?'

'I'm going to break the news about Waites to Marcia Tracy. She knew him and she knows this Hanson, the kid who was leading the teen-gang yesterday. She's got to know something I don't. If I find anything out I'll let you know.'

'Thanks. When will that be?'

'I'm coming up to see my wife in the hospital, See you after, say around four this afternoon.'

His single eyebrow came down gloomily. 'Yeah, may's well. I'm supposed to be off at three but I don't see that happening today.'

I put Sam back in the car and drove up to Marcia Tracy's cottage. Her Mercedes was parked in the shade and she was lying on a blanket in the sun, wearing a one-piece swimsuit without straps. She had a good body, lean and well-shaped. She was an attractive sight and I felt the normal male excitement. Her radio was beside her, playing what sounded like Mozart.

Her eyes were closed but she turned her head when I opened the car door, then sat up, hugging her arms around her knees. She looked relaxed and languorous and I got the feeling that she had no idea of the big things that had happened since we had spoken last.

'What is it now?' she asked, snapping off the radio.

'I'm afraid I have some disturbing news, Ms Tracy.'

'Oh?' She cocked her head, surprised by my formality. 'What happened to Colombo and "just one more thing, ma'am"?'

'Mr Waites was killed last night. At the hotel in town here.'

She gave a half shriek. 'What are you saying?'

'I'm sorry to have to tell you but I've just come from there. Somebody stabbed him.'

She stood up in one fluid movement, holding one hand over her mouth. 'Oh my God.'

She was genuinely shocked but there were no tears in her eyes. A very contained woman. 'Who did it?'

'We're trying to find out. So far we don't have any idea, but there are some fingerprints in his room. We're hoping they'll help.'

She took a deep breath, then another. 'Come inside,' she commanded and led me to the verandah. 'Sit down.'

We both sat and she composed herself for a further few seconds, then asked, 'Why did you come to see me?'

'I knew you were friends with him. You drove him to the gas station yesterday. I wondered if you knew anything about him that might help us.'

'He was my lawyer,' she said tightly.

'Yes. You said that before. But I find he's a criminal lawyer. Do you have call for a criminal lawyer in your business?'

Her face tightened even further. 'And just what do you know about my business?'

'Not much. Just what you've told me, but I don't know of any business outside of crime that needs a criminal lawyer.'

She glared at me, her lips pursed, a study in anger. 'I was charged with a driving offence. He represented me.'

'When was that?' It kept it conversational, I didn't believe her.

'How should I know? A while back. He got me off.'

'And that's it? He acted for you and you remained

friendly and when he ended up in Murphy's Harbour, you
knew he was here and gave him a hand when his wife
walked out and her girlfriend was murdered?'

'What are you saying?' It was a hiss.

'I'm asking, not saying. I've got a murder to investigate
and I don't know much about the guy except that he knew
you. So I came to see you.'

'I've told you all I know about him.'

'Then why did you ask me in? You could have told me
to go away without inviting me in.'

She shuddered suddenly and I saw that the skin on her
arms was drawn up in tiny goosebumps. 'I'm frightened.'

'It's unlikely anyone else locally is in danger.'

'How can you say that? You don't know who killed him.'

I played my second card. 'Might have been his dealer.'

Her eyes flashed. 'Are you saying John used drugs?'

'Yes.'

She didn't reply and I let her sit for a few seconds longer.
'So does that guy Hanson we talked about yesterday. I
found him high and murderous on something, probably
PCP.'

She stood up, taut and tanned. If Fred hadn't been part
of my life I would have wanted to get to know her a lot
better. 'How many more bombs are you going to drop on
me?'

'I was hoping you could help me a little. You didn't tell
me a lot that was useful last time we talked.'

'I know very little about Eric Hanson.' She waved one
hand airily. I got the feeling she was happier talking about
Hanson than about the dead lawyer. 'Oh, his work, of
course. He's more intelligent than the usual run of actors.
Most of them are unbelievably dumb.'

'I gather he was doing some kind of research yesterday,
when he rode with that gang. When I saw you together I
assumed that he was auditioning or whatever for some
movie you were making.'

She was in control of herself now. She bent to the cigarette box and took one out. I'd left my matchbook on the table and there was one last match in it. She lit her cigarette and dropped the burnt match in the ashtray as she drew smoke deep into her lungs. 'You mentioned something like that last night. If Hanson's in trouble I guess I'll level with you. Yes, I'm trying to get a new movie together. It's about teen-gangs. He's a little old for the lead but he's good. He could handle it.'

'You'll have to scratch him now. He could do a couple of years for what he's charged with.' I was fishing, but she made no answer and I had a new insight. 'Is that why you retained Waites? To keep people out of jail when they were working on a movie of yours?'

She struck a pose, perhaps unconciously but very stagey, jutting one hip and cupping her right elbow in her left hand, holding her cigarette up next to her face, looking at me quizzically. 'There's some of that goes on,' she said. 'Especially with drugs. There's too much drug use today and sometimes people get caught. If it shuts down a production a lot of people stand to lose money.'

'Has Waites ever represented Hanson?'

'I don't know. Hanson has never worked for me.'

The conversation was headed for another stalemate so I changed my tack, making it more personal. 'I have no right to ask you this but I've got a lot of things breaking at the same time. Can I ask you to help me, please?'

'Ah-ah. Humility.' She sounded triumphant. I just smiled. I'd been polite throughout all my talks with her but apparently I hadn't tugged my forelock often enough.

'Well, yes, I guess you'd say that. I wondered if John Waites ever discussed his private life with you.'

She drew on her cigarette and resumed her pose. 'Not in detail. Why d'you ask?'

'From talking to him yesterday I got the impression that he was pretty annoyed with his wife. He's—was—a button-down yuppie lawyer. She's kind of a bohemian, lets everything go to hell while she paints. That's what he said. On top of which, he didn't seem too broken up when he thought she was dead.'

She looked at me without saying anything, then suddenly stubbed her cigarette. 'It's early, but I'm going to have a drink. Would you like something?'

'No, thank you. I'm working.'

'Suit yourself.' She padded off into the house and I heard ice cubes clinking and she returned with a deep, dark drink. She sat down and raised the glass. 'To his memory.'

I nodded and waited, there was more to her grief than friendship. I was starting to believe that Waites had been one of her lovers. He was in the right area, rich and important in his field, an equal of sorts. But her next words surprised me.

'I guess you'll find out some time so I might as well tell you. John was my second husband.'

CHAPTER 7

If she was expecting me to reel back, slapping my forehead at the shocking revelation, she was disappointed. I'd already seen that she and Waites were close and Fred had told me she had a couple of exes. The news figured. But to humour her I showed polite surprise with a question. 'How come you got on so well? Most people stay away from their exes.'

'I'm not most people,' she said defiantly.

'I can see that, Ms Tracy. Tell me, please. Did John Waites bring his wife up here because of you?'

'I happened to mention that the Lodge seemed like neutral ground for them, fancy enough for her, passable for him, that's all.'

'But both you and Mr Waites knew the other would be here?'

'Yes.' She was brisk again. 'This was to be business as well as pleasure, As always, I have a few problems with this new production and his advice was useful. We figured he could spend some time discussing things with me while his wife painted.'

'And did that happen?'

'He came over a couple of times. She'd promised him she would play golf but she forgot all about it once she got here. She had her goddamn easel and paints in the car and she set them up on the beach and that made her deaf and blind. He could have laid the cocktail waitress on the sand in front of her and she wouldn't have seen it.'

She was starting to loosen up now and I eased into the reason I'd come here. 'How badly did she bug him? I mean, he sounded really ticked off about her when I spoke to him yesterday.'

She answered as if it were a social question with nothing to do with the wife's disappearance. 'Her art was starting to get to him. I think he figured she would change when she married, that she'd relegate her painting to just a hobby. I guess he felt a bit like a guy who's married an alcoholic. She had him, what could she possibly want more than that? You know.' She waved one hand vaguely. 'He didn't realize that everything else, including him, came second to her paint-box.'

'Is she any good?'

She sipped her drink and gave a grudging nod. 'I guess. She's some kind of impressionist. Since she married John, her work brings big prices in Toronto.'

'Didn't that please him? He seemed like a man who wanted success.'

'He was. But it had to be his own success. That's what came between him and me. As long as I was hanging on by my fingernails he felt confident. When I made *Family*

Pride and then *Bugaboo* and started making real money, things fell apart.'

'And where did he meet this girl? I imagine she's younger than he was.'

'Not a lot. She's thirty. And I know exactly where he met her. It was at the studio. At a wrap party for *Family Pride*. She came with the cameraman.'

'And John made the moves on her.'

She looked at me through narrowed eyes. 'I can tell you didn't like him. He wasn't your type, was he? Too sophisticated.'

'I only met him twice, both at bad times.' It wasn't the whole answer. Waites had not been a guy I wanted to spend time with.

'Women adored him,' she said softly. 'He didn't bother wooing, he was too confident. He radiated power. Without half trying he could seduce any woman he wanted.'

'And he worked his magic on this girl?'

'He didn't. Not at first, and it infuriated him. I saw him with her and kidded him about losing his touch.' She smiled, but not fondly. 'A dumb thing to do. He decided she was a challenge and he went to work on her the way she worked on her painting. In the end she said yes, not because she wanted him particularly, I never thought so anyway, but because he was always there.'

'And where were you while all this was going on?'

She gave a little jerk of her head and reached for the cigarette box. I recognized it as a defence mechanism. 'You could say I had plans of my own. And anyway, I was away a lot. We shot *Bugaboo* in the Rockies and I was out there on location for three months. I'm a producer, not a housewife.'

Listening to her made me glad that Fred had pretty well given up acting. A wife who disappears for three months at a time to the other end of the country is not my idea of the perfect mate. I'm a chauvinist, OK, but I hoped I'd never

be sitting home with the baby while Fred was three thousand miles away smiling at a camera.

'And when you got home, what happened?'

'He'd moved out. He'd been living with her for a week.
So I had a meeting with him, not her, I didn't want to see
her, ever. And we agreed to a divorce.'

'Why did he marry her? If all he wanted to do was prove
he was wonderful he could have moved on.'

She lit her cigarette and blew smoke thoughtfully. 'I
asked him the same thing. He didn't have an answer, but
I think I did. She made him feel incomplete. Not sexually
or in a male sense, but intellectually. I guess she had the
same kind of power that he did, in a different way. She
never really surrendered to him. She slept with him but it
wasn't as important as her painting. He wanted to possess
her, the way he might have owned one of her paintings.'

'If she was making good money as an artist she didn't
need him, surely?'

'She's been making good money only since her marriage
to John. Before then she was making a couple of hundred
dollars a time in some crummy gallery in Soho, that's in
New York in case you didn't know.' I did, as it happened.
Once on liberty I had spent a weekend with a girl a lot like
this Marcia Tracy sounded, in her studio in Soho. But Ms
Tracy was still explaining. 'He pulled some strings, lined
up some buyers for her and arranged for a fancy gallery to
show her work. It sold out. Maybe it's a bubble that will
burst now he's gone. Maybe she's good. I don't know. I
don't understand pictures unless they move.'

This was all good background but it wasn't advancing
my investigation, so I pressed a little harder. 'Is that where
she came from, New York?'

'No. She was from Wisconsin or some deadly place like
that. She studied in New York and moved there. From there
she came up to Toronto with the cameraman I told you
about.'

I'd been hoping for an address but obviously she didn't have one to give me, so I asked the next question, hoping it wouldn't stop her talking. 'Do you think maybe he wanted her dead?'

That blew it. She stood up, carefully setting down her cigarette first. 'John was not the ideal husband.' she said carefully. 'But he was no murderer, if that's what you're asking.'

'Did he talk about her to you these last few days while they were staying at the Lodge?'

'No.' She made a move towards the door. 'And this discussion is over. You're trying to get me to say he wanted to kill her. He didn't and I won't. Please go.'

'Sure. I have one last question, please. Did you know he had a cocaine habit?'

'No, I did not.' She was fierce now, angry enough that she might easily have been lying, but she wanted me out so I went.

'Thank you for your help. Will you be staying up here for a while?'

'Are you telling me not to leave town?'

'I thought I asked a polite question, Ms Tracy,' I said as I stepped down into the sunshine.

'I'll give you a polite answer. I haven't decided yet. How does that suit you?'

'It'll have to do. I'll be in touch.' I clicked my tongue to Sam who was lying in the shade, beside her car and walked out to my own car. She lay down on her blanket again and turned up the radio. She had not brought her drink with her, I noticed.

On my way back to the station I called in at the Lodge and spoke to Holland. He said he would supervise the movement of Waites' body to Toronto for forensic work and I was able to go back to the station to do the paperwork. I typed up the report on Waites' death and copies of the statements Holland and I had taken from the people in the

Lodge. And after that I also recorded the gang swarming and the killing of Horn's dog.

I'm a better typist these days since Fred bought me a book and made me put masking tape on the keys so I had to follow the book to find them. It worked and I'm faster but this job still took me until one-thirty and there was no time to go home and change before visiting the hospital.

By the time I'd picked up the roses and a box of candies for the nurses it was two-thirty and I reached Fred's room at feeding time. I've seen a lot of things in my life but nothing so far has topped the thrill of watching Fred with the baby.

In uniform I felt like a bull in a china shop but Fred put me at ease. She was over her ordeal, feeling strong and well. She would be coming home in two days, she told me. I said 'good' while I juggled my workload in my head. I had a lot to do and it wouldn't ease up until I had at least located Moira Waites.

'You're being very quiet about all this, dear,' Fred said as she gently put the baby over her shoulder and patted her back. 'What's been happening while I've been in here multiplying?'

I gave her a scaled-down version of events and she looked sober. 'Are the OPP going to help you on this? A murder involving a man from Toronto, you can't handle that on your own. You'll need help from a lot of people.'

'It's heavy right now, but it'll settle down soon.'

'While things are so busy for you maybe you should stay at the Harbour and work on it, rather than drive up here all the time.' She's a good woman, a real cop's wife, understanding that the job has to come first sometimes.

'Maybe, if you don't mind, I'll put off coming again until tomorrow afternoon. We've had some gang trouble on Main Street and I'd like to show a little more presence for a day or two, people are getting spooked.'

The baby gave a tiny burp and Fred wiped her mouth

and told her she was clever girl. The woman in the next bed was watching us like a visitor to a zoo. I guess she hadn't realized that policemen procreate just like real people. After a while the nurse came and took the baby back to the nursery and Fred got up and walked around there with me to peer through the window and watch our firstborn yelling as lustily as the rest of them. 'The nurses tell me she's a screamer,' Fred said, hanging on to my arm. 'Can you handle that?'

'For you and her I could handle anything at all.'

At a quarter to four I left, after she'd made me promise to stay away until the next day at least. I was anxious to get on with my investigation so I didn't need any urging. I returned to the car and let Sam have a stretch, then drove up to the police station.

Holland was in the detective office with his feet on the desk and a cup of coffee. He told me where the machine was and I grabbed a cup for myself, remembering that I'd had no lunch so far. The way things were breaking and with Fred away I was going to lose weight. 'Coupla things,' he said, after he'd asked the expected questions about Fred and the baby. 'First off, Stinson found prints on the glasses from the room. One set was the deceased's. The other set isn't on record, so far as the computer in Toronto has been able to check. And they're not Hanson's either.'

'That's another theory shot to hell,' I said. 'I'd been hoping we'd find they belonged to Kershaw, that escaped con.'

Holland shook his head. 'No dice. The guy in Toronto checked Kershaw's prints individually. It's not him.'

'So what's the second thing?'

'Second thing is that a hotshot lawyer from Toronto came into town and sprung the kid you arrested last night, this Hanson.'

'What was his name?'

'Hers. A Ms Freund. Works for the same firm as this

Waites guy. She gave me one of their cards and Waites is on the list as a partner.'

'I just found out that Waites' firm works for a movie producer, Marcia Tracy, she's staying at her own place in Murphy's Harbour. He was on a retainer to cover the company's butt if any of their people got in legal trouble.'

'This Hanson kid works for her?' Holland was only half interested, he hadn't been with me to see the way all the strings in my caseload led back to Marcia Tracy.

'Not yet, apparently. She's considering him for a part in a movie but maybe he knew about Waites from that, talking to other actors, stuff like that.'

'Maybe.' Holland was looking smug, holding the most interesting news for last, I guessed. 'There's one more thing.'

'Helpful, I hope.'

'Could be. Could tie the both homicides together in a neat knot. We found prints on the car, that Honda Accord. No ID of course, because they're the same as the prints on the glass in Waites' room.'

We sat and sipped our coffee, staring at each other sightlessly. The whole thing was tying together. After a little thought I had an idea. 'Hey, have you checked the Jeffries' house for prints? Could be that he's the guy responsible. Just maybe he found out, say, that Waites was boffing his wife. He kills the wife and puts her in Waites' car so we figure Waites is behind it. Then, for whatever reason, he goes to see Waites and kills him.'

'Doesn't hold water,' Holland argued reasonably. 'If some guy came to my house after, God forbid, his wife had been murdered in my car, I wouldn't send out for drinks.'

'Waites was yuppie. Who knows how guys like him think?'

Holland was still unhappy. 'You know the rules of evidence as well as I do. I can't print Jeffries without arresting him or having his consent.'

'No sign of him anywhere?'

'Naah.' Holland finished his coffee and scrunched up the cup, tossing it at the garbage can. It missed and he grunted and picked it up. 'I've done everything I can but unless we go nationwide with this thing we can't stake out every car rental, every ticket agency, for him or the Waites broad to show.'

'And it's his car that the teen-gang used to buzz Murphy's Harbour.' I thought out loud. 'Maybe we should concentrate on finding that car. It'll be a mass of finger-prints by now but we might find his in it somewhere.'

'It's an idea.' He swung his feet down. 'I'll put the car out as wanted for investigation in a homicide. That'll wake up the troops more than it just being stolen.'

'Good idea. Now, while I'm here, I have to file a state-ment about the Hanson arrest. Can you get me a type-writer?'

He sat me down with a machine and I did my thing and he witnessed it and I was on my own. By now it was six in the evening and I was hungry enough to take a bite out of Sam but I drove back to Murphy's Harbour to eat. The presence of the car on Main Street would remind the good folks where their taxes were going.

It was a good to be back at the Harbour in any case. I like the spot. It's been home for three years and they're good people. Right now, on a bright summer evening, it was at its best with the shadows lengthening across Main Street and everyone moving slowly in the warmth. I sat at the window of the restaurant and ate a good dinner. Yung Luk is a gourmet cook if you let him do things his way and I had his Thai soup and Szechuan beef while most of the other customers ate fish and chips. Then I paid and took Sam for a stroll around town.

I went into the grocery and the bait store. Both owners were glad to see me. They'd already heard about Waites' death so I didn't have to explain where I'd been all day, but I got the usual small-town feeling that they wished I'd give them more attention and quit showboating, which is the way people look at a murder investigation when they're not involved.

It was seven o'clock and night was coming down on the town. The two lights on Main Street were on already with their usual halo of mosquitoes, and so was the big light at the dock of the Marina.

All the berths at the Marina were full, and, as I always do, I started my evening patrol at their hotel, the Lakeside Tavern. I went in by the back door and ambled through the kitchen with Sam at my side. The cook had a hamburger someone had sent back as too well done and he gave it to me for Sam who crunched it down and wagged his tail.

Amy Vanderheyden was at the desk in the back and she greeted me happily and bent to pat Sam, the only dog allowed in there. She chirruped happily about Fred and the baby and tutted about Waites' death and I smiled and nodded and looked around. The usual crowd of boaters and cottagers were in for dinner and the trumpet, piano, drums band was playing 'Don't cry for me, Argentina' well enough that a couple of Moms and Pops were pushing one another around the dance floor. A typical Thursday night in Murphy's Harbour, except for the homicides I was working on.

The Vanderheydens' daughter, Beckie, was waiting table, flirting happily. She's a good-looking blonde of sixteen and like all smalltown girls she's waiting for someone from Hollywood to drive into town and discover her. But she has her Dutch parents' level-headedness and when she saw me she excused herself from the table and bustled over.

'Hi, Chief. Congratulations on the baby.'

'Thank you, Beckie. How's things with you?'

'Good,' she said, then put her hand on my arm, which surprised me, she's not forward. 'Chief, you know those kids who ripped off the grocery today?'

'I wish I did. I'm looking for them.'

'I saw one of them a while back. Mom sent me to the
store for some Parmesan cheese and I saw the biggest one,
he was on his own and I think he was going into the
Murphy's Arms.'

'That's the kid with the dark hair, around five-nine?'

'That's the one. I heard tell that he killed some Indian
lady's dog. He's got some nerve, coming back to town after
that.'

'He sure has. Thanks very much, Beckie.' I nodded to
her mother and left the place quickly, getting back in my
car for the short ride to the town's other hotel. It's below
the lock, a standard beer joint with draught beer and no
food facilities, the place our locals do their drinking.

Again I went in through the back door. No kitchen here,
just a corridor with the beer storeroom to one side behind
a solid steel door. I came out behind the bar where Eddie
the barkeep was running the beer tap full steam, moving
one glass after another under the spout without turning it
off. He looked at me and made an offering gesture with a
glass but I shook my head. 'Maybe later, thanks, Eddie.
I'm looking for a kid in here.'

Eddie completed his order and turned off the tap, wiping
his hands on his apron as his waiter strode away. 'Under
age, is he?'

'No sweat. That's not why I want him.' I looked around,
recognizing most of the crowd. And then I saw the boy. He
was sitting alone with a beer in front of him, smoking a
cigarette. He had the pack stuck in the sleeve of his T-shirt,
the same T-shirt he had worn when he killed the Horns'
dog. I studied him for almost a minute. He seemed nervous,
probably because he was under age but also because he
was out of his element. These were real people around him,
guys who worked hard and came home tired. He didn't. I
could tell that from this distance. He had to buy his muscles
at Hermann's Gym.

He was watching the door, and that worked in my favour as I moved towards him between the tables. I was half way there before he saw me and bolted for the door. I didn't give chase. Instead I told Sam 'Track' and he bounded after him, grabbing the heel of his right shoe so that he tripped and sprawled headlong. Before he could sit up Sam was over him, snarling an inch from his face.

Then noise in the bar stopped as if someone had switched off the sound on a TV. Then ony guy shouted, 'Go get 'im, Sam,' and everyone cheered and I knew they were on my side, Sam's at least, and that was just as good.

I've taken the same psychology courses as any policeman these days and I even took a couple at college when I came out of the Marines. So I knew the worst punishment for this kid was to hurt his pride.

I did it by pulling his arms behind him and snapping the cuffs on his wrists. He went scarlet with shame but I was glad. He'd caused a lot of distress for the Horns. Now it was his turn.

'You're under arrest for malicious damage, assault on a woman and for causing undue pain and suffering to an animal,' I told him. Then I pulled out the card from my notebook and read him the formal caution and the rest of the Charter of Rights ritual. I did it loudly enough that the beer drinkers all heard and the kid's eyes filled with tears of frustration. Then I eased him up on his feet and bent to fuss Sam and tell him he was a good dog. He does a lot of my work for me and earns me the biggest chunk of the respect our locals have for their law enforcement system. A couple of them cheered, and one of them, bolder than the others, dared to reach out and pat Sam's head.

'This the guy who killed that man at Pickerel Point?' he asked and I just smiled like the cat who swallowed the canary. 'He's in custody, I'm taking him in, if you'd get the door, please.'

'Yeah, sure.' He bustled ahead of me and I touched the

boy between the shoulder-blades and sent him ahead. The crowd followed as I put him into the police car and drove off. I checked them in my mirror to see if they were going to follow down to the station but they just broke up again and went back in for another beer. Good. I didn't need an audience.

At the station I went in the back way, confronting my prisoner with the reality of law-breaking. The place isn't shocking, unless you're in handcuffs. There are four one-man cells along the back wall. Each one has solid walls and a cage front. They contain a bare plank platform, a toilet and a hand basin. That's it.

In the space in front of the cells there's a wooden desk and a chair. I unlocked the handcuffs and said, 'Sit.'

He sat, rubbing his wrists, not looking at me. His flush had gone now and he was pale under his tan.

'Turn your pockets inside out, lay all your possessions on the table.'

He sat there and said, 'I want to see a lawyer.'

'You'll get one phone call when we're through here.'

He didn't move. His face had drawn itself into a pout. He was frightened but proud.

I opened the top drawer of the desk and took out the arrests book and a pen. 'I'm just going to say this once more. Empty your pockets.'

'Or what? You gonna kick the shit out of me?' Even scared, his voice was schooled. He didn't say 'outa'.

I hissed at Sam and he snarled and thrust his muzzle an inch from the boy's knees. The kid licked his lips. 'I'm telling my lawyer you did this to me,' he said, but he was fumbling in his pockets as he spoke.

'Easy, boy,' I told Sam and he sat on his haunches while the kid stood up and turned his pockets inside out. All he had was a clasp knife and money, a few coins and a bundle of bills. I patted him down and checked there was nothing hidden in his socks or back pocket. 'Cigarettes too,' I said.

Angrily he took the pack from his sleeve and tossed them on the desk. 'Now take off your belt and shoelaces. And your watch, that goes with your other stuff.'

'Why are you taking my belt and laces?' he asked as he did it.

'So you won't hang yourself with them.'

'Why would I do that?'

'Happens all the time. What's your name?'

He looked at me and then away. 'I don't have to tell you.'

'It's all the same to me. Suit yourself.' I counted his money. 'You have twenty-eight dollars and fourteen cents. One Buck clasp knife. One yellow-metal wristwatch, Rolex on dial. One pack of Export A cigarettes.' I made the entry in my arrest book. *John Doe, 17-19 years old, 5ft 9ins., black hair, brown eyes. Wearing Levi jeans, Reebok running shoes. Charged with* . . . I wrote in the charges and looked up, putting the top on the pen, looking as satisfied as I could manage. I wanted him cracked. 'Right. Now you wanted a phone call. Come with me.'

In the front of the office I sat him on a stool and picked up the phone. 'What number do you want to call.'

His mouth was working as he weighed his alternatives. No doubt he knew a little law, knew that he could wait until I called a bail hearing and then leave town. That would give him a chance to explain his problems to his parents face to face, to cut down on the shock they were going to experience if he rang them now. 'You got a pizza place in this town?' he asked.

'No. Is that the only call you want to make?'

'Yeah.' His decision made he was tough again. 'Yeah. So stick me in your slammer. See if I care.'

'First I'm going to get a statement from you,' I said easily. 'Sit down there.' I indicated the chair beside the desk.

He sat down, crossing his legs, folding his arms, a closed book.

I ignored him and pulled out an occurrence form and started typing. He watched me, breathing very shallow.

'Right, now.' I lifted the top of the paper and read to him. 'John Doe, you are arrested on the following charges. You have been given the caution and advised of your rights under Canada's Charter of Rights and Freedoms. Now I'm going to ask you to make a statement. Name?'

He almost fell for it. 'Phil, he said and then stopped, angry at himself. 'You've got it down there, John Doe.'

'Right, Phil. How did you come into town tonight?'

'I'm not saying. I was here, OK?'

'Dumb,' I said cheerfully. 'If you'd stayed out of town I might never have found you. You'd have been free to swarm more places, kill a couple of more dogs maybe.'

'I don't know what you're talking about.'

'Listen, son. You're in deep trouble. Right now you're thinking that if you get out of here you can run away and I'll never find you. But here's a hot flash. I'm not letting you out until I know who you are and where you're from. So all you're doing is making your parents even angrier at you than they are now.'

'You don't know anything,' he said. 'In the morning you have to deliver me to a court somewhere. When you do I'll be bailed out and you're left holding a bag of fresh air.'

'So your daddy's a lawyer, is he?'

That silenced him. It didn't break him down but he was starting to realize that he'd lost.

'You could get away with this still, you know. Or most of it. I know that Hanson set you up. Did he give you the car you came here in this afternoon?'

'I don't know any Hanson.'

'Fine. I'll ask you again later. Right now you're going in the cells.' I stood up, leaving the half-completed form in the typewriter. 'Let's go.'

He stood up. I could see that his confidence was evaporating. There was no audience for his bravery. It was just him and me, and Sam, a solemn, silent presence. He needed somebody there to appreciate what he was doing, otherwise he was going to lose confidence in himself entirely. I figured he'd be ready to talk to me in about an hour's time. It would seem like an eternity to him.

I put him in the cell furthest from the door, the most isolated-seeming in the place, clanked the door shut and locked it. Then I did the hardest thing yet. I left him, without finding out where he had found the Jeffries' car, and walked out of the back door, locking the deadbolt behind me.

I got back in the car and drove into town again, trying to work out where the kid could have come from. I was surprised by the fact that he had not been carrying a driver's licence or any other ID. Probably he was under nineteen and had left his wallet in the car that brought him, not wanting to be embarrassed if he was asked for proof of age. It also meant that one of the vehicles in town was his. Maybe, if luck was on my side, it would be the Jeffries' Magic Wagon.

But I couldn't see it anywhere in town, so I took a slow drive up and around my whole patch, checking the cars parked at every cottage and the guest houses and our few lodges. It took me an hour and a half, counting a ten-minute stop at home to feed Sam and heat myself a cup of day-old coffee in the microwave I'd put in since marrying Fred.

At close to ten I was back in town again, shaking the door handles on all the lock-up premises. Everything was secure and I walked Sam back to the car just as a new Subaru four-wheel-drive pulled up. It stopped beside me and George Horn stuck his hand out of the window. 'Hi, Reid.'

We shook hands. 'Hi, George. Good to see you. Been home yet?'

'Yeah. My mom's pretty shaken up. The new puppy helped, thanks for the tip.'

'Welcome. She'll be glad to hear I've got the kid in the cells.'

'Good. What's his name?' He got out of the car, a slim tall man, neat in his dark city suit.

'He won't say but his first name is Phil.'

George was thoughtful. 'You'll have to release him tomorrow after a bail hearing.'

'Not if I don't get a name and address. He can't win.'

'Who did he call when you let him use the phone?'

I told him about the bravado and George shook his head. 'Watching too much TV.'

'Yeah. I wish he'd open up. When he came to town and hassled your mother he was driving a car belonging to the husband of the dead woman, Carolyn Jeffries. We've had another murder in town and I want that car badly. I want to trace Jeffries or Waites' wife. I think they're together and they left town in that car.'

'And the kid won't talk?'

'Not a word. Figures he's a hard man.'

George pursed his mouth, as angry as I've seen him. 'He's a little prick, killing poor old Muskie like that.'

'Well, I'm not about to give him the third degree but I want to crack him open. I plan on trying him again when I get back in.'

'Leave it with me,' George said. 'Give me fifteen minutes and I'll be at the station.'

'I can't let you take him apart, George, much as you'd like to.'

'I won't.' He looked at me very straight. In the harsh street light his face looked chiselled. 'You trust me, don't you?'

'You know that. You saved my ass last summer. I still owe you for that one.'

'Trust me,' he said. 'I won't do anything illegal, I

promise. Borderline unethical but nothing that will get me thrown out of law. I don't want to end up back on the pumps at the Marina.'

'What are you going to do?'

'You'll see,' he said. 'And afterwards I'll come in and tell you what we found out in Toronto.'

He got back into his car and drove down over the bridge to the hotel where he parked and went into the phone-box. Then I put Sam in my car and drove back to the station.

This time I went in through the front door and spent a minute or so checking the teletype and generally advertising my presence. When I was sure my prisoner knew I was back I went through to the cells, carrying a pop can as if I was just enjoying a cold drink.

He was standing against the bars of his cell and he spoke at once. 'I want that phone call now.'

'You refused your chance.'

'I was confused, you didn't explain it to me properly.' He was tense but still acting tough. He would be an unpleasant adult, I figured, a bullying boss and a bastard around women.

'If you want to tell me your name and answer a few questions I'm prepared to let you make a call, even though I don't have to,' I said.

He slammed the bars with his hand. 'You go shove it,' he said. 'I've waited this long. I can wait all night.'

'Suit yourself.' I shut the door and returned to my desk where I sat and read the teletypes. Nothing on it was new to me. The OPP had reissued the description of Jeffries and Moira Waites and the Magic Wagon, specifying they were wanted in connection with a homicide, but there was nothing else of interest on the list. I finished it and waited a few minutes more until George came in.

He came the front way and called out 'Good evening, Chief,' loud enough that the prisoner could hear out back.

'Good evening, sir, what can I do for you?'

He winked at me and pushed a nine by ten envelope across the desk. 'Your info,' he mouthed. Then he said out loud. 'I'm visiting in the neighbourhood and I saw you arresting a man at the Murphy's Arms Hotel earlier.'

'Yes. I did.'

George's face was perfectly straight. He said, 'I happen to be an attorney and as you don't have one in this village of yours, I thought perhaps he might need one.'

'I've heard of lawyers chasing ambulances but this is a new low, if you ask me.'

'Nobody asked you, Chief. Please keep your opinions to yourself and ask your prisoner if he wants to talk to a lawyer.'

I went to the back door and opened it with a slam. 'You, kid. There's a lawyer in town. He's asking if you want to talk to him.'

He had heard every word of our conversation and he was standing at the bars grinning a mile wide. 'Yeah. I do. Bring him in. Like I can't come out there, right?'

I turned and called George. 'He'll see you.'

George came through and I got a chance to see him move. He's about six feet tall, and lean. In his suit and white shirt he looked like authority on the move. He came in and pulled out a card which he handed to the boy. Then he turned to me. 'Please leave us alone and shut the door.' His tone was snooty and I glared at him for the kid's benefit but did it, slamming the door.

They were out there five minutes while I looked at the information George had brought me. It contained brief biographies of Marcia Tracy, Waites and Hanson. I read Tracy's first.

She was thirty-eight, formerly married to the banker Dalton, from whom she had inherited the cottage, then to Waites. That ended in divorce one year before. She had been arrested once, for impaired driving but had gotten off. Waites had defended her. She had been born in Toronto and had taken the television course at Ryerson, the big polytechnical institute in Toronto, and worked at a number of jobs before founding her own production company on the death of her first husband. A bracketed note said that his death had been investigated but eventually the inquest had declared it accidental. In George's neat handwriting was the note. 'I have more, will tell you.' At that point she had inherited his insurance and estate and used the money to open her business. She had married Waites six months after her husband's death. For five years she had struggled to keep her company afloat but had then had a couple of successes, *Family Pride* and *Bugaboo*.

Her divorce from Waites had been uncontested and there had been no division of family property.

At this point in my reading George came back to the doorway and spoke to me in the same loud voice, not his normal tone. 'Did you realize that my client is a juvenile?'

'I didn't realize he was your client?'

'Well, he is. And he is also seventeen years old and you've got him locked into an adult facility.'

'He's alone, in no danger.'

'At the moment, no. But if you get busy and these cells are filled, who knows what terrible things could happen. I want him released immediately into my charge.'

'I'm not letting him go until I have his name and address. I have to notify his parents and I want to make sure he returns here for a preliminary hearing tomorrow at noon.'

'I'll give you the name. That will have to be enough. I'll take responsibility for him after that.'

'I don't know you from a hole in the ground. How do I even know you're a lawyer, not some other rounder from that gang of his?'

'My card,' he said and handed it to me with the shadow of a wink. I read it. John Noble, insurance broker.

'OK, then. I'll have to let him go. Once I know his name.'

'Phillip Freund.' he spelt it for me. The name tickled my memory but nothing caught.

'And you'll have him back here tomorrow?'

'Yes. I'm going to drive him to where he's staying and I'll pick him up and deliver him back for a hearing. When will that be?'

'I can get the magistrate here for noon.'

'Right. Let him out.'

I took out the key and unlocked the cell. Even with George working whatever he was doing I hated to let the kid go. He thanked my by saying, 'Still feel like a big-shot? Eh, copper?'

'This isn't over yet, Phil,' I told him. 'Wait for the last laugh.'

CHAPTER 8

The kid couldn't resist giving me the finger as he reached the door. I ignored him and sat down, wondering just how George was planning to smarten him up. For a moment I almost went out after them and brought the boy back, but reason won. If I held him and got an investigation team down from Parry Sound the boy would just toughen up. He would know that the bigger the police department the less chance there was that anything physical would happen to him. And if they succeeded in opening him up by sweet talk, they would probably have their findings thrown out of court later. The lawyer his parents could afford to retain for him would argue that we hadn't observed the boy's rights.

I shook my head and hoped that George had seen a way around it all. It would be clean, even if the legality was a little rocky. I was confident of that. George had come a long way from the Reserve. He wouldn't blow it all. His personal loss would be unbearable, but even worse would be the way all his doubters would shake their heads and mutter about not being able to trust an Indian even when he'd been to college.

Slowly I sat down again and opened Waites' file. It didn't tell me a lot that was useful. He was a high profile guy, for a man in his early thirties. He had a way of swaying juries and had built a reputation for making the police look foolish, which delighted the newspapers but didn't endear him to me. It's always easy for a lawyer, with the advantages of hindsight and unlimited time, to examine an investigation and find some petty thing that a cop didn't consider in the half-second in which he had to decide before pulling his gun or breaking down a door. I'm not a vigilante but I'm more concerned with justice than law. In my view, lawyers mostly don't care about justice, they use the law as a fine-tooth comb to try to drag their clients out of trouble.

Waites' personal file was slim. He had graduated from Osgoode Hall, Canada's foremost law school, the one George Horn had aced, articled at his father's firm although Waites senior had been dead by that time. He had been admitted to the bar in '79. According to George's notes, the firm's best defence lawyer had suffered a stroke the following year and Waites had been moved into the second spot, taking over as the firm's top criminal man in '86, the year after he'd lost to me over Kershaw. Since then he had won a number of shaky cases and had a good circle of satisfied clients, including a Colombian cocaine dealer and a couple of murderers, all of whom probably felt they owed him a lot more than the money he'd cost them. George had noted that he was known as a womanizer and had been married twice, the first time to Marcia Tracy.

Hanson's file had some surprises although nothing was helpful in the case. His real name was Eric Kowalski. His father was a garbageman in Toronto. He had appeared in a number of plays around Toronto and had studied with a

woman called Poirier whom George described as the high
priestess of The Method. His reviews had been good and
he had appeared in a number of TV commercials. On two
occasions he had worked for Marcia Tracy but according
to George's notes, had been only an extra with no speaking
part. He was twenty-eight years old and lived with a woman
fifteen years his senior. She was a sound engineer for CBC,
our national TV network. Her name was Hanson and no
doubt he had taken it as his own because it sounded less
ethnic.

I closed the file and was sitting with my feet on my desk,
thinking about it when a car drove up outside. I swung my
feet down and waited. A moment later the car drove away
and the front door of the office opened. George came in,
smiling. 'Can you believe it?' he asked cheerfully. 'I stopped
at Kinski's gas station on the highway, left the kid inside
while I went in to buy some pop and some sonofabitch stole
my car, with the kid in it.'

I played the game by his rules. 'Any idea who it was?'

'No. The guy on the pump said there were three Indian-
looking guys in a pickup truck. Two of them got out and
got into my car and drove off, just like that.'

'Where's the kid?'

'That's the funny part. They took him with them.'

'They're not going to punch him out, are they?'

'No,' he said sincerely. 'They're Indian. They won't
touch him.'

'I just hope the hell you know what you're doing, George.
You want me to report your car missing?'

He looked at his watch and yawned. 'A bit late tonight,'
he said. 'Why don't you make a note of it and we'll look
for it when you drop me off at home. You know what
Indians are like. They've probably gone back to the
Reserve.'

'Does your mom know what you're doing?'

'She's too busy making a fuss of her new dog. I got her

a German short-hair. Pretty little guy but it'll grow big enough that kids with baseball bats won't take after it like they did with Muskie.'

'And your dad can train it for hunting. Good idea.' I wanted to talk about Freund, wanted to know where the Jeffries' Magic Wagon was, but that wasn't going to happen tonight. Instead of pushing it I asked him about the information he'd brought me.

'You made a note on the Tracy file, something about her first husband's death.'

'Yeah.' He sat down the other side of the desk and I put my feet back up. Like most North Americans I'm more comfortable that way. Like every Indian, he isn't. He sat back in his chair and said, 'One of the guys at the office remembered the case. It seems there was talk that his wife, this Marcia Tracy, was running around a lot, screwing actors and the owner of the production house where she was working. According to my source, there was some kind of scandal brewing and Dalton, that's the husband, had hired a private detective to follow her. Then one night he died. Just like that. The coroner said he'd had a couple of Scotches before going to bed and had taken sleeping pills. Seems his heart was a little touchy and the combination finished him.'

'You think she knocked him off?'

'The inquest ruled it accidental. There were some who thought it might have been a suicide, or even murder. According to the transcript, the housekeeper said there had been bad blood between the two of them and Dalton had been talking divorce to her, that's the housekeeper.'

'I guess Marcia would have been out on her ear if the old guy had divorced her.'

George shook his head. 'Not entirely. That was after the Family Law Reform Act. She was entitled to half the house and so on, but it wouldn't have been cut and dried. And the way it ended she got a cool half-mill in life insurance, on top of everything else.'

'Sounds to me like a hell of a good motive for feeding him a few drinks and some extra pills.'

'The jury didn't buy it. She came across as the grieving, misunderstood widow. She was young, by their standards anyway, around thirty, a career woman. The way the guy at the office remembers, that went over big with the jury, there were a couple of what he calls bra-burners on it. Anyway, they found it accidental and the whole thing was dropped.'

'And six months later she marries Waites.'

He nodded. 'Yeah. Then they divorce, he remarries, all three of them come up here and the wife vanishes and he winds up dead. You've got to wonder if something from the past didn't crop up.' He paused, 'Oh, one thing more, from the present. I learned that she's got money troubles. She had a couple of big successes but her last few movies have been crap. Now she's trying to raise money for the next one and nobody's coming forward.'

'So she's strapped. That's interesting. And we already have the feeling that she killed her husband for money. I wonder how this ties together with what's happening here?'

George shrugged. 'Unless she's got insurance on the dead woman, I don't see how it can help her.'

'There must be something,' I said, 'but we won't know until we've got more. I have to talk to Moira Waites and her boyfriend. I guess he's her boyfriend, this guy Jeffries whose wife ended up dead in the lake.'

'You'll get your chance in the morning. The kid'll be back and he'll talk up a storm.'

'Nobody's going to rough him up, George? You know I can't sit still for that.'

'Nor can I.' He stood up. 'You may not want to hear it but the case I'm working on right now in Toronto is about a policeman who hammered some wife-beater. Good old frontier justice, right? Except that the reason the wife was being beaten up was because she was having an affair with the same copper. He's looking at five years and I'm going to see he gets it.'

'That's the only way to play it. Right down the middle.'

He paid me a compliment. 'If every cop worked the same as you, Reid, life would be a lot nicer.'

I swung my feet down. 'So I guess the sweet talk is so you can get a ride home.'

''Preciate it, please.'

'OK. Come on, Sam.' I switched the lights off, except for the blue light over the door outside, and led Sam and George out to the police car.

It was after eleven by now and the Reserve was in darkness. George invited me in but I refused. I planned to spin down the highway a few miles each way, looking for the Magic Wagon. Then I'd take one last pass around the Harbour and hit the sack.

I did it all and found nothing and after midnight I pulled in at my house and let Sam out of the car to seek. He found nobody but he showed a lot of interest in the space around my house, so I went around it with him, flashing my light everywhere to see if someone had broken in. It looked intact so I opened the front door and let him go first. Again he found nothing and I fed him and let him out for a minute, then cleaned my teeth and went to bed.

The phone rang at four-thirty. I grabbed it on the first ring. 'Police, Murphy's Harbour.'

It was George. 'Sorry to drag you out so early, Reid. Our neighbour, Jim Buck, he says he was fishing last night up at Loon Lake. Says there's a car on the road looks like mine. Didn't get the number. I wondered if you wanted to give me a ride up, see if we could find it, scratch it off your stolen list.'

'I'll be over there in fifteen.' I hung up and went to the bathroom for the world's quickest shower and shave. Then

I took Sam and drove to George's place. Everyone was up
and his mother came to the door to see George off. She
stood there under the porch light with the puppy under her
arm and she waved at me and held the puppy up. I called
out hi and drove away with George.

'I guess Jim Buck is resting up,' I said easily. 'His lights
weren't on.'

'I guess. He's been up all night fishing,' George said.
'Got some nice pickerel, couple around four pound.'

'Was he with the kid all night?'

'He was fishing, but his brother's still up there,' George
said.

'What happened?'

'I'm not sure. Why don't you ask Freund? My guess is
he'll be talkative.' George flopped his head sideways, sleeping or pretending to.

Loon Lake is on a side-road to begin with and then a
further eight or nine miles into the bush on an overgrown
logging road. At night, on foot, you would never find your
way down there unless you were born here and knew every
tree. I made no comment and a few miles in we came to a
fork. My headlights played over George's car, covered with
dew.

'Good as new,' he said happily. 'Isn't that lucky?'

I looked at him. 'Now I wonder which of these roads a
man might try first, looking for the kid?'

'That one looks good.' George pointed.

'Did anybody stay with the boy?'

'Don't know what you mean,' he said, getting out. 'But,
come to think of it, Jim said that his brother Jack wasn't
home yet.'

'I'll call you later.' I drove off up the logging trail until
a deadfall blocked it completely, then got out and turned
Sam loose to seek. It was still dark and I carried a flashlight
with me but didn't turn it on, letting my night vision

develop on its own. It would be light within another hour and I could manage until then.

Sam ran in and out of the bush all the way, then he checked and looked up before bounding away again. It was jackpine here, low to the ground and tangled, second growth. I didn't try to penetrate it, knowing that the boy wouldn't have gone into the bush here, he must have blundered off the trail further up where the trees were better spaced and he lost the trail in the darkness. I went on, looking for a likely spot.

I found one, a couple of hundred yards further on and turned off in the direction Sam had taken. A moment later I heard his bark, about a quarter of a mile ahead among the trees. They were thicker here so I made sure to blaze myself a trail I could follow out, snapping off branches and leaving them hanging at eye level. It made more noise than I liked but I didn't think the boy would notice. The only thing he was hearing was Sam, who would be standing in front of him, giving tongue the way he's trained to. It would sound to a kid as if Sam were out for blood.

I reached him a few minutes later. He was up in a tree, sitting with his knees drawn up uncomfortably. I shone my light on him and saw his face was scratched with branches and he had been crying.

'Easy,' I told Sam. Then to the kid: 'What the hell happened to you?'

'Keep him away,' he sobbed.

'He's the one who found you. You ought to be grateful. Come on down, he won't bite.'

I kept my light on him, watching as he made a quick attempt to dry his eyes on the front of his T-shirt, then turned and shinned clumsily down. Most kids would have hung from a branch and dropped but he hadn't worked things out that far. He climbed all the way down and came over to me.

'Thank you,' he said and tried to shake my hand.

I didn't shake. 'What happened?'

'A bunch of Indians stole the car, They put me out here.'

'Here?' I played dumb. 'How in hell did they drive here?'

'Close,' he said. 'There was a trail. They were talking Indian. I couldn't understand. Then they opened the car door and shoved me out. I was lost. It was dark. And the mosquitoes. Oh my God.'

'No sweat. I found the car. This is a popular fishing spot, I've found stolen cars before up here. And I figured I'd take a look for you, in case you'd wandered off and got lost.'

'I heard a bear,' he said. 'There's bears here.'

'Yeah. Lots of them. Well, I can take you out now, or I can leave my dog keeping you up that tree and go away. Which would you like?'

'Take me out,' he said. 'You wouldn't leave me, would you?'

'Why should I help you? You haven't helped me.'

'I will. I promise I will.' He was almost wetting himself with fear.

'I'll think about it.' I sat down on a log, keeping my light on his face. 'Depends on you. Now tell me where you found the car you came to the Harbour in yesterday.'

'On a side-road, you know, off the highway. We were down there in that old heap of Eric's an' we knew you would recognize it if we came back. So we were looking for another car and we found one.'

'Unlocked with the keys in it?'

'No. It was locked. But Cy, that's one of the kids, he's done things with cars before. He said guys sometimes leave cars with the key hidden somewhere. It was up the tailpipe.'

That meant the car had been left for a second user.

'Could you show me the place where you found this car?'

'It was on Ellis Lane. I remember a signboard when we came out again.'

'And you left the car there?'

'No. Cy drove it away. He knew where he could sell it, he said.'

He continued to talk but I was thinking. I'd seen the car after supper at the motel where I'd found Hanson.

'What time did you find the car? The wagon?'

'Around noon. We used it to come back to your town for the swarming.'

I was working it out. Perhaps this Cy had been in cahoots with Hanson, had been another plant, maybe another actor. He had taken the car to get away from the gang and return it to Hanson. After all, I had seen the car at the motel late at night. In fact, maybe Cy knew in advance where the Magic Wagon would be hidden, knew that the keys would be with it. Which meant I had to find him and talk to him.

Freund was anxious to come clean. It was a good sign and I was still learning from him, so I let him continue.

'And Cy had gone by then?'

'Yeah. I told you. Like, most of us were just out for laughs. But he was looking to make some money. I mean, he's bad.'

'So are you. You killed a woman's dog, pushed her down, and then went and trashed a store. Is that your idea of a laugh?'

He bit his lip. I kept the flashlight on his face, even though it was starting to grow light around us. He probably wasn't aware of it in the glare. After a moment he spoke, in a trembly voice. 'I didn't want to. Really. But the kids were on my case. They said I shouldn't be the leader. Cy knew about cars. He had more guts'n me. When he came back he should take over. I had to do something heavy.'

'She'd had that dog twelve years. It was a member of the family just about, and you prove something by whacking it with a club. I ought to walk out and leave you here.'

'Don't do that!' He almost screamed it. 'Don't leave me here! I'll make it up to her. I promise.'

'I can't let you off.'

He gave at that point and wept like a baby for about a minute. I turned the light off and stood up. George's treatment had worked, maybe better than it needed to. The kid had started out with a low opinion of himself and now he felt like a hole in the ground. But I was a half-inch further ahead in the case.

'Where's the wagon now? The one you drove to the Harbour in.'

'I don't know. The guys were going to pick me up later, like, after I'd had a beer. Like, even killing the dog didn't impress them. They dared me to go in the bar in Murphy's Harbour. They said I wouldn't have the guts to go into your town and break the law again. I had to do it. They went off somewhere. They were going to come back for me and then we were going home.'

'You keep saying "they". Who do you mean? Was Cy back by then?'

'Yes. He was driving. He said he'd pick me up after and we'd all go home.'

That gave me a first entry to my search for the mysterious Cy. 'So Cy set up a rendezvous with you, before he left?'

'Yes. He said to pick him up at the Honey Harbour road. He said he knew a guy there who would buy the car.'

Honey Harbour is close to the motel where I'd found the old Ford. Probably he'd returned the car to Hanson and then walked the half mile back down the highway. I asked him, 'What does this Cy look like? What was he wearing?'

He gave me a pretty thorough description and I noted it and then asked my last question. 'Where's home?'

'I live in Toronto but I'm staying at Wasaga Beach. That's where we were all from, What must've happened is the guys came back and found out about you busting me and they took off there with the car.'

'Let's go.' I stood up and moved out, using the light for the first part of the way to check on the trail I'd left. Within a couple of minutes we were back at the roadway and I left the light off and marched briskly back to the car.

He kept up with me, taking the occasional little extra step to stay alongside. I threw him a question. 'What does your dad do?'

'He doesn't live with us. My mom's a lawyer. She's gonna kill me.' He was calm again now but frightened down to the soles of his feet. 'She's big on animal rights. Always talking about fur coats and experiments and stuff like that. When she hears what I did, she'll hit the roof.'

'And then you'll feel almost as bad as Mrs Horn did yesterday. That's almost fair. Add in a couple of hundred hours of community work and you'll be close to paying back what you owe.'

'Oh God,' he said and then nothing.

We reached the car and this time I sat him in the front. He didn't need any further humiliation. He'd grown up overnight.

He showed me where they had found the wagon. It was a lonely section of road, half a mile from the lake shore and with no cottages around it. I knew there was a cluster of them at the bottom end but this wasn't in my jurisdiction and it was still too early to stir up a bunch of holiday-makers. I decided I'd tell Holland and let the OPP men make a canvass to see if Jeffries and the woman had been down there. Probably not. Jeffries and Moira Waites had most likely changed cars here. And that meant they could be anywhere at all.

As I headed back to Murphy's Harbour I thought about Freund. He needed help. He wasn't goint to get it from his mother. She'd provide expensive legal counsel for him to hide behind but he'd never be free in his own head unless he stood up for himself now.

'Listen,' I said at last. 'I know the woman you hurt. She's a good person. I figure if you went to her and apologized she'd drop the charges against you.'

'Go and see her?' His mother had done a job on him. He sounded terrified.

'If you face up to her you're facing up to what you've done. It'll be over. Otherwise you're going to feel like a dork every time you look in the mirror.'

He didn't speak for a long time. Then he said, 'All right. Could you take me there, please?'

'Sure. She lives on the Reserve.'

His head whipped around. 'You mean she's an Indian?'

'Didn't you notice when you were shoving her over?'

'No. I mean, she looked just like anybody else.'

'Right.' I said. He had a lot to learn and Jean Horn would be a good teacher. I said nothing else until we pulled up in front of their neat little bungalow. It's not fancy by city standards but it's tidy and Jean has as much garden as she can squeeze out of the sandy soil. It was full of tomatoes and corn and cucumbers and Jean was out there weeding, the puppy gambolling around her feet.

She stopped and looked up as I drove in. 'Recognize her?' I asked and Freund nodded, gulping quietly.

'Her name is Mrs Horn. Go and talk to her.'

I sat there while he got out and went up to the gate, moving slowly, gathering his courage. She straightened up and looked at him without speaking. He went over to her, inching carefully between the rows of vegetables, watching his feet at every step. Then he stood in front of her, his back to me so I couldn't see his face. I watched Jean. She said nothing for a long time then bent down to pick up the puppy and I saw Freund make a swipe at his eyes with his sleeve. She handed the puppy to him and he stood stroking it, letting it lick his face.

After a minute or so Jean took the dog back and set it down, then came over to the car. I got out. ''Morning, Jean. Whaddya think? About the charges?'

'If I charge him, he's got a record,' she said. 'Forget it.'

I stuck my hand out to her. 'Thanks, Jean. I know where George gets his heart from.'

She shrugged and shook hands. 'He says he wants to make it up to me. I don' want his mother's money.'

'Looks to me like the house could use some painting,' I said 'And I know Peter would sooner be fishing.'

She laughed out loud. 'Guess where he is now?'

'Have the kid do it. He'll feel better for it.'

'I'll ask him,' she said. 'I got some coffee on. Had breakfast?'

'Not yet.'

'Come on,' she said. 'An' let Sam out, if the puppy won't rag him too bad.'

I let Sam out and she put the puppy down and it went crazy with delight, circling and yapping at Sam, trying to get a game started. I rubbed Sam behind the ear. 'Go on,' I said and he knew he was off duty and played with the puppy as if it were his kid brother.

Freund had come out of the vegetable patch and he came up to us. He looked a little more comfortable but without any of the smugness he'd shown the night before.

I looked him in the eye. 'Mrs Horn has agreed to drop all charges,' I said. 'But there's a condition attached.'

'I don' mind,' he said eagerly, then, 'Thank you, Mrs Horn. I was a jerk.'

'Yeah. Well how are you with a paintbrush?' I asked him.

'Never tried,' he said, surprised.

'This is where you learn. The house needs painting.'

'I'll get the paint,' Jean said. 'I don't want money off you.'

'When can I start?' He looked as if he'd just won the Oscar.

'After breakfast,' she said. 'Come on. You need to wash up as well an' I'll put some alcohol on those scratches.'

He turned his head away for a moment, composing himself. 'Thank you,' he said.

I went in after them and Jean brought the puppy inside so that Sam could get a rest. He needed it. A puppy will wear out any full-grown dog the way a toddler can wear out an adult, I thought, and pondered my own future. Life was going to be busy.

We washed up and Jean painted the kid's scratches with rubbing alcohol and she made a big breakfast. It was a treat for me as well. Fred had been watching her weight the last month or so and meals had become fairly spartan around our place. She had offered to cook me other things but I'd said no, and hadn't done it myself because I know she's got a good appetite of her own and I couldn't expect her to stay on a diet if I was living it up.

At around seven I drove back to town, leaving the kid with Jean Horn who was going to start him scraping the house before painting. He had a couple of days' work ahead of him and he looked very pleased with the prospect. He said he was going to ring his mother first, before she left for her office. Apparently he was supposed to be staying with friends at Wasaga Beach. The friend was some college kid whose own parents commuted to the cottage at the weekend, so there had been no panic about his being away overnight. But now it was time to check in and let his mother know what was happening. He wasn't too pleased with the protest but I figured it would be easier than it had been to confront Jean Horn.

The bait store was open and I had a word with Perrault, then checked the rest of my properties, looking for breakins. We don't get many, even in summer when the town is swollen to five times its size with holiday-makers, but this morning we had.

The back door of the grocery was open. It hadn't taken much. The door must have been the same age as the rest of the building and was dried out and brittle. Somebody had put their shoulder into it and forced the rusty old hinge screws out of their sockets.

I told Sam 'seek' and sent him in ahead of me, knowing it was an unnecessary precaution. The break-in had been done overnight no doubt and the guy was long gone.

Sure enough, the place was empty. The cash register had its drawer hanging out, as it was always left overnight and the safe in the front window was in place. Nothing seemed disturbed but I rang the owner and waited until he showed up five minutes later.

He looked around and swore, then checked to see if anything was missing. 'If it's candy it was kids,' he told me. 'But I don't see kids busting the door in. They just shoplift.'

'How about food?' I asked him. 'Any of that gone?'

He looked at me, eyes narrowed. 'I'll check. Hold on.' I followed him as he went around the food section, a tiny deli counter and a display of cheeses in the dairy case.

'Yeah,' he said at last. 'There's a coupla salami and a box of good Cheddar gone. And some bread. How did you guess that?'

'There's an inmate on the run from Joyceville,' I told him. 'I've got an idea he's up around here somewhere. It could be him.'

It was Kershaw, I figured. He had found his way to Murphy's Harbour and I wondered when he would find his way to me.

CHAPTER 9

There wasn't much to go on. The store has so many people through it that there was no way Sam could pick out the shop-breaker's scent. I tried it anyway, letting him sniff where the man must have stood to rifle the two food counters and he did it, then led me to the owner who was

standing at the back door, checking the damage. I tried
Sam again at the back door but he couldn't pick up a scent,
so I gave up.

The owner was angry. 'Sonofabitch. Twice in two days.
My insurance is gonna go crazy,' he said. 'Lookit. Forced
the door right off the goddamn hinges.'

'Get a steel door put in,' I advised him. 'I'll try to find
this guy and if and when I do you can go after him for
damages. But he won't have any money or he wouldn't
have been stealing food.'

'You're right. Dammit. I'd sell this place if anybody'd
buy it off me. Hell, Chief. This is too much. You gotta keep
a better lid on things. Two losses in one day. That's not
why we pay a police chief.'

'If it makes you feel any better, I've caught the kid who
did the swarming yesterday, He's over at Horns', painting
their house. He said he'll make the damage good.'

'Well, I guess that's something,' he said grumpily. 'Sorry
I sounded off.'

'Sorry about the crime wave. But I know who I'm looking
for. If I find him I'll get him to pay for the damage.'

'Yeah. OK.' He waved me off. 'I know you do a good
job. It's just I'm thinkin' why me? OK?'

'OK. See you later, Jack.'

I called Sam and went out to check the rest of the properties. Nothing had been touched. I was especially careful
around the liquor store. Kershaw hadn't been the one who
got the bottle of Scotch the night before and after five years
inside he would want a drink. But the locks were all in
place, so I drove down to the station and went in.

The phone rang almost immediately and I picked it up.
'Murphy's Harbour Police.'

'My name is Mrs Freund, may I speak to an Officer
Bennett?' No please.

'I'm Bennett, Mrs Freund.'

'My son just phoned. I find he's been coerced into doing manual labour for some family of Indians.'

There were so many things to argue with that I didn't bother. 'Did he tell you why?' I asked politely.

'He said he'd got himself into trouble and the woman was letting him do this for her instead of preferring charges.'

'Did he tell you the nature of the trouble?'

'Nothing she wants to prosecute him for, so it can't be much. I feel this is some ruse to obtain his labour. Why should a boy be permitted to demean himself in this manner? That's what I want to know.'

'You think work is demeaning?' Two can be as snooty as one.

'In case you haven't heard about it in your township, Canadians have certain civil liberties.'

'And in case you haven't heard about it in Toronto, assault of a woman, plus other offences, is enough to get even a first offender a criminal record.'

She shouted now. 'I want to speak to your superior.'

'I'm the Chief, Mrs Freund. What's your complaint?'

'My complaint is that my son has apparently been tried and found guilty without a hearing.'

'If you'd like a hearing I'll be glad to arrange one. Come on up to the police station at Murphy's Harbour and you can conduct your own. Unless you persist in your attitude, Philip will get off without a criminal record. How does that sound?'

There was a long silence. Her pride was all banged up but she was an intelligent woman. 'What are the precise charges?'

'Didn't your son tell you?'

'His exact words were "I pushed a lady over and did some other things".' Her voice became lower. 'What kind of things? Were they sexual?'

'No. They were not directed at any person. But they were criminal. The plaintiff has very generously agreed to drop the charges. She doesn't even want money. Instead she has agreed to let him work out his indebtedness. He's glad of the chance. I know him fairly well by now. Maybe better than you do in some ways.'

That didn't sit well but she swallowed her anger. 'I'll be up there at noon. Will you be there?'

'I'll try, but I'm in the middle of a homicide investigation. I'd prefer it, and so would your son, if you just stayed where you were and let him work things out. He'll be a better man for it.'

'He's just a boy,' she almost screamed.

'Today. Tomorrow he'll be a man, a better man if he does what he's set out to do.'

'That's a matter of opinion.'

She was weakening but she sounded like a reasonable person. 'This has to be your call, whether or not to let him continue. I hope you'll consider your actions very carefully and bear in mind that he's got feelings of his own.'

She put the phone down without speaking and I hung up and called Parry Sound. Sergeant Holland was in his office and I filled him in on the location where the Magic Wagon had been found. We mulled things over carefully for a while and decided that we needed to speak to Cy, the gang member who had known about cars. 'I wish we hadn't let that Hanson guy go so fast,' Holland said. 'No choice, of course, but it's starting to look like he knows something about the Jeffries woman. I'll ring Toronto, have one of their detectives chase up Hanson there. And we'll look for this Cy.'

'I've given you the description. It matches one of the kids I saw in town first time the gang came here. The Freund boy may be able to give you something more. He's over at the Reservation, painting the house for the woman whose dog he killed.'

'You figure you can trust him?'

'Yeah.' I hadn't give him any details, the fewer people

knew about it, the safer George's reputation would be in future. None of the Indians would say anything, that left the secret with me. I wanted to keep it that way.

'Well, I'll send a couple of guys down to Ellis Lane to talk to the locals. On the way down there they can talk to Freund.'

Hearing him speak the name triggered my memory with a click. 'Freund? Isn't that the lawyer who sprung Hanson yesterday?'

'Yes. Dammit, I must be asleep. How can I get in touch with her? You got her number?'

'No. But she's coming here at noon. And you can call the Horns and get her number off her son.'

'I'll take care of it,' he said. 'I want to talk to Hanson. Should have kept him in custody but we couldn't.'

'OK. I'll leave it with you. I've got a lot on my own plate here. We've got a shop-breaker in town and I figure it has to be a fugitive. Seems to me we may have that guy Kershaw up here. Plus I'm still waiting for the guy in the next room to Waites to make a statement. I'll head up to Pickerel Point Lodge and talk to him.'

'OK. I'll keep you posted when we hear from forensics in Toronto or if we round up this Cy kid, or Hanson.'

I thanked him and hung up feeling useless. Detective work is largely a matter of sifting reports, of questioning dozens, even hundreds of people and looking for patterns of similarity in their stories. It's easiest when you have dozens of men asking the questions and a computer to compare their findings. Alone, I was going to be lucky to find anything useful in the Waites case. And I was starting to worry about Kershaw. I had a feeling he was my shop-breaker and that he was holed up in the bush close to town, waiting for a chance to get even with me. By now he might have picked up a gun somewhere so he could stay back out of sight and drop me when I wasn't expecting it.

The prospect was scary but I spent two whole years in

Viet Nam under the same threat and had come out intact except for busted-up arms from the booby-trap that had killed the guy ahead of me on the trail. I'd also been shot since, the last time a year ago. But now I had a family to consider. That made it different.

I spent a while on the telephone, first calling Joyceville for a current picture of Kershaw. The only one they had was his admission photograph, five years out of date at least but they promised to fax it to me. I could photocopy it and spread it around town, that might help a little. I also phoned Fred in the hospital. She was waiting for the baby to be brought around for her morning feed. She sounded bright and cheerful but admitted that she didn't feel quite as energetic this morning as she had the day before. I arranged to visit her in the afternoon, then left the station, turning the phone to the radio.

I drove around the town first. It was a picture-postcard morning. The sunlight was lying over everything like gilt on antique furniture and people were moving slowly, muscles slackened by the warmth. The kids were rambunctious, of course, a bunch of them were running and swimming on the tiny beach beside the marina and the usual teens were impressing one another beside the bridge. I drove over and up to Pickerel Point.

The guest I'd wanted to talk to was in the lounge. He asked me to come outside and I thought he might have something to say that would be important. He had not called me, he admitted, because he was embarrassed. I had to reassure him that what he said would be kept in confidence before he allowed that he had not been in his own room at all that evening. He had been elsewhere.

I looked at him, a lean city-dweller in his late fifties, brown from his week of fishing but nervous. He was going through a divorce, he explained. He had come to the lodge to fish, nothing more, but he had struck up a friendship with a lady, he used the word with care, he was obviously smitten and wanted to keep her out of any hint of scandal. She was divorced, younger than he by some considerable amount, etc, etc. It's one of the older stories in the world but he figured he'd written it for the first time so I went along, then quietly checked with his date.

She wasn't a bombshell, a quiet, pleasant woman in her forties, a birdwatcher, she said, who had come here for a few days' birding. Everything checked out so I thanked her and wished her luck and left, driving idly around the lake road, examining all the empty cottages. There are a number, even in the height of the season, which stand empty all week. This was Friday morning and the owners would be coming up from Toronto after the rush-hour for their weekends. In the meantime I wanted to be sure that nobody had broken into any of them, especially now that we had a shopbreaker in town. It would have been ideal for him, the perfect place to lie low for a couple of days. He would be on the move by now, ahead of the owners' return, but if luck ran my way, I might find where he had stayed and track him with Sam's help.

There were only a few. I'd covered them all earlier in the week but I tried the doors and checked around again. There were no broken windows or signs of any forcing having been done so I went on until I came to Ms Tracy's place.

Her car had gone. She might have retreated to Toronto, I thought, or perhaps just gone out for a while but I parked the car and got out, bringing Sam with me.

The air-conditioning was still humming in the back window so it seemed as if she was still in residence. The verandah was open but the front door was locked and there were no signs of anything having been forced. I would have headed back to the car except that Sam began to growl. Most owners immediately shush their dogs, but that's a civilian reaction. I just stood back and watched him for a moment. It might have been a skunk or porcupine under the house, that would have triggered him, but he didn't make an approach. He growled low in his throat for about a half minute, under the rear window where the air-conditioner kept humming. And then he slowly tilted his head and howled, so softly that it was almost imperceptible but it made the hair stand up on the back of my neck. It was his response to something I wasn't hearing or seeing. And whatever it was, it was inside the cottage.

I told him 'Good boy' and went around the place again, checking the doors. They were locked and I stood for a moment sniffing for smoke. Fire would have upset him. Or perhaps Marcia Tracy had left her radio on and they were playing some song that had high-pitched tones in it. If that was the case, it would end in a little while and so would Sam's reaction.

I went back and checked him. He was still howling. Then he stopped and barked sharply. And that was the deciding factor. I'd seen him howl at music before, but nothing had ever made him bark. He was hearing something that his training told him was trouble.

I didn't wait any longer. The back door had a glass pane in it and I took out my stick and knocked it in. The noise was shocking but Sam did not react. He continued to howl, and then bark. I stood at the broken window and looked in. I was looking into the kitchen. Nothing seemed out of place and I stood and listened carefully, hearing nothing at first, and then, very faint, a human noise, a moan.

I whistled Sam and reached through to unlatch the door. There were bolts in it, in addition to the lock and I had to lean in over the broken glass and tap them open with my stick. Then I let Sam in and followed as he bounded out through the kitchen door and straight to the back bedroom.

He bounced on stiff legs, barking furiously. I was a second behind him and saw what had distressed him. Marcia Tracy was lying naked across the bed, unconcious and bleeding, her face a swollen mask.

'Easy,' I told Sam. 'Good boy.' He relaxed and I gath-

ered the woman's arms to her sides and wrapped her up in
the bedclothes. She made no sign of awareness so I left her
and called Dr McQuaig. He was out, at the hospital in
Parry Sound, but his wife was home and she's a nurse. She
said she would come right over and warned me not to try
to give the woman anything to drink or to move her. I was
to call the ambulance at once. I know enough about first
aid for her advice to be redundant but I said OK and
dialled the ambulance number. The dispatcher told me they
would be there in half an hour. Next I phoned the Parry
Sound OPP and gave them the licence number of the missing Mercedes which I had in my notebook from two days
before. The driver should be approached with care and
should be held, I told them. Also the arresting officer should
take a good look at the man's knuckles and check for blood
on his clothing. The corporal said he would put it on the
air and I hung up and went to look in on Ms Tracy and
see if she was moving.

She wasn't conscious but she was breathing and I bathed
her face with cold water, hoping she would come around.
She didn't and I knelt there, hopelessly, sponging her face
and waiting for Mrs McQuaig. She arrived in five minutes,
a rangy, capable Scotswoman who swept in and knelt
beside me.

'The poor wee thing's taken a pounding,' she said. 'Was
she like this when you found her?'

'Out cold. She's naked under the bedding.'

'Had she been raped?'

'I've no idea. I covered her up right away to keep her
warm.'

'That was guid,' she said in her soft Highland voice. 'She
was punched,' she said firmly. 'I've seen the same injuries
at Glasgow Royal on a Saturday night often enough. The
man who did it has marks on his knuckles, most like. Any
idea who it is?'

'There was nobody here. If you'll stay with her I'll look

around, see if he left anything left that Sam can get a scent from. But her car's gone. He likely took that.'

'Do it,' she said. 'If she comes to I'll call you.'

I left her and looked around carefully. Not much seemed to have been touched in the place. Ms Tracy's robe and a nightdress were lying on the floor at the entrance to the bedroom. The nightdress was a practical-looking item of flowered cotton. She had not been expecting an assignation, I judged. It was torn at the throat, the way a man might have ripped at it in his haste. On the kitchen table I found the remains of her breakfast, a coffee cup and half a grapefruit. There was no second cup and the kitchen was neat. It looked as if she had been finishing breakfast when the man arrived. It had not been a social call or she would have taken down another cup, the percolator was full.

I checked her purse. It was turned upside down on the couch in the living-room, the contents, cosmetics and her cheque-book, lying there. Her keys were gone and there was no money or credit cards. Whoever had attacked her had robbed her and gone. He may have raped her first, we wouldn't know unless the doctor at Parry Sound took a swab, but judging by the torn nightdress I figured the attack must have had a sexual content.

I led Sam back into the bedroom and let him sniff around the rug and the end of the bedclothes, then turned him loose with the command 'Track'. He ran to the front door and when I let him out he went directly to the point where I had last seen her car parked. Then he stopped and began casting around. I watched, wondering if he would find the man's arrival track. If he had come out of the woods I would follow him back to see where he had come from, probably the place he had spent the night. There might be something there that was useful. But he only went a few yards further down the driveway and then doubled back to the front porch.

I put him over it again and he repeated the performance,

step for step. It meant that the man's track began and ended on the driveway, which meant he had come in a car, which again meant that he had not been alone, someone must have driven off after leaving him here. In my eyes that meant that Kershaw had not been the guy.

As I stood there I heard the wail of the ambulance siren coming up the road and I waited and waved them in. The paramedics jumped out and got their gurney and a board. One of them was a big serious-looking woman and she led the way, bossing the other one with a succession of curt commands. He was an older man, around fifty, and he followed her without a word, rolling his eyes at me helplessly.

'In the bedroom,' I told them and they trotted in and took over from Mrs McQuaig.

'Did you find her?' the woman asked her.

'No, Chief Bennett did.' Mrs McQuaig narrowed her eyes. She was used to respect and this woman wasn't giving any out.

'Was she like this?' The woman asked as she strapped an oxygen mask on Ms Tracy's face.

'I wrapped her up and wiped her face. I have the swab here.'

The woman unwrapped Ms Tracy and she and her assistant carefully got the board in place, supporting Ms Tracy's neck and wrapping her carefully in their own blankets.

'Are you coming with us?' the woman asked. So far her assistant hadn't uttered a word.

'Yes. I'll follow in the police car. Use your siren and get her up there pronto.'

'We'll do our job. Just do yours,' she said.

I picked up the swab, a bundle of paper towels I had used to wipe Ms Tracy's face with, and went into the kitchen for a plastic bag. 'You won't need that,' the woman said bossily.

'You do your job and leave mine to me,' I said.

She snorted. 'Come on, George, we haven't got all day.'
She led the way with the gurney.

I turned to Mrs McQuaig. 'I want to be there when she
comes around. Could you do me a favour please and wait
here until I get back? I want to fingerprint this place later
and I don't want anyone else in here.'

'What if the guy comes back?' She asked the question
without fear, the way she might have asked for a weather
forecast.

'Wait in your car on the road. If anyone drives in, get
the licence number and drive to Pickerel Point and call
me on the phone. Same thing if anyone goes into the
bush behind the house. If there's no answer, call the
Parry Sound OPP. I'll be back in about an hour. It's a
lot to ask, but could you take it on, please? I don't have
anybody else.'

'Sure,' she said grimly.

'Thank you, Alice.' I touched her on the shoulder and
left with my plastic bag in my hand, and took off after the
ambulance.

The man was driving, taking out his frustration, I
guessed, wailing his siren and winding the ambulance up
pretty good for such a narrow road. But speed was important, I had a lot to do once I'd spoken to the doctors and
installed an OPP man at the hospital to speak to Ms Tracy
when she came to.

We sped up the highway and reached the hospital within
twenty minutes, faster than I'd driven it with Fred on her
way to Emergency. There was a doctor waiting for us and
he took charge at once. I followed him into the examining
room, carrying my plastic bag.

He worked quickly, checking her vital signs, then sending
her in for a head X-ray. While we waited for the plate I
had a chance to speak to him. 'These are the paper towels
I used to wash her face. If the man who did this cut his

knuckles, his blood may be here as well. Is there any way of checking the group?'

He was young and had the oddly cropped beard that you usually see only on Mennonites, an earnest guy. He took the bag in one hand and looked at the bloody mess inside. 'It won't be simple but I'll try. I'll only use part of it for my test. If I don't get anything we can send the rest to the forensics place in Toronto.'

'Thank you, Doctor. Also, I want to speak to her as soon as she comes to.'

'Right.' The X-ray technician brought in the plate she had just exposed and he nodded thanks and clipped it on to a light board. He looked at it for a long time, then shook his head, puzzled. 'I'm not a neurologist but I can't see anything wrong, structurally.'

'What does that mean?'

He looked at me, tapping his teeth with his right thumbnail. 'It means that the wounds are superficial. And in every case like that I've ever seen that means she should be conscious by now.'

'You think she should be able to talk to us now?'

He nodded thoughtfully. 'I think maybe there's something else, like, say, she's ingested something that's anæsthetized her.'

'Like what?'

He pondered some more. 'It's impossible to say. She doesn't smell of alcohol but other than that it could be any kind of depressant, an illegal drug of some kind, maybe heroin.'

I thought about that for a moment, remembering how reluctant she had been to talk to me. 'Is there a chance that she's just acting unconcious so I can't talk to her?'

'Is that likely?' He frowned now. In a rural hospital like this he wouldn't have treated many crime victims, he wouldn't know how suspicious a cop can be.

'It's a possibility. There's a lot going on down on my

patch, her ex-husband was murdered there and she's involved in a couple of things that make me suspicious.'

'Well then—' he straightened up and flicked off the light on the panel—'we'd better check that out.'

CHAPTER 10

As a former hockey player I'd thought the doctor might have used smelling salts under her nose to bring her around, but he wasn't about to do anything so rough and ready. Instead he went back to her and leaned over, close to her ear, and said loudly, 'Can you hear me?' He repeated it a couple of times, then glanced up at me and said, 'I don't think she's conscious,' and to her, 'I'm going to take a sample of your blood to test for drugs. You'll feel a little jab.' He swabbed her arm and took a vial of blood, wiped her arm again and put a Band-Aid on the mark.

A nurse came in and took the blood sample away. I told him, 'There were signs of a scuffle at the scene, Doctor. I think she might have been sexually assaulted. Can you examine her for that, please?'

'If you like. Turn your back,' he said primly. When the nurse returned he told her, 'Betty, I have to make a test to see if this woman has been assaulted. Get a swab, will you, please. In fact, get three of them, we'll do this right.'

I turned and stared at a blood pressure machine on the wall until he said, 'All right, Officer.'

I turned back and he nodded. 'There are signs of recent sexual activity. It doesn't necessarily signify violence but it may.'

'Can you label the swabs for me, please? I'll have to send them to forensics.'

'Right.' He sent the nurse for plastic bags and he marked each swab and I initialled and sealed them in his presence and hung on to them. He said, 'I'm sure she would never have allowed me to take those swabs if she were conscious. That's good enough for me.'

I held up one hand. 'You're the expert, Doctor. I'll ask the Parry Sound guys to leave a policeman with her. When she comes around she can talk to him.'

'Good. In that case I'll get her assigned a bed. She'll probably be in the intensive care unit if you want to leave now.'

'A detective from the Parry Sound unit is going to meet me here. I'll stay with her until then.'

There was a tap at the door and he called, 'Come in.'

Holland came in. ''Morning, Dr Baer, 'mornin', Betty. I'm here to talk to Chief Bennett, can I take him away a while?'

'Of course.' The doctor seemed relieved.

The nurse smiled and said, 'Chief Bennett. You're our new father, aren't you?'

'Yes. I'd like to visit my wife after I've spoken to Sergeant Holland, if that's OK.'

'I'm sure it will be.' She didn't seem hung up about visiting hours.

Holland led me outside. 'Let me get this straight. That woman's the ex-wife of this Waites guy?'

'Right. Someone beat her up, raped her probably, then locked her place and took the car.'

'Could be this Kershaw guy who's on the lam from Joyceville. He's not been picked up yet.'

'If it is, he's with someone else. Sam tracked him to the driveway and lost him. He must have arrived by car.'

He scratched his chin, making a rasping noise where he'd missed a few whiskers that morning. 'You sure set a lot of store by that dog's nose.'

'He does a good job, never been wrong yet.'

'Yeah, well. We've got the car on the air. When'd you think this happened?'

'She'd had breakfast but hadn't washed up yet. So the guy hasn't had more than a couple of hours.'

'That's a hundred, maybe a hundred and fifty miles. Hell, he could be half way to the States now.'

'The guys at the border would find him if he tries to cross. I specified that in my call. Also I've mentioned that her credit cards are missing.'

'Have you reported that?'

'No. I came right up here as soon as the ambulance arrived. I'll take a minute and do it next.'

'Good. That could get us somewhere. If the guy's dumb enough to use the card.'

We talked a little longer and he promised to have a uniformed man detailed to sit with Ms Tracy and take a statement when she came around. In the meantime there was nothing else to do but notify the credit card companies that her cards had been stolen by a man we wanted on a major felony charge. With their computer working for us we would soon have a location if the thief tried to use one of the cards.

The companies were easier to deal with than the government. But not by much. I wasn't sure which cards she had and I was forced to do some bullying before the clerks at the other end of the line would tell me whether she was a customer. And then I had to speak to supervisors before I could get them to promise cooperation if the cards were used. It took half an hour before I was free to go upstairs to visit Fred.

She was dozing when I got to the room and I sat by her bed for about ten minutes before she opened her eyes with a start and saw me. She wasn't so limber today but she was just as cheerful as ever and we went around to the nursery and looked at the baby, who was asleep. It was pleasant, feeling like a civilian for a few minutes, and I tried to keep my mind off the case I was working on but Fred soon saw through me.

'You've got a lot on your mind, haven't you?' she said as
I took her back to her room.

'Yes, there's a whole complicated case going on right now
at the Harbour and I'm up to my rear end,' I admitted.

'First things first,' she said. 'Why don't you go back down
there and get on with your job? I'm fine here. I'll be out
tomorrow and we can take it from there.'

I found out what time I could pick her up and she kissed
me gently and I left, dropping in on Ms Tracy's room on
the way out. She was still unconscious but there was a
policeman with her, reading a paperback book. He had a
tape-recorder with him and he seemed a capable guy. I
chatted with him for a minute, giving him a few details that
would help him to talk to her, then left and drove back to
the Tracy place to relieve Mrs McQuaig.

She was sitting in her car across the road from the Tracy
place, listening to classical music. Nobody had come back,
she told me and I thanked her and she left.

I took the fingerprint kit out of my car and went inside,
leaving Sam to 'keep' outside. He picked himself a shady
spot under a tree and sat there, watchfully.

Now I had time I examined the house properly, seeking
anything I might have missed in my haste to get Ms Tracy
to hospital. First I checked the kitchen. She had probably
been here when the man arrived, eating her grapefruit. I
tried to put myself in her place. She had been alone, otherwise two coffee cups would have been in use, so she must
have heard the car drive up and gone to the front door.
Then she must have recognized the caller. Otherwise she
would not have let him in. She was alone, in her housecoat.
After the things that had happened at Murphy's Harbour
in the last couple of days most women would either have
ignored a stranger until they had got dressed or else spoken
to him through the closed door. That meant her attacker
was no stranger to her.

That much was good news. When she recovered consciousness she could give us a name. Dandy. I could issue a warrant for the guy and when we got him it might even help in my search for Waites' killer, or the man who had beaned Mrs Jeffries and stuffed her into the trunk of the Waites Honda. Maybe.

In the meantime I did the job thoroughly. First I examined her housecoat and nightgown for blood traces. There were none. So the attacker had stripped her first, possibly raped her first, before he beat her up. On that thought I examined the bedding. There was blood on the pillows and the top of the sheet but it was only smears, there was no spotting as there might have been if the attack had taken place as she lay there. So I looked all around the room, and then I found bloodstains on the wall beside the door. I checked the height, remembering how tall Ms Tracy was, about five-eight. The marks were an inch or two lower, as if someone had rammed her head into the wall.

I thought about that for a long time, putting the fact together with the placement of the injuries on her face. It made sense. The upper part of her face had the worst damage, mostly around the eyes.

There didn't seem much for it but to wait until she woke up and gave us a statement, but in the meantime I dug out a few flakes of bloodstained plaster board and put them in an evidence bag. I also made detailed notes of the location of the bloodstains and entered them in my notebook, together with a sketch of their appearance. Then I examined the bed again and this time found bloodstains on the heavy old alarm clock on the bedside table. There was a fingerprint on the glass, clearly delineated in blood. I got my kit out and lifted it on tape, then dusted the rest of the clock, finding another print on the back.

Next I checked the bathroom and the kitchen for signs that the man had washed his hands there after the attack. Unless he had been crazy that would have been his logical move before leaving the house. I found nothing visible.

Perhaps a forensics team might, in the sludge of the U-trap under the sink, but that was out of my league so I concentrated on trying to pick up other prints. I lifted a set off her coffee cup and then her lipstick cartridge and then had to admit I was stumped. There was nothing else I could do on my own.

Before I left I called the hardware store on the highway and had them send a guy up with a sheet of glass to fix the back door. I also asked him to bring a padlock and hasp for the front door. Without Ms Tracy's keys I would have had to leave the place open if I was to look in here again before she returned.

He came right up, a chatty kid of about nineteen who tried to find out what happened. I told him the place had been broken into and the owner had asked me to install a lock. That satisfied his curiosity. Break-ins don't happen often but he just muttered about goddamn kids while he quickly and efficiently closed the place up. By the time he had finished it was noon and I drove back to the police station with Sam.

There was a Cadillac parked outside with a woman in it. Mrs Freund, I remembered. I got out and went over to her. 'Sorry if I've kept you waiting. I had another emergency this morning.'

She didn't acknowledge my answer. 'Where's Phillip?' she asked.

'He's up at the house he's painting. Does he know you're coming?'

'I thought you would have brought him here as you promised.' She was glad of the chance to attack me, but my shoulders are broad. If you want popularity you join a rock group, not a police department. I looked her over. She was forty-fiveish, smartly dressed in a linen suit, carrying a briefcase. She was handsome rather than pretty, a brunette, heavier than she might have been for her height but attractive for all that. Her appearance shouted 'money'.

'I've just been investigating an assault case. It took precedence over our rendezvous. Come inside, please.'

I unlocked the station and led her inside. She looked around contemptuously but said nothing. I let her through the counter and offered her a chair. She shook her head but I sat down anyway. I was in charge here.

'What, precisely, is my son charged with?'

'At the moment, thanks to the generosity of the woman he assaulted, there are no charges outstanding. However, if you choose to open all this up again, he faces a slate of charges.'

'What are they?'

'Assault, first, as mentioned. He pushed a middle-aged woman down on the ground. Secondly, drinking under age. Thirdly, theft and public mischief. Fourth, having a weapon dangerous to the public peace. Fifth, and this one won't sit well with you he tells me, causing unnecessary pain and suffering to a dog.'

She went pale under her tan. 'What happened, Officer?'

'Why don't you sit down, Mrs Freund?' I suggested again. 'Would you like a glass of water?'

'No, thank you. I don't need water,' she said but she sat, holding her briefcase on her lap.

'Your son got mixed up with a youth gang,' I told her. 'It's a gang I very much want to track down because it's involved with another case. The leader of the gang is Eric Hanson, the man you represented in Parry Sound yesterday.'

She was startled. 'Hanson works for a client of my firm. He's in his twenties, far too old to be involved in some kid stuff gang business.'

'He's dropped out of sight. I want to talk to him. Do you know where he was going when you had him released?'

'No. But the Parry Sound police have his Toronto address. That's good enough, surely.'

'He's not there, we're told. I wondered if you knew where he might have gone.'

She shook her head. 'I represented him at the bail hearing. Acting on the facts as I saw them, I was able to get him released on his own recognizance. He's to show up again for a court appearance on Monday next. I expect he'll be there. In the meantime I imagine he's taking some time to think things over.'

'I hope you're right. But in addition to the charges against him he's the guy behind your own son's trouble.'

'How so?' Her face was grim. She would be a tough opponent in court, I imagined.

'He's auditioning for some film part. He put together a gang of disaffected kids. Twice over the last two days they swarmed properties on Main Street here. On the second occasion, your son was carrying a baseball bat with which he killed a dog. The owner tried to hold him but he pushed her over and assisted in the swarming of the store before she could get up to help. He got away. Then later he came back into town and went into the beverage room where he was drinking beer when I arrested him.'

She pursed her lips, breathing heavily. I waited for her to speak. When she did it was so low I could hardly hear her. 'This would never have happened if he had a real father.'

'It would never have happened if your son had not been ripe for recruiting. And what makes it all the more complex is that the film this Hanson is trying to get into is one your client, Ms Tracy, is producing.'

'I know nothing of her work. She was John Waites' client. I merely acted for him as he was on vacation.'

'You know he's been murdered?'

'I learned that yesterday at the police station in Parry Sound. It was a shock to me.'

'I think maybe Hanson can help us understand what's going on. And just to complicate things further, Ms Tracy was assaulted this morning. She's unconscious in Parry Sound hospital.'

'Good God.' She shook her head as if the information had wedged itself somehow in her receptors. 'This all makes Phillip's problems seen very small.'

'They can be small. If you just let him go on the way he's going today. He's making amends and building some self-confidence.'

'You know these people well, do you?'

'Very well. Their son's a lawyer with the Crown Attorney's office in Toronto. They're exceptional people. I'd trust them with anything.'

Surprisingly her next comment wasn't about the tangle of problems around us. She spoke very softly. 'It hasn't been easy, bringing him up on my own.'

I wanted her help. Maybe she could find Hanson for us, or get Ms Tracy to fill us in on whatever was going on. I chose my words carefully. 'I think you'll be comforted to know that he's changed from the first time I met him. I think he was trying on the rebellion thing and he's found it doesn't suit him. He's a changed boy.'

Without warning she started to sob. It was so out of character with her businesslike clothes and manner that I was startled. I got up and handed her the office box of tissues and then went out to the cells and ran her a glass of cold water. By the time I brought it back to her she was in control of herself and she took the glass gratefully and sipped. I sat and waited until she set it down and spoke again.

'I've been on my own with Phillip since he was twelve,' she said. 'I do what I can but there's no male example in his life. I know it's not healthy but what can I do?'

'What happened to your husband?' I didn't really care but it seemed like a humane question. I figured she would chat for a few minutes and then I could shoo her back where she'd come from so that her son could keep on painting and growing himself some backbone.

Her answer shocked me. 'He was a criminal,' she said. 'He was sent to prison for ten years.'

'Does Phillip know this?'

'No. I told him his father had left me and we moved away from the area where we'd been living before. None of our neighbours knows any more than I've told them.'

'That's five years ago. Your husband should be getting out soon.' I wondered what he'd done. Ten years is a savage sentence for anything less than murder. He must be a hard case. Maybe her concern was for the fact that he would be back on the street in the near future.

'We're divorced now.'

'Then your only concern has to be your son.' Way to go, Dear Abby. 'If you like I can take you up to see him, but if you want my honest opinion, it would be better if he stayed there until he's finished his job. A couple of days should do it.'

She blinked a couple of times before speaking but her voice had regained its strength. 'You seem like a very sensible man. If you believe this is best for him, I'll go along with you.' She stood up. 'Thank you for being so considerate. I take it that you personally have dropped the drinking under age charge?'

'Yes. It's trivial, most kids try it.'

She held out her hand and I shook it as she went on. 'I'd like to compensate the woman. What do you suggest?'

'She told me that she didn't want your money. She's pleased that Phillip came and apologized to her and she's happy to have her house painted. I'd leave it at that.'

'Perhaps I might pay for the paint?' She badly wanted to do something tangible but I knew Jean Horn better than she did. 'I think the best thing you could do is write to her. Thank her for dropping charges and for giving your son a chance to make amends.'

She considered that for a moment and then nodded. 'Yes, that sounds best. 'Now, what about the stores my son swarmed?'

'They don't want to press charges but they're business people and they lost money.'

'Where are they?' She was toughening up again now, facing the fact that she would look bad over the next little while, the mother of a delinquent.

I told her and she said, 'Will you tell Phillip that I came to see you? Tell him to call when he's finished his work and I'll pick him up.'

'Will do. And might I ask you a favour in return?'

She was at the door. 'I think I can guess. You want me to let you know if I learn the whereabouts of Hanson.'

'Right. And if you should talk to Ms Tracy, perhaps you could ask her to be more helpful. She knows personally now that this business is serious.'

'I won't be seeing her, I have to go back to court this afternoon. But if I can help, I promise I will.'

'Thanks very much, Mrs Freund.'

She paused with one hand on the doorknob. 'It's not Mrs. It's Ms Freund. I dropped my husband's name when he went to prison.'

'Good idea,' I said. She seemed like a sensible woman, obviously successful, in charge of herself. She didn't need the handle some criminal had hung on her.

'I thought so,' she said. 'And I never liked the name Kershaw anyway.'

It knocked the wind out of me. 'Kershaw? You mean George Kershaw, The guy who was sent down for bank robbery in nineteen eighty-five?'

'Yes.' She looked at me very hard. 'And I did follow the case even then, Officer. And I know he was arrested by a man called Bennett. Was that you?'

'It's a small world,' I said and thought that it was getting smaller by the hour.

'I understand he made a break from a day pass,' she said.

'We'll get him and he'll be back inside for the rest of his sentence.'

She didn't answer right away and I wondered if I'd offended her, but at last she said, 'I hope so,' and left.

After she was gone I sat down to think about the case. Something more than coincidence was at work here. I pulled out a piece of paper and drew a bunch of circles, one for each of the names involved in the case, Waites, Tracy, Hanson, Cy, Freund/Kershaw jr, Kershaw sr. Each of them was linked to at least one of the others. Then there were Mrs Waites, the vanished woman, Mrs Jeffries, the first victim, and her husband the store-keeper. They were all part of another, secondary group, tied to the first by the presence of Waites.

It was tantalizing but it proved nothing. What we needed was to sit down with one of the principals and ask questions. So far that wasn't possible. Waites was dead. Marcia Tracy was dead to the world. Hanson and the other kid, Cy, had vanished. The case was cold and getting colder.

It's four years since I worked in Toronto, I quit after the scuffle with a bunch of bikers that saw me arrested for manslaughter and cost me my marriage, but I've maintained contact with some of the detectives I used to deal with and now seemed a good time to renew auld lang syne.

I tried Elmer Svenson first but he was out of his office so I rang my old partner, Irv Goodman. He works in the fraud squad and spends a lot of time in his office, going over the books of companies suspected of some kind of scam. He answered the phone cheerfully and asked how things were. 'Must be nice, sitting around in the sunshine. How's Fred? She had the baby yet?'

I filled him in and he wished me *mazel tov* and after I'd inquired about Dianne and the kids we got down to busi-

ness. 'I've had two homicides here and they're tied in with
a kid in Toronto, an actor.'

'Name?' Irv doesn't waste time.

'Eric Hanson, born Kowalski. He lives with a woman
called Hanson who works at CBC. The address is Apartment 3065, 413 Delaney, do you know it? Seems to me that
used to be a parking lot.'

'Not the last two years, it's a chi-chi condo now, lake
views and all that good stuff. What's he done?'

I filled him in and he asked a few questions, until he had
the facts shuffled in his own way. Then he said, 'What are
you doing?'

'I'm waiting for the Tracy woman to come round. She
might be able to tell us something, although there's no
guarantee that the guy who beat her up has anything to do
with the case. I just figure he might.'

'Anything else about Hanson might be useful?'

'Yeah, he was driving an old Ford, licence number 197
HKH, registered to a guy called Patton, in Scarborough.
That might help.'

Irv noted the number and then said, 'Even if you find
him it still sounds like a long shot. What are the OPP
doing?'

'They're trying to trace Jeffries and Waites' wife, widow
now, I guess. But from what I make of it, those two're holed
up somewhere, could be they've got the blinds drawn and
they're jumping on one another's bones, not knowing
what's going on, or maybe they're part of this and they're
hiding out.'

'And what do you want out of Hanson? Haven't the OPP
called out detectives to check him out?'

'Maybe. But I want to know how come he roped in the
Kershaw kid for his gang. That can't be pure coincidence.'

'You think Kershaw did the killings?'

'It's a good bet. Waites could have sprung Kershaw and
asked him to kill his wife. Kershaw killed the wrong woman.

Then somebody, maybe Kershaw, killed Waites. All that would make its own kind of sense, but I can't understand why this Hanson kid would drum up a gang that just happened to include Kershaw's son, and use the gang to make trouble in Murphy's Harbour.'

Irv was silent for a long time but I didn't add anything, At last he said, 'So it figures that Hanson is part of the scam, whatever it is, maybe a trick to keep you occupied while Kershaw does his thing.'

'Sounds screwy, I know, but there has to be a pattern here.' I hadn't mentioned Kershaw's old threat to me but Irv has a long memory.'

'What I remember of Kershaw, he was planning to get even with you when he got out, that right?'

'They all say that.'

'Yeah.' Irv was thoughtful. 'But they don't all walk away from day passes at the same time that a whole other thing is going down where you live. I'd watch your back for a while, old buddy.'

'Sam does that for me, but thanks for the warning.'

'Yeah, well, I haven't had lunch yet so I'll grab a couple hours, go talk to this Hanson, or his lady if I can't find him.'

'Thanks, Irv. There's times I miss having a load of other guys on the team.'

'You wouldn't miss this bullshit,' he said devoutly. 'I haven't seen the sun all week, been hanging over a bunch of books since last Friday, that's eight days nonstop.'

'Your own fault for getting an education,' I kidded and he laughed and hung up.

I was busy for the next hour, parcelling up my evidence, the swabs and fingerprints from the Tracy case, and arranging to ship them to the forensics centre in Toronto. Then I drove out to Kinski's gas station from which George's car had been stolen the night before. Paul said he would hand the package to the express company driver and asked if I'd found George's car. I told him yes and he shook his head. 'Goddamn Indians. Ask me, you can't trust any of 'em.'

'No harm done,' I said. 'I found the car, not a scratch on it. Those kids yesterday ripped up the seats and stole the tape-player, this wasn't touched.'

He'd been expecting a full agreement but he grunted and left it at that. I went from there to the Horns' house. George's car was in the driveway but I could see Phillip painting the house, doing a neat job on it, not slopping the paint or getting himself messy. And the house was growing brighter by the minute.

He stopped when he saw me and waved with his brush. 'Hi, Chief, whaddya think?'

'Looks good,' I said. Sam had come with me and Phillip came down the ladder and patted him on the head. Then he looked up at me and asked the hard question. 'I just found out that my lawyer is Mrs Horn's son. Did you know that?'

'Yes.' Tell the truth and shame the devil my father used to say.

He shook his head ruefully. 'Jeez. Am I dumb! I thought he was doing me a favour.'

'He was. All the charges have been dropped. I was just talking to your mother.'

'What did she say?' He was nervous again now, his acne blooming.

'It's all over. She isn't going to interfere. She said she'd pick you up when you called that the job was finished.'

'I don't think I'll get it done today,' he said. 'Mrs Horn says I can stay here tonight.'

'How do you feel about that?'

He was angry now, at himself. 'I feel like a jerk. That's how. These people are nice.'

I laughed. 'You're not the first guy to feel that way. I was a hell-raiser myself at your age.'

'Yeah?' He seemed relieved. 'Like, what did you do?'

'I took my dad's car on a joyride when I was fifteen. Went off the road and dinged the hell out of it.'

Now it was his turn to laugh. 'What happened?'

I shook my head. 'The old man was one of a kind. He was madder'n a snake but he didn't hit me. He made me work with him until we'd got it back into shape. Then he picked up some parts from God knows where and helped me build a dirtbike to ride until I was old enough to drive.'

'He sounds like a great guy.' The boy looked wistful. 'You still see a lot of him?'

'He was a miner. The stope collapsed on him and his partner the year I turned eighteen.'

The boy's eyes filled with tears. 'Aaah, hell.' he said.

'Listen, I wanted to ask you a couple of questions, about these other kids you were with. You mind talking?'

'No. I already spoke to the OPP guys.'

'OK. I've found out that Eric, the sparkplug of the gang, he's an actor, he's older than he looks, twenty-eight. I figure he's trying out for a part in a movie and he put the gang together for some kind of experience, research, whatever.'

He thought about this without speaking for a while. 'I'm trying to remember how it was,' he said at last. 'Like, I was hanging around the beach, scoping out the girls, you know. Only none of them would talk to me. I was from somewhere else. They were all local. You know how it is.'

I nodded and he went on, 'So anyway, there were three of us guys, I guess I was the oldest. We hung around together and then this Cy kind of tagged on.'

'Had you seen him around before?'

'No. He just turned up one day and hung around. He made us laugh. Said the broads were all a bunch of dogs, we'd likely get AIDS or herpes if we went with them.'

The police text on the genesis of gangs came back to me. A company of rejects. Bull's-eye. 'So how long was it before Eric showed up?'

Phillip thought for a moment. 'Not long. Next day, I

guess. He drove up in an old clunker, that Ford we were driving, remember? Cy started calling him names and Eric karate-kicked him, knocked him over. Then he picked him up and asked if we'd like a beer. So we said sure and he took us in his car and bought a two-four and we all had a couple bottles. That was the first day.'

'Then what happened?' It sounded more and more as if Cy had been an accomplice. The karate kick could have been an actor's trick, delivered on cue, with no force but seen as terrible if the guy on the other end fell over. I didn't think Hanson knew martial arts. He hadn't seemed competent on either of the occasions I had tangled with him.

'That was two days before we came up here. The next day we kibitzed around on the beach at Wasaga, like, we broke up the volleyball game and just generally acted like goofs. Then Eric said this was boring. Why didn't we head off somewhere and have some fun.'

'And that was when you drove up to Murphy's Harbour? Did you stop anywhere else on the way?'

'No, except to buy some beer. Like, I was bored with the drive. There's all kinds of places we could have stopped but Eric said he was looking for the perfect place. And he pulled in here.'

'Did he say why Murphy's Harbour was perfect?'

'Yeah. He said there was just one cop here, we wouldn't have any fuss with police.'

So he'd done his homework. 'Was Cy his number two man?'

'No.' Phillip ducked his head. 'No, like, Eric said I should be his lieutenant. He said I was smart and Cy was dumb.'

'And what did Cy say about that?'

'He kinda sulked but the other kids called him crybaby so he just shrugged and said, OK, go on, see if he cared.'

'Did it ever occur to you that the two of them, Eric and Cy, had set this thing up between them?'

Phillip thought hard about it, rolling his lower jaw forward the way some people do when they're concentrating. 'Come to think of it, yeah. The day after Eric kicked him, Cy took his shirt off and there was no bruise on his chest, where the kick landed. The kids saw it and they all said he was—' he hesistated and said—'you know, a pussy, that Eric hadn't hurt him at all. But now you say it, maybe Eric really hadn't hurt him, maybe it was all some kind of show they were putting on.'

'Eric is an actor,' I told him. 'He's a professional. He gets paid to make people believe he's telling the truth when he says things.'

'Then maybe it was all a show,' Phillip said bitterly. 'And I fell for it and killed poor old Muskie for a coupla goddamn phonies.'

'I went and killed people in a war for a bunch of goddamn phonies,' I told him. 'But you can see why I want to find Eric, or Cy.'

'I'll think about it,' he promised. 'If I think of anything that can help you I'll let you know.'

'Good. It's important, Phil. I'm counting on you.'

It was one-thirty when I left him and I drove back into town and had a hamburger and Coke at the restaurant, then went back to the office to check the Fax machine.

The authorities at the prison had sent the photograph of Kershaw. It was less than perfect but it gave an idea of the general look of the man, together with a physical description. I pasted it down on a sheet of paper and typed, '*Wanted for escaping from custody and for theft. Believed to be in this area. If seen, do not approach, ring the police station at Murphy's Harbour or the OPP at Parry Sound,*' and put both phone numbers below.

The bank has a photocopier so I went in and made a couple of dozen copies. The manager took one and taped it to the wall where customers would see it and didn't charge me for the other copies. Then I made a circuit of town, leaving one in at the stores and bars and the marina and campsites and the two locks.

Around four o'clock I was finished and came back to the office and telephoned Holland. He told me Ms Tracy was still out but he had some results from forensics in Toronto. Waites had a trace of cocaine in his blood and an alcohol level that suggested he'd taken about two drinks. Death had been caused by the stab wound to the chest which had severed his aorta. The cut to his throat had been made first. It was bad but, given immediate treatment, he might have survived it.

'Anything on the fingerprints?'

'Nothing helpful. Whoever used the glass in his room is not on record. The only thing they'll say is that the guy who made the prints has smallish hands.'

'Does that fit with what you know about this Jeffries character?'

'I hear he's around five-nine and kinda scrawny. No idea of his hand size.'

'I'd sure like to talk to him. I wonder where in hell he's got to?'

'Well, he's not been seen down Ellis Lane. My guys turned it over down there. A couple of people had seen the grey car there, the wagon. It was seen eight a.m. yesterday morning and was gone by two in the afternoon.'

'I wonder if he went down there as soon as he left Parry Sound? Maybe had a rendezvous with another car and changed it there.'

'Yeah, well, how would the other driver have left? You figure someone would deliver a car and then walk away? The grey wagon was left there, remember.'

We both had ideas at the same time. I said, 'Maybe I could bring Sam up to the Jeffries house and pick up something with his scent on it. Then I'll have Sam track around at Ellis Lane. He might be able to show something we've missed.'

'Worth a try, I guess,' Holland said without enthusiasm. 'I was thinkin' maybe those kids have switched the licence plate on the grey wagon. I'm going to put it on the air that guys should check the licence of every wagon they see.'

'Right. Might be worth doing the same thing with Ms Tracy's Mercedes. If Kershaw took it, he'll change the plates for sure.'

'I'll get on it,' he said.

'Good. Meanwhile I've got a Metro Toronto detective checking on this Hanson character, see if he can shed a little light on what's happening.'

'Oh, that was the other thing,' Holland concluded. 'The package in his room was PCP, angel dust, and the same thing was found in his blood.'

We thought about it some more and promised to call each other if we got anything new. He also promised to send a man down to the Jeffries place and bring a pair of his shoes to the station in Parry Sound so I could get Sam looking for him.

When we'd finished the call I hung up and called Irv Goodman. He was pressed for time. 'The inspector wants my findings on these books by the morning, that's why I didn't call back. I was going to call around eight, when I'm done here. But I did find out two things.'

'Good, what were they?'

'Well, first, he and this Hanson woman split up a coupla weeks back. She doesn't know where he is. That's the big thing, so we're lost for a way to find him.'

'Pity, but OK, what was the second thing?'

'The reason they split up.' Irv said. 'Seems his lady found out he was having a fling with some other woman, a film producer. She, that's the girlfriend, figures it's just a professional thing. The producer is older than him, although that doesn't mean much, hell, this Hanson woman is forty-five if she's a day.'

'Professional—you mean he was sleeping with the producer to get a job?'

'Wait, I didn't tell you the best bit.' Irv chuckled. 'The job he's after is something about being the honcho of a street gang.'

'And the producer is Marcia Tracy of Northlands Productions.'

'Absolutely,' Irv said happily. 'How d'ya like that?'

'It's tying up tighter and tighter,' I said.

'There's one other thing, something I dug out of her accountant, guy I did a favour for one time. And this could be vital. It seems this Tracy woman is in financial trouble. She had a coupla successes, but that was a year or two back. Now she's had four stinkers in a row and she can't get backing for her new movie.'

I didn't mention George's version of the same story. 'So she's in trouble?'

'Big trouble. She's mortgaged everything to get this new movie off the ground. If it doesn't go through, she's in a hole.'

'I don't see how it fits exactly. But it's a damn good motive for what's going on up here.'

We jawed a while longer and I thanked him, then hung up and the phone rang again. 'Hello, is that Chief Bennett?'

'Yes, go ahead, please.'

'This is Dr Baer. The woman has come round. Can you come in and talk to the Parry Sound officer, please.'

'Be there right away. Thank you, Doctor.'

I ran for the car and wailed up the highway. At the hospital I went straight up to Ms Tracy's room. The doctor was there, and the constable, who nodded to me. 'She knows the guy,' he said. 'His name's Hanson.'

CHAPTER 11

I took my hat off and went over to the bed. Ms Tracy looked at me, moving her head painfully. 'I understand you found me.'

'My dog. He heard you over the noise of your air-conditioner.'

'Thank you,' she said.

'How are you feeling?' I wanted her to see me as the good guy, not the hardnose she had thought me earlier.

'I feel like death warmed over,' she said, and tried to smile.

'Nothing permanent's been done. The doctor will fix you up so there isn't a mark within a week.'

I sat down on the chair beside the bed and winked at the doctor. He took the hint and left. 'I'd like to catch the guy who did this to you. He belongs inside.'

'It was Eric Hanson.' She said it angrily. 'He raped me and beat me up.'

'We'll get him, I promise you. Tell me what happened.'

'I was just finishing my breakfast when he knocked on the door.'

'Was he alone?'

That made her frown. 'Yes, why do you ask that?'

'Did you hear a car drive up before he knocked? Or did you get the impression he'd walked?'

'I didn't hear a car.' The question has confused her. I wondered whether she had rehearsed her story or was still not functioning properly. 'Why do you think he came in a car?'

'It might have helped if I knew, that's all. Go on, please.'

'Well, he came in and I asked if he'd like a cup of coffee

but he said no. He wanted to know if I'd finished casting
my movie.'

'And what did you say?'

'I told him yes and he asked if he'd got the part he was
angling for. And I told him I still hadn't made up my
mind.'

'Were you telling him he hadn't got the job?'

She frowned and the effort tugged at the plasters on her
face, making her gasp with the shock. I waited and at last
she said, 'He's too old. There's an American boy, a dancer,
if I can get him he'll be perfect for it.'

'And what happened then?'

She turned her head away on the pillow for a moment
and when she looked at me again there were tears in her
eyes. 'He got angry. He started to shout at me and I told
him to leave.'

'And then what?' I asked the question gently, as if I
believed those tears in her eyes were real. Her story was
coming out too well, as if she had rehearsed it. Tears might
have been part of the rehearsal. Drama was her life's work,
after all.

'And he attacked you.'

She nodded dumbly, then wiped her eyes on the edge of
the sheet. 'He and I had been close before. He'd always
seemed so courteous.'

'What did he do?'

'He grabbed at me and called me a bitch. He said I'd
only wanted him for sex.' She sniffled. 'He said I was too
old to get a man for myself, that I used my position to take
advantage of young men who would never bother with me
otherwise.'

'And then what?'

'Then he tore my nightgown off and pushed me down on
the floor and raped me. He kept on asking how I liked being
used, the way I'd used him.'

It was possible but she was telling it too well. I've talked to a lot of women who've been assaulted. They don't lay things out as straight as this usually.

I played along anyway. 'Nice guy. And did he beat you up then?'

'Yes. While he was, you know, on top of me, he was hitting me.'

'Did you hit him back? Is his face marked?'

'I tried but he held my hands. He's very strong.'

I heard a movement behind me but I didn't turn, I wanted her to think that her story had my whole attention. Then Holland came and stood the other side of the bed. He said nothing and she ignored him and went on.

'And what happened then? Did you pass out?'

'I guess so,' she said. She looked away, at Holland, and then back. 'I'm not sure. I was hurt. I think he picked me up and kind of dragged me through to the bedroom. I don't remember.'

'Did he hit you with anything other than his fists?'

She shook her head regretfully. 'He hit me again but I was numb, I don't know whether he used anything else. Is it important? Look what he did to me.'

Holland was anxious. I could feel his excitement across the space between us but he didn't speak, he's a professional, this was my investigation.

'Did you know he took your car and rifled your purse, took whatever money you had and your credit cards?'

'I passed out,' she said and then, 'Look, I'm thirty-seven years old. I've been through a lot in my life but I've never had anything like this happen to me before. I was in shock.'

'OK. Thank you for your help, Ms Tracy. We've already put out a description of your car as being stolen. We'll circulate Hanson's picture. Do you have one at your house?'

'No.' She seemed sure of that. 'There's one in the file in my office in Toronto. Or you can get one from his agent. I gave you his name yesterday.'

'I'll get right on to it,' I said. 'You'd better rest now.

We'll leave the policeman here so you'll feel safe. Then tomorrow, when you're rested, maybe we could talk about this some more.'

'Oh God,' she groaned. 'Oh well, I guess so, if you must. I just want you to catch him.'

'So do we, Ms Tracy. Thank you for your help.' I stood up and smiled at her, then nodded to Holland who took the hint and came out of the room with me.

'Got the bastard dead to rights,' he said happily. 'Description, complaint, hell, we can even get a photograph.'

'She's lying,' I said.

That stopped him cold. 'Lying? Don't look to me like she's lying.'

'That's not the way the attack happened. If it was an attack.'

'What are you smokin'?' He was angry. 'What makes you so all-fired sure she's not telling it like it was?'

'Couple of things. First her story. It's hard to believe a guy could hold both her hands and rape her at the same time he's punching her in the face like that.'

'It's possible,' Holland said. 'He's a big kid. I saw him. He's six feet anyway, one seventy-five.'

'Sure it's possible. But I've seen the room where it happened. There are no bloodstains on the floor where she says she was attacked, but there's blood on the wall at face height. Whoever attacked her rammed her head into the wall a few times. She'd have remembered that. And there's blood on the alarm clock next to her bed. Somebody hit her a few licks with that for good measure.'

'But like she said. She was dazed, she doesn't remember.'

'Ask the doctor, if you like. He said he couldn't see any clinical reason why she should have been unconscious when she came in. She may be faking this whole thing. There's a chance that Hanson did call on her, that he did even drive away in her car. He may even have screwed her but I don't think a few clumps in the head in the middle of all the sexual activity would account for her being so dazed that she didn't remember having her head banged into the wall later.'

Holland wasn't convinced. He cocked his head thoughtfully. 'What's your version, then?'

'I think she's lying. I'm not sure why. Could be that Hanson got snaky when she told him he hadn't got the part he was after in her movie. He may even have raped her, although a lawyer would get him off. According to my latest update, he's split up with his steady girlfriend over his affair with this woman.'

'So he's her boyfriend.' Now Holland understood what I was saying. 'They had an argument. He threatened to get nasty so she wants to get him sent down, just to punish him.'

'Exactly. It's even possible she banged her own face on the wall a few times, maybe even hit herself in the face with her clock.'

'But then what? You say the house was all locked up. Would she have locked herself in, where nobody would find her? That doesn't make sense to me.'

That was a fact which had bothered me as well and I turned my full attention to it. 'Maybe she didn't intend for me to find her,' I thought out loud. 'Maybe she was expecting some other guy, someone who would have found her banged up and gotten mad and taken after the guy she said had done it to her.'

'Yeah, but what about her car and keys being missing?' Holland was coasting now, shooting down my theory with cold hard facts. 'You mean she drove her car off somewhere, dumped her keys and money and then came back to her house and banged herself around so some strange guy, some Mr X, would feel sorry for her and climb on his white horse and go out to set things right? Come on, Reid. That's not the way it works.'

'I've sent the clock and some prints I found to Toronto for comparison. I'll know better when I hear back. Meantime we should find Hanson. He's tied up in this whole thing, the Jeffries killing, this assault, recruiting the Freund kid into a gang. I want him.'

'Put him on the air, then,' Holland said. 'And chase up this agent of his, get a photograph.'

'Right.' I recalled my reason for driving up here. 'Did you get something from Jeffries' place for my dog to track from?'

'Yeah. There's a pair of running shoes in my car. You want 'em now?'

'May's well. I'll make the calls. Could you leave them for me, please?'

Holland chuckled indulgently. 'This is a good scam you got goin', Reid. Whenever nothing's breaking, call in the dog and take a nice long walk in the fresh air.'

'He earns his keep,' I said. Sam had done more for me than the entire OPP in my years at the Harbour.

'OK. Call from the front desk. I'll see you there.'

We went out to the front and I made my calls. First to the OPP office to circulate Hanson's description and then to Toronto to ask the Headquarters detectives to pick up his photograph from his agent and get it out to all police departments on the Fax. Holland came back while I was calling and dropped a pair of running shoes in front of me in a plastic grocery store bag. They were pretty funky and I figured Sam would have no trouble picking up Jeffries' scent from them.

I glanced outside and noticed that the sun was low. I had only about an hour left before dark but I didn't leave right away. I went upstairs quickly to have a word with Fred. It didn't seem right to leave without doing that. She was lying back on the bed, but she sat up happily when I came in. I kissed her. 'Hi, love. How are you feeling?'

'Can't wait to come home,' she said. 'The nurse tells me

I'll feel weak for a day to two but I can do that at home, can't I, just as easily as I can here.'

'What time can I spring you?'

'Any time after nine. Can you make it?'

'Hey, no sweat. I've even cleaned the place up.'

'Made our bed, I guess you mean.' She smiled. 'You need to make up the crib and all the other things. There's three of us now.'

'Bossy,' I said. 'You rest up and I'll be here at nine.'

She winked at me and I left and went out to the car, carrying Jeffries' running shoes.

By the time I reached Ellis Lane and found the spot where the grey wagon had been parked it was dropping dark. But I took my flashlight out of the glove box and then gave Sam a good whiff of the shoes and set him loose. He ran back and forth with his nose to the ground and finally came to a point about twenty yards off, where he stopped. It was as I'd thought. Jeffries had left his car there and driven away in something else. So that was one good theory proven, to no advantage. I fussed him and let him try again but he just covered the same ground, so I called him off and drove back to Murphy's Harbour with him on the front seat and the bag with the running shoes in it between us.

As I drove I found thoughts coming at me from every angle. I was responding to the road at one level and at another I could see Fred. And on another plane I was thinking about the case and realized suddenly that the running shoes next to me were small, no more than an eight or nine. The man who had killed Waites had small hands. The fingerprint guy had been sure of that. Maybe it had been Jeffries.

I headed for the second entrance to the Harbour and drove straight to the Lodge. Mrs James was surprised to see me but she opened the door to Waites' room and left me there with Sam and the pair of running shoes. I shut the door and took out one of the shoes. I gave it to Sam to sniff and then told him, 'Track.'

He put his nose down and began to run around the room. He went into the bathroom and barked at the edge of the tub and then he ran to the bedside where the depression in the pillows still showed where a man had sat, and barked again. And finally he checked and went over to the fire-escape rope that lay coiled in the corner, anchored to a bolt in the window-frame and barked again.

I called him off and fussed him as if he were a puppy, rubbing his great head and telling him he was a good boy while he whined happily. 'You're a better cop than I am, Sam,' I whispered. 'You've told me who killed John Waites. Now all we have to do is find him.'

CHAPTER 12

I took Sam downstairs and checked under the window. The scent hadn't lasted as well in the open air but eventually he tracked around the blind side of the building and out to the parking lot. Jeffries must have driven away from that point.

Mrs James was still working and she told me that nobody of Jeffries' description had rented the room that she could remember, nor had she seen him visiting. She would check with her staff.

It was a downer but I got a similar response when I phoned the OPP with my news. Holland was off duty and I had to talk to another detective. He wasn't excited. He was working on a break-in at a local gas station. It was small potatoes but he had a good chance of solving it. He promised to put my message on the air. It might help, he said, without enthusiasm. Reminding me that we didn't know where the guy was or what he was driving.

That thought sent me back to Ms Tracy's house. She had known Waites and his wife and the story of their marriage, maybe she also know the Jeffries in person. It was a slim chance but I was grasping at straws by now.

She was away so I gave up and drove downtown to check on the Friday evening activities. It was warm and the air was full of a smalltown charm that made you think of summer nights long ago when there would have been women in long white dresses enjoying the evening air and the sound of a mandolin ringing across the water. That night there were only the usual teenagers with a radio playing something by Reba McIntyre. I made my rounds of the properties, then drove home for supper.

I let Sam check around the place first and when he found nothing I went in and foraged. There wasn't a lot in the fridge but I made a sandwich and a pot of coffee and called the hospital. Fred was feeling good and we chatted while the coffee perked. She was excited about coming home and gave me a shopping list.

We said good night and I sat with my coffee, thinking about the case. There were four people who could tell us useful things. One of them would turn up soon, I hoped. The odds were good on Hanson. It was his ambition in life to be well known. He would show up somewhere. And Moira Waites would be back painting, trying to sell. Jeffries might be different. If he'd killed Waites he would be keeping his head down and might already have left the country.

That left Kershaw. I didn't know much about him beyond the facts of his arrest. He'd sworn to get even but that was talk. Now he was out he would put freedom above revenge, I figured. He could find work. As long as he didn't work for anybody who needed his Social Insurance Number for the payroll he could give himself a new identity and disappear.

But would he? I thought back to the arrest. He had been high on cocaine, his lawyer had insisted. Previously he had been of good character. I remember the smiles exchanged between the cops involved when his lawyer came up with that chestnut. But he had looked respectable enough, had come to court in a good suit and tie, looking more like a banker than the raving gunman I had been obliged to shoot. And his wife was a lawyer. What had driven him to holding up a bank? Cocaine was the easy answer but it didn't satisfy me.

On impulse I called my sister's house. She was in but Elmer was still working. He had a new shooting to investigate, some Vietnamese had shot down the owner of a restaurant in front of his customers that afternoon. She sighed at that and wondered what kind of city Toronto was turning into.

'World-class. Isn't that what the politicians keep boasting? Now you've got world-class crime to go along with the theatre and all the cultural stuff,' I suggested.

'I figure I'm too young to be pining for the old days, but I can't help it,' she said. 'Anyway, how's Fred and the baby?'

I told her they were coming home next day and she made approving noises and then Elmer came in. She put him on and he told me about the case. 'The witnesses swear the kid was no more than fifteen, sixteen. I'm telling you, Reid, it's the pits these days.'

'How about taking your mind off it for a minute or two?'

'You need some help,' he said. ''S long's I don't have to go out of that door again tonight, that's fine.'

'Just from memory, maybe. Remember this guy Kershaw, the bank robber on the lam from Joyceville?'

'Yeah, he's still out. What about him?'

'Well, he seems to be tied in to what's happening up here and I was trying to work out any connection. I know he held up a bank, shot the manager and took a hostage. I'm wondering why.'

'He was a cokehead, wasn't he?'

'Yeah, but he had a lot going for him. He was wealthy. He wasn't the kind of guy who would rob banks to support his habit. He would have pulled some white-collar scam, mortgaged the house, something.'

Elmer was quiet for a moment, then he said, 'Chuck Grady was in the detective office back then. I'll give him a call, see if he can remember anything.'

'That'd be good of you, Elmer. It would help if Chuck knew what Kershaw did for a living in those days, anything to give me a line on why he was robbing banks.'

'If I can get him tonight, I will; otherwise tomorrow morning, that be OK?'

'That'd be great. Hope it doesn't mess up your evening, what's left of it?'

'I don't have anything on. There's an AA meeting at nine but I'm too late now. I've started painting, ya'know. I never had a hobby in the old days and a lot of they guys say you need something to do, otherwise you start getting itchy without a drink.'

'That's not a problem any more, is it?'

'Been dry for three years by the grace of God,' he said 'But it helps take my mind off work. I'm just a dauber.'

'Then get daubing. And take care, OK?'

'You too,' he said and hung up.

As I was washing the dishes, the phone rang. It was Jean Horn. 'Hi, Reid, I wondered how Fred was, when she's coming home.'

I told her and she said, 'That's why I called. I was wondering if you'd like me to come over and smarten the place up before she gets back?'

'I've kept it pretty good, thanks, Jean.'

She laughed. 'I'm not talking about having the dishes washed. You need food and flowers. I'll bet you've got nothing in the fridge but a couple of cans of beer, am I right?'

'Well, I must admit, except for half a head of lettuce, yes. But Fred's given me a list.'

'You've got enough to do without going grocery shopping,' she said. 'How about I come by in the morning, around nine?'

'That would be very kind of you. I'll drop you off a key and some cash.'

'Good. Come by any time before ten and we'll be up.'

It was nine-fifteen so I drove over there right away. George and Phil Freund were outside under the porch light, filleting a couple of big bass. The kid was beside himself with excitement. 'Look at that, Chief,' he said. 'Three pounds. I caught him.'

'With a Fireplug, I bet.'

George laughed. 'You an' your plugs, Reid. I'm Indian, I don't use plugs.'

'Used a little frog,' Freund said happily. 'Caught the bait, then caught the fish. We're having it for breakfast.'

'Nice going,' I said. It was starting to look as if Eric Hanson had done this kid a favour when he brought him into the gang. 'I've come to see your mother, George.'

'Go on in. They're watching TV,' he said, still working with his knife. I tapped on the door and Jean called me in. She was in front of the television, knitting. The puppy was asleep by her feet. Her husband was across from her in his chair, head lolling as he dozed.

I gave her my spare housekey and some cash which she resisted at first, and then asked her about Freund. 'He's a good kid, Reid. I don't know why he did what he did yesterday.'

'His mother came up to see me today. She's been raising the boy on her own. His father's gone. She's not short of a buck, she's a lawyer, but there's been no man around to set the boy an example.'

'Him and George get on just fine,' she said. 'And he learns real well. He caught that bass out there.'

'His mother appreciates what you're doing,' I told her. 'And so do I.'

'Yeah. Well,' she said. 'You want some coffee?'

'No, thanks, I just had supper. I'm going to check around town again and then hit the sack, more coffee would keep me awake.'

She laughed. 'Better get all the sleep you can before Fred gets home with the baby. Then you'll know about losing sleep.'

'You're a big comfort. But thanks for the help. I know Fred will be grateful.'

I left, still worrying about the case. There was so much to do. Somebody should be canvassing every motel, every lodge and rooming-house for a hundred miles around, but the OPP didn't have enough men. The best they could do was a telephone cavass, missing half of the places for sure. We needed real manpower like I'd been part of in Toronto. There we could put a team of guys together to check everything, witnesses, past addresses, parking tickets, all the hundreds of tricks needed to come up with a lead. On my own I was like an ant trying to measure the pyramids.

I was glooming quietly when the break came, a phone call, switched to my radio. I took the mike. 'Murphy's Harbour Police.'

'Parry Sound OPP. Got something for you. A woman's been abducted from a motel on Sideline 12, the Bonanza.'

'I know it. When?'

"Bout five minutes ago. The owner says a man grabbed her and pulled her into a car.'

'On my way. Are your guys coming?'

'Yes. Be on the lookout for a small blue car. Driver around six feet, one-ninety, dark hair, That's all she had.'

'She?' If this was the missing woman's car the registration should have been on the check-in card.

'The owner. Says it looked expensive.'

'I wonder if it's the missing Mercedes?' I said. 'On my way.'

I hung up and hammered out along the side-road and back to the highway, heading south five miles to Sideline 12. It was too dark to check the colour of cars coming the other way. Maybe one of them was the car I wanted but I concentrated on getting to the Waterfall.

It was a middlebrow place, a long, low building set hopefully in a spot cleared of trees but otherwise devoid of attractions. A good place to go bankrupt.

A woman was standing in the middle of the lot, beside a suitcase which was lying as if it had just been dropped there. She ran towards me when she saw the flashing lights.

'Officer, he went that way.' She pointed back the way I had come. Nothing had passed me as I drove the side-road so I asked, 'What happened?'

'I was in the office and I saw a car parked out here. Then I saw a man running to it, carrying this.' She tapped the suitcase with her foot.

'Did he drop it and take off? What about the woman?'

'She ran after him, screaming. I couldn't make out what she was saying but she caught up with him and he dropped the case and hit her in the head.'

'Then what? Did you shout?'

Now she stopped, licking her lips nervously. 'Well, not exactly.'

'What did you do?'

'Well, I was robbed once, so I keep a shotgun under the counter. I pulled it out and fired it.'

I frowned inwardly. This isn't Dodge City, people don't use shotguns to keep the peace, but I was glad she had.

'Then what happened?'

'He just pulled her into the car.'

'Did he try to pick up his case?'

She cut the story to its bare bones. 'I shot again and he took off like a bat outa hell.'

She had broken the law but I wasn't going to cast the first stone. She might also have broken our case open.

'Did you see the licence? Any part of it, just one or two numbers?'

'He had his lights off, I couldn't see anything.'

'Did you recognize the woman?'

'It looked like Ms Baker from unit nine.'

'Let's look inside. Do you have a key?'

'Yes.' She pulled it out. 'What about this?' She nudged the suitcase.

'I'll put it back in the room. It figures he's stolen it from there.'

I picked it up with the flat of my hands. It was full and heavy but I managed and took it to the door of unit nine.

She tried the door. It was ajar. 'Don't touch it, please, and stay outside, if you would,' I told her and whistled for Sam. He was at my side in an instant and I shoved the door with the back of my hand and told him 'Seek'.

He snaked by me and around the bed, which was unmade. On the far side he checked and began barking, his head low to the ground.

I followed him in, taking a moment to shove the bathroom door open and glance in. There was no light but the room was small and I could see that it was empty. Then I turned to Sam and saw what he was barking at. Beside the bed lay the body of a small, bearded man, head lolling on a broken neck.

CHAPTER 13

The owner asked, 'What is it?' in a nervous voice.

I whirled to her. 'Don't touch anything. Stay there, please.'

'What's going on?' Her voice was shaky with fear. 'Something smells bad.'

'There's a body here, it's a man. Stand outside, please.'

She gave a low, frightened wail and stepped out, holding on to the doorjamb for support. I crouched and felt for a pulse in the man's neck. There wasn't one, of course, but the body was still warm. I hushed Sam and stood up, looking around at the room. The bed was unmade. There were a few personal things, women's lotions and a hairbrush, on the chest of drawers. A brown grip with the lid flopped down stood on the canvas stand in the corner. I looked in and saw it was full of women's clothing. That reminded me of the other case and I went outside and brought it in, again lifting it with the flat of my hands on either side so as not to get prints on it. I stood it beside the door.

'Can I use your phone?'

'It's at the office.' She was breathing fast and shallow, hyperventilating. But I needed answers. 'What did he look like?'

'Big. Your size. I couldn't see his clothes except that he had dark pants and a light shirt. He wasn't wearing a jacket. And I think he had dark hair.'

'Thank you. Now relax. Hold your breath for a while if you can.'

She drew in a big breath and held it as she led me to the office. I ran ahead of her and dialled the Parry Sound OPP.

The man on the desk told me they had two cars on the way. One of them a patrol car, should be there any moment, the other had the inspector in it. That was good news. It meant they had jumped the same mental hurdle I had and suspected that the affair was tied in with our homicide investigations. 'Get on the horn. Tell him there's a dead man here, looks as if it could be Jeffries. And the guy who did it is around six-one, one-ninety. He has dark hair, a light shirt, dark pants, no jacket.'

'Will do,' he said.

I looked up at the owner. 'Can you remember anything at all about the car?'

'It was blue, I think. But it was too dark to tell properly.'

'Dark blue, light blue?'

'Dark. A small sedan, looked foreign.'

I passed the information on to the dispatcher and hung up. The owner had settled down again now, here in her own familiar surroundings. I put her more at ease. 'Play down the shotgun when you talk to the OPP. You're not supposed to use it, but I'm glad you did.'

'It didn't stop him taking her,' she said ruefully.

'The case he left behind will be useful. We'll find him. Now, could you tell me your name, please?'

'Joyce,' she said, 'Joyce Graham. What do you want to know?'

'OK, Joyce. What did the woman look like?'

She hadn't seen the woman herself but remembered from her daughter who had registered her that she had arrived alone, without a car, saying a friend had dropped her off and that her husband would be in later. That had been the previous day.

'Can I talk to your daughter, please?'

'She's at a party, I'll call her.' She picked up the telephone.

'Don't say anything about the body. We don't want a crowd of people here cluttering the place up.'

'Right.' She dialled and when the phone was picked up I could hear the music through the phone from four feet away. She had a tense little conversation with the daughter, who didn't want to come home, but eventually she agreed and Mrs Graham hung up. 'She's on her way.'

'Fine. Now tell me, have you been into the room at all since yesterday?'

'No. I offered to clean up this morning but they told me they didn't want it, so I left them alone.'

'Them. Did you see the man?'

'Yes, a little guy with a beard. He said his wife was in the shower. Polite but not friendly if you know what I mean.'

'Did he sound American?'

'Yes, Michigan or some place, I thought.'

'And did they have a car here?'

'No. I wondered how he'd got here but they'd paid for two days in cash so I didn't push it.'

I stood a moment, thinking. It was no use rushing back down to the highway. The car had a twenty-minute start. It was up to the OPP to stop it. Maybe they'd put road-blocks out if they could spare the manpower, but even if they did, he'd probably turn off when he saw the line-up and vanish down some side-road. In daylight it might be possible to find it from their helicopter but until then he was lost to us.

'I'm going back to the room,' I told her. 'There's a couple of cars coming. Show them the room, and let me know when your daughter gets here.'

'Right.' She nodded. 'I'll put some coffee on.'

I went back to the room and looked at the body. Whoever had killed him had been strong; aside from that, no clues. But the suitcase drew me. Jeffries, if this was Jeffries, had been killed for the case. What was in it?

I heard a car siren and went to the door of the room. The car pulled up in front of me and a woman officer got out. I could see that a number of the doors had opened now and anxious-looking people were poking their heads out.

The policewoman came over. I knew her slightly and said, 'Hi, Elaine, step in.'

She came in. 'I heard there's a body.'

'Over here. Mind where you step.'

'Right.' She followed me and looked down at the body. 'That's Stu Jeffries,' she said. 'I was in his store once to get a picture framed.'

'The woman with him was taken away. The guy was after that suitcase.'

'Wonder what's in it?' She looked over at it, glad to look away from the body.

'When the inspector comes we'll open it. For now, the best thing we can do is canvass the other units, see if any of them saw anything.'

'Right. I'll start at the far end. Can you secure this place and take the other end?'

'Yeah.' I stepped out after her and placed Sam in front of the door, telling him to keep.

I went to the other end of the building and checked with all the occupants. They were all anxious to help but in the end they had nothing new to contribute. They all mentioned hearing shots and one of them said that there had not been a car parked in front of unit nine. So Jeffries and the woman had been stranded here. It made me wonder who had dropped them off. Had someone picked them up from where they had left their Magic Wagon and brought them here? Another mystery.

Elaine and I met to compare notes, just as the inspector arrived, a guy called Dupuy, a good copper. He was driving the car and he had the crime scene man with him. Stinson looked as if he'd been dragged out of a party somewhere and there was a smell of beer on the night air, but the inspector wasn't commenting.

Elaine and I were briefing them on what we'd found when a car pulled in and a young woman got out. The motel owner was standing in the shadows and she scurried out and brought the woman over to us. 'This is my daughter, Aileen, she was here when Ms Baker checked in yesterday.'

Dupuy took over. 'Thank you for coming to see us, Aileen. What can you tell us about Ms Baker? What did she look like? Did you see anybody with her, any visitors?'

It turned out that the girl didn't know much more than

her mother had already told me. She had a description of the woman, who sounded like a twin for the body I'd found in the car trunk. The only thing she could add was that she had an American accent. That gibed with what I'd heard about Moira Waites.

Dupuy left Stinson to talk to the woman and we went to the room. He wrinkled his nose. 'Smells like his bowels gave out.'

'His neck's been broken. It happens, I guess.'

We went and looked at the body. Dupuy crouched and checked the angle of the neck. 'It would take a strong man to do that.'

'Kershaw, the guy on the lam from Joyceville, I'm sure he's up here. His name has come up in my inquiries. This could have been him.'

'What makes you think that?' Dupuy asked, not looking at me, his eyes flicking around the room.

I told him about Waites having been his lawyer and very tentatively aired my theory that Waites might have arranged for Kershaw to kill his wife.

'Sounds farfetched,' Dupuy said, but not dismissively. 'We need more than a theory. Does his description match the guy the owner saw?'

'As far as it goes, yes.'

'Well, that's something. We'll know when we've printed everything in here.'

'He was trying to steal this suitcase,' I said. 'I lifted it back in, by the sides, flat-handed. Other than that it's untouched.'

'I'll get Stinson to open it for us and we'll search it.' He left the room and came back with his assistant, who was pulling on a pair of surgical gloves.

'Might be best if we searched the room first, Inspector. If this thing's locked, maybe the key's in the deceased's pockets.'

'OK, dust the outside while we look around,' Dupuy

ordered and Stinson set to work while we started investigating the scene. We chalkmarked the location of the body and had Stinson take all the essential shots. Then we rolled the body over and examined it closely. Aside from the broken neck there were no apparent wounds. The hair was pulled up from the scalp as if the killer had grabbed him by the hair. 'How did he break the neck that way?' Dupuy wondered.

'That's an unarmed combat trick, left arm around the throat, then roll the head forward, using the left elbow as a fulcrum under the jaw to snap the neck,' I said. 'It's quick and quiet.'

'Where would a guy learn that?' Dupuy asked. 'That's not the kind of trick you learn at a storefront karate class.'

'It's standard unarmed combat training. Maybe he learned it in jail from some ex-soldier.'

'What was he in for, refresh me.' Dupuy frowned.

'Bank robbery, took a hostage.'

'He sounds like a real rounder. This could be his work,' Dupuy said. 'We're going to need guys. I'll make a call. You look around but don't move anything.'

He went to the phone and I started checking the floor and all the exposed places. There wasn't anything unusual. In the bathroom I found an electric razor but aside from that everything was feminine, shampoos and lotions. There was a purse on the night table. I was holding it when Dupuy came back.

'What a time for this to happen,' he said angrily. 'A third of my people are on leave. I've had to call guys in from days off, the Midland detatchment is setting up road blocks to the south, I've got one guy blocking Highway 69 outside Parry Sound and I've sent Elaine up to help him. I've been on to Toronto and they're putting a team together but they won't be here until morning. And I've called Holland. He's getting back to the office.'

'You can count on me as long as it takes, Inspector.'

'Thank you. What did you find so far?'

'Not much, except for this purse.'

'OK, take a look in it,' he said.

It was a big, practical purse, some kind of woven raffia construction, and inside it was the usual jumble. But there were two wallets. I took them out one at a time. The first had ID and cards in the name of Carolyn Jeffries, along with a few dollars. The second one belonged to Moira Waites. It had three hundred and forty-six dollars in Canadian cash and a US hundred-dollar bill.

I showed them silently to Dupuy. He shook his head. 'Why would she keep both sets of ID?' He looked at the drivers' licences side by side. 'They look near enough alike that she could have used the Jeffries woman's credit cards, I guess.'

'That must have been it,' I agreed. 'But she must have known it would have made her the prime suspect for killing Mrs Jeffries if we found her with both IDs.'

Dupuy had been a cop long enough to see the argument with that. 'She could have pleaded ignorance, just keeping the wallet for her friend when she saw her. It wouldn't have put her away, would it?'

'I guess not.' I finished searching the purse but found nothing that helped.

At last Dupuy said, 'You go ahead and search the rest of the room. Dave and I will search the body.'

He waved me on and I opened all the drawers. There was nothing much in any of them but under the sink in the bathroom I found a bottle of J. & B. Scotch, half consumed.

'Can we get some prints off this bottle?' I asked. 'It could be the one from Waites' room.'

Dupuy looked at it. 'That's the brand that was taken from Waites' room, right?'

'Right. And the suitcase has Waites' monogram on it as well. So we've wrapped up one homicide.'

'Yeah, the one that's not on my duty sheet,' he said

ruefully. 'Big deal.' He called Stinson in to print the bottle and while he did that, Dupuy and I stripped the bed, finding nothing hidden. Then we looked into the closets and the open suitcase. It was filled with woman's clothes. 'Did you notice that Jeffries doesn't have anything of his own here,' I said. 'The suitcase Dave's working on was taken from Waites' room. That's Waites' monogram.'

'You're saying that this guy didn't know he was going to be away overnight?' Dupuy asked, pointing a toe at the body.

'Seems that way. And I wonder why? What was he involved with the first day that stopped him going home again?'

'He didn't have to,' Dupuy said. 'He's about the same size as Waites. Maybe that's why he stole the suitcase when he killed the guy. Gave him a whole new wardrobe. Yet the woman had clothes. She was expecting to be away from home for a while, he wasn't. Maybe she knew something he didn't when they left.'

'The woman who was abducted isn't his wife. His wife was killed in that drowned car. This woman is Moira Waites. She was away from home when she left Waites,' I explained. 'Waites told me that she took everything when she left in his car, the one her friend was found dead in.'

'Is this everything she took?' Dupuy asked? 'One suitcase?'

'No, I don't think it is. She's a painter. She would have had cavases, paints, all that stuff, but it's not here.'

'Must be in her car,' he said.

'But there's no car. And the owner of this place says she came on foot.'

'I wonder if she left it up at the Jeffries place?'

'I didn't notice it yesterday but it's worth looking at again. And it's also worth watching the house, see if she heads back there.'

'It's a long shot but I'll get Holland on to that,' Dupuy

said, and scratched his head wearily. 'I can't find any pattern at all in this. Three people who know one another, including a husband and wife, all killed, and clues left all over the goddamn province. Waites' golf clubs up near Honey Harbour. Waites' suitcase here. Waites' car used in the first woman's death. And this guy—' he flipped a hand at the corpse—'flitting around out of sight for two days, then turning up dead in a motel with Waites' widow. What's goin' down?'

'I can't work it out. But there's more to it than that, even. The Tracy woman and the Hanson kid are all part of the same daisy chain. She was married to Waites. The actor was working for her, or trying to. She gets beaten up, says Hanson did it. Hanson disappears.'

'Is there something we're missing there?' Dupuy asked. He was tired and out of his depth. Although he had been a cop longer than I and held a good rank, he didn't have the same experience with homicide and was wary about making moves that might look dumb.

I wasn't out to carve him so I said, 'Don't forget Kershaw. Waites was his lawyer. I still figure that Waites sprung him to kill his wife. And on top of that, it's Kershaw's son who ended up in the gang that Hanson put together. This isn't just random. There's a pattern OK, even if we don't see it.'

'I think I'll have Holland go talk to this Tracy woman in hospital. Maybe she can tell us something new.'

'Good idea. You want me to go ahead in here while you call?'

'Yeah, sure.' Dupuy nodded and walked out. I worked on for another five minutes before he came back. 'Caught him at the station, he's going over there now,' he said, then added, 'She couldn't have done this, she's in hospital.'

'No, she didn't do it, Inspector. But she crops up everywhere we look.'

'You're right. We'll finish up here.' Dupuy waved his

hand at the half-unpacked suitcase. 'There's not much more
and I'll bring the cases with me when I come back to the
station.'

We went back to the suitcases, sorting through the
woman's case first. It had nothing useful in it, just a variety
of simple but colourful clothing that reminded me of
Waites' description of his wife's wardrobe. An arty type.

We took everything out and searched all the internal
pockets and compartments but there was nothing there. An
innocent piece of luggage that had belonged to a woman
with nothing to hide. It gave us no clue.

We repacked the case and checked the dresses hanging
in the closet. There was nothing in them but the labels from
some womens' store in Toronto. I folded them into the
suitcase and we searched the body. It proved once and for
all that he had killed Waites. In the pockets we found ID
in the names of Jeffries along with six hundred and eighty
dollars cash and then, in another pocket, all Waites' credit
cards. We looked at one another without speaking when we
pulled these out. Waites' murder was solved, but I wasn't
going to quit looking until I found Moira Waites and knew
who had driven Carolyn Jeffries off the rock into the lake.

In the bottom of his right-hand pocket we found the
suitcase key and we opened it up. It had an immediate
bonus for us, a neat little zippered briefcase inside on top of
the clothes. Dupuy took it out and looked at me knowingly.
'Maybe now we'll have something.'

I was anxious to examine it but he played the senior
officer, opening it and taking out a manilla folder. He
frowned at the cover. 'Street boy,' he read. 'What the hell
does that mean?'

'It's likely the name of Ms Tracy's movie.'

He looked at me disbelievingly and opened the file. I was
trying to read over his shoulder and he tilted the paper
towards me a fraction to make it easier. I saw that the top

sheet was a financial statement of some kind, columns of figures and names.

'Breakdown of projected costs,' Dupuy said. 'Jesus, how much does it cost to make a movie?'

I wanted him to hurry up. Maybe he knew more about figures than I did, most people do, but I was deeper into the case than he was, I would see something important faster than he. But he read it through with painful thoroughness, then passed it to me. I sat on the bed and re-read it. The various cost projections were itemized. Script, lead actors, a million dollars allotted there, no wonder Hanson had been so anxious to get the part, balance of cast, location costs, wardrobe and on and on. Nothing useful. A total cost of 6.3 million.

Then Dupuy handed me the second page. This was a summary of the fund-raising efforts. She had assembled only five million dollars, including a promise from the Canadian Film Development Corporation. which had a question-mark pencilled against it. There was also a pencilled note at the bottom. '1 mill. possible on delivery.'

'What's that mean?' Dupuy asked.

'Beats me. Maybe it's a film term of some kind, or maybe it means she has to deliver something to get the million.' I was baffled, as he was. None of the people or companies listed had any significance to me. 'I'd just say that if she can't find another one million three hundred thousand dollars, the project's off.'

Dupuy had spent his career in small towns but he was not a dull man. 'They raise this kind of money routinely, don't they?'

'My wife's the expert. She says it's always a struggle and Ms Tracy told me she's having problems with the production. That means money, I guess.'

'Still doesn't tell us anything,' he said. 'This is just business, this guy Waites was a lawyer, it figures he would have business stuff with him.'

'What are the other papers?'

He leafed through them. 'Names, presumably of people she plans to hit up for the money. List of actors. Then there's some kind of story, says "treatment" on it.'

He took his time reading through the papers, passing them to me very slowly. None of the names rang a bell. They were mostly individual names, together with their companies which were again simply collections of names, no indication what the companies did, although I could tell from the addresses in Toronto's Bay and King Streets business area that they were all prestigious outfits.

Then he handed me the next sheet, a production summary. It had a listing which began with the director and the technical people and most of these slots had names inked in. Then came the cast and the first inked in name was Eric Hanson.

'This doesn't gibe with what she told me in hospital today,' I said. 'Hanson's name is inked in. She said he wasn't getting the part and that's why he attacked her.'

'She could have changed her mind,' Dupuy said tentatively.

'Sure, she could. But when you figure he's been acting out the part of bad boy in my jurisdiction, you wonder whether he was paying her off for the part.'

'Does that make sense?' Dupuy shook his head. 'Do guys go to that kind of length to get parts in movies?'

'Anything short of killing, if the part's big enough.'

'Well—' he breathed a long sigh—'your wife's the actress, not mine. Maybe you know. Anyway, read this.'

He handed me the last item, the treatment. I read it through quickly. It involved a teenager who got tangled up in a gang, starting with a disaffected group of kids in a high school. They carried out swarmings and a couple of beatings and then graduated to drug sales. The boy started having second thoughts and when he was told to commit a murder he tried to get out. With the gang after him, he hid out in an apartment belonging to a woman in her thirties. She and he have an affair and she straightens him out and he moves in with her.

'Pretty kinky stuff,' Dupuy said.

'It could appeal to women without a guy in their lives.'

'Are there enough of them to make a picture sell?' His small town background was showing now.

'Toronto is down by the head with single women. It's a good idea, they can enjoy watching someone their age end up with a young stud with a heart of gold. I figure this Tracy woman is pretty smart.'

'If she's so smart, how come she hasn't raised the money she needs?'

'Beats the hell out of me,' I admitted. 'But it's routine as far as I know. What interests me more is that the plot kind of matches up with the actor, Eric Hanson, and the way he moved in on Ms Tracy. That much is true to the script.'

'You think he killed this guy?' he flipped his hand at the body that we had been walking around as if it were some piece of furniture.

'My bet is Kershaw, but Hanson is big enough.'

'I'll call Holland and get him to ask Tracy about all this,' Dupuy said. 'And I'll have them collect the body, then we can finish looking at this stuff and close up until the morning.'

'Right. You want me to go on looking through the case?'

'May's well.' He left with the folder and I crouched by the case and dug deeper into it. It was full of clothes, all of them casual but expensive, but I remembered the cocaine we had found in Waites' room and I shook out each item to make sure it didn't have a package concealed inside it. None of them did and I got to the bottom of the case without finding anything.

I crouched there for a while longer, looking at the case blankly. Nothing useful, except maybe the file on Tracy's movie. And yet I had a feeling that there was more. There had to be. A man had been killed for this case. It had to contain something important. There was only one angle we hadn't checked, and one quick way to find out if I was right.

I went outside and called Sam. He bounded over to me and I fussed him, then calmed him and led him into the room. He looked over at the body but gave no reaction and I played the last card I had. I've trained him to be a one-man police department. Even though I don't get many drug cases I worked with the OPP dog trainer on developing his nose for drugs. Normally he doesn't react to anything he's not told to, but now I gave him his cue.

'It has to be a good solid hint,' the trainer had advised me. 'Like, normally we put a different collar on a dog when he's sniffing drugs, that alerts him. But you can do it with a command word. But make it unusual. Don't say anything ordinary.' So I held up one finger to Sam and used the code word, a memory of my own past. 'Mei Kong.'

He stiffened and turned away, searching. He sniffed the body on the floor, then left it and turned his attention to the pile of clothing, beginning to growl low in his throat. Finally he reached the suitcase and began to bark, furious now, scratching at the bottom of the case with his front feet as if he were trying to dig a hole through it.

Behind me I heard the door open and I turned to see Dupuy in the doorway. 'What the hell's going on here?' he shouted angrily.

'A new twist,' I told him. 'My dog has just shown me there's a stash of drugs hidden in this suitcase.'

CHAPTER 14

I told Sam 'Easy' and bent down to rub his head and let him know I was proud of him. It had been months since

I'd tested his drug-sniffing skills, but he had performed as if he did it every day and given us something new to go on.

Dupuy was unconvinced. 'You sure about this?' He was examining the case. 'This thing looks perfectly normal.'

'Must be a hidden compartment,' I told him. 'It needs examining by the drug squad.'

He picked the case up and shook it, holding it up by his ear, an instinctive, useless test. 'Doesn't look like it,' he said again. I took out my pocket knife and probed the bottom of the case. It was lined with a paisley cloth and the surface underneath was firm, aluminium probably. 'Want me to cut it?'

'Why not? The owner won't complain.'

I put the case on the floor and pressed on the tip of the knife blade. It gave, easing through the thin metal. I started sawing back on it, cutting a slit on the inside of the lid. White powder leaked through the crack. 'Here it is.' I showed him and he shook his head in disbelief.

'How in hell did they pack that thing? It looks like it went in there when the case was made.'

'Maybe it did. I don't know. But it's there. What do you want to do now?'

'I figure we wrap up here and I'll take this back to the station.'

'We should watch this place tonight,' I said. 'The guy who killed Jeffries may come back to get this.'

'I know,' Dupuy said impatiently. 'I'm going to leave a man here. Can you hold on until he arrives?'

'Sure. Soon's the body's gone I'll lock up, turn out the lights and sit out of sight somewhere, watching.'

Dupuy bent over the case. 'The guy who was chased off must have known this was full of dope.'

'Which means he must have been tight with Waites.'

'Maybe your idea is good after all,' Dupuy said carefully. 'Maybe Waites' wife knew about the dope as well and was going to blow the whistle.'

'That's a solid motive for killing her.'

'Maybe.' We looked at one another, thinking hard. He was beginning to see the case the way I did. Like me, he felt flooded with useless information. We had everything except answers.

I thought for a moment. 'Sergeant Holland should be told about this now, while he's having a talk with the Tracy woman.'

'I guess I'll go see if he's there yet,' Dupuy said. 'The meat wagon's on its way. Can you stay here till then?'

'No problem. Then I'll wait for your man to arrive. Tell him to flick his lights twice so I'll know it's him.'

'I will. And thanks.' He left Waites' clothes piled where I had folded them and took the suitcase with him, closing it carefully first. 'Talk to my guy before you leave.'

'Right.'

He walked out and I sat on the edge of the bed, stroking Sam's head absently. There were so many connections staring us in the face. But how did they fit? This latest angle, for instance, the drugs. Dupuy was right, the way the case was filled made it very professional. But who was behind it? The suitcase belonged to Waites. Had he known about the drugs? Or had they been put in there before he bought it? And when had he bought it? And why was it with him in Murphy's Harbour? And why had Jeffries taken it when he killed Waites? Had he taken it just for the clothes it contained, or had he known it was packed with dope? And where had Waites been taking it in the first place?

I thought about that aspect for a while. We're further from Montreal than from Toronto, so he couldn't have been intending to ship it there. On the other hand, we're closer to Sault Ste Marie where there's a crossing into the States. Perhaps Waites had intended to send it over the border there. But why hadn't he done so already? He'd been in Murphy's Harbour almost a week. And that was when I had another idea, the reciprocal course. Maybe he had

arrived here with a clean suitcase and someone had filled
it for him. Maybe he had to sell it in Toronto. Maybe
the stash in his golf shoes had been some kind of advance
payment for his involvement.

That raised the question of who his supplier had been.
He was tight with Ms Tracy. But if she were the source,
surely her contacts would have been in Toronto. That was
where she spent ninety-nine per cent of her time.

I was roused by the sound of a vehicle outside and then
a tap on the door. I called, 'Come in,' and the door opened
to admit a couple of ambulance men. 'We're here for the
body,' one of them said. He was young and elaborately
casual, his hair cut bowl fashion, long on top, almost shaved
at the sides, out of character with the formality of his
uniform.

'He's here.' I pointed and they brought in their stretcher
and stood looking down at the dead man. 'Well, thank God
he ain't heavy,' the other one said. He was older, with the
red face and explosive skin of a heavy drinker. 'Last call
we got was this heavy old broad up three flights of stairs.
Goddamn near killed me getting her down.'

'You're lucky this time,' I told him. 'Try not to scuff up
the chalk mark.'

'No problem,' the young one said. He wrinkled his nose.
'Jeez. How can you guys work in a stink like this?' I said
nothing and they rolled the body on to the stretcher and
left, joking back and forth to show what hard nuts they
were.

I switched off the light and left the room, driving my car
around the back of the unit, out of sight of the road, then
took Sam and went out to the front of the unit, close to the
entrance. I made myself comfortable with Sam beside me,
waiting. No cars passed. At this time of night the side-road
was used only by the locals and they were in bed. At last a
car approached, from the direction of the highway. As he

pulled in he flicked his lights and he pulled in at a vacant spot down the front of the unit.

The driver turned and wound his window down as I approached. There was enough starlight for me to see that he looked young. A uniformed man, I guessed, press-ganged into plainclothes stakeout work in his own car. He spoke first. 'How're you tonight?' the tough-guy mask of a green copper.

'Good. You? You know what's on?'

'Yeah. The inspector briefed me.'

'Good. We want this guy, if he comes back.'

He looked at me contemptuously, without speaking. Who the hell was I to tell him anything? He was chewing gum, I noticed, and I hoped he could handle the job. The man we wanted might come back on foot and if this guy got bored and turned on his radio Kershaw or whoever it was would be spooked.

I asked him to call his office and let them know I'd left, then collected the car and drove back up to the harbour. It was after midnight but there were still cars parked in front of both drinking spots so I looked into both places. The crowd had thinned in each of them but there was no sign of Kershaw or Hanson. I checked all my properties one last time and waited in the car for half an hour, until the bars both closed and the last customers drove out then took one last trip to the station to check for messages.

There were a couple of Faxes and about a yard of entries on the teletype which I read first. Nothing new. More details of the case, the descriptions of Kershaw and Moira Waites and Hanson and the make and number of Ms Tracy's Mercedes, all issued by the Parry Sound dispatcher.

I went over to the phone to check the Fax machine and while I picked up the messages I pressed the prepro-grammed button to get the OPP. The desk man told me that Sergeant Holland was talking to the inspector and put me through. I glanced at the Fax messages as I waited. The top one was a circular, inviting me to save big bucks on a new Chevrolet. I crumpled it up as Dupuy answered.

'Bennett?'

'Right, Inspector. I wondered what Bill learned from Tracy.'

'Nothing,' he said. 'Let me put him on.'

There was a rustle as the phone changed hands, the distant burble of voices in the room and then Holland said, 'She'd gone, Reid. Signed herself out.'

'Dressed in what? She was naked when we brought her in.'

'She called the Salvation Army. They brought her in some clothes.' Holland was thinking now. He obviously hadn't analysed the details before this.

'Where did she go? She didn't have either money or a car.'

'The Sally Ann captain gave her a few bucks. She took a cab from the hospital. We're following up on it now but she's gone like a wild goose in winter.'

'There's a bus for Toronto at midnight. Gets to the highway here around quarter to one. I guess you checked that. Other than that she must have taken a room someplace.'

'We're checking but we've only got one man on patrol, the other guys are on the road block.'

'Did the doctor have anything to say about her condition?'

'Just one thing. Apparently you'd asked him to take a blood test for drugs. He didn't find anything.'

'Did he say she was faking the coma?'

'Wouldn't commit himself on that one.' Holland humphed tiredly. 'Gave me the usual medical double-talk, that the degree of loss of consciousness did not tally with his experience of her kind of injuries. Nothing we could take to court.'

'You need me to come up and help? I'll check her house first.'

'There was a muffled consultation and then Holland said, 'No. The inspector says we all need a break. She's not a suspect. I was just going to talk to her for background. He says the hell with it, we'll chase her up tomorrow.'

'Suits me, it's been a long day. I'll take a ride by her house on my way home, though.' I realized how tired I was, finding to my surprise that I had sat down without thinking about it and was leafing through the other Fax sheets as I talked, hardly seeing what I was reading.

Holland made some answer but a word in the next Fax sheet caught my eye and I missed his comment. The word was 'Kershaw'. I said, 'Hold on a second, there's a Fax here might help.'

I read it quickly. It was from my sister's house. She had installed a machine so she could work at home sometimes when the kids were off school. The message was from Elmer Svensen.

Reid. Talked to Chuck about Kershaw. He says K. was running an investment brokerage, small stuff. He thinks K. had dipped into the money, $2-3 hundred thou. His bet went sour and he tried the bank caper. Seems there was a shipment of negotiables coming in that day and he knew about it. Not a standard robbery. Also, Chuck says the investment that failed was a movie. Does this help? There was no charge laid on the scam, his wife made the losses good.

'Listen to this.' I told Holland. 'The circle keeps on getting smaller and smaller.' I read him the Fax and waited.

He said, 'Yeah. Could tie in, I guess, if it was Tracy's movie.' He didn't sound enthusiastic and I knew why when he went on. 'Alla this stuff's older'n hell. I don't see how it helps to know what happened six, seven years back. We got three warm corpses to worry about. We've got reporters up the yin-yang here. Everyone's wantin' to know when we're gonna make an arrest and we keep comin' up with stale stuff.'

I took a moment to get my excitement down to his speed. He didn't see the connections the way I did. It all seemed academic to him with media people chasing him for action. By the morning the media would be down here, bugging me when they realized that the OPP didn't have any sexy answers. Then I might feel like he did.

'It ties in,' I said slowly. 'From where I sit, and I'm sitting because I'm just as pooped as the rest of you, we've got some kind of reunion of rounders. First one of them we can get hold of, including the Tracy woman, and this thing's gonna come to pieces in our hand. You'll be promoted, Dupuy will get to be Prime Minister and I'll get my week's pay.'

He knew I was right but his agreement was feeble. 'I know, Reid, but we got three people, four if you count this Kershaw guy, all of them can untie this thing for us and one or other of 'em's gonna turn up soon. I say we call it a night.'

I could imagine Dupuy sitting across from him, nodding agreement. An arrest would profit them. They belonged to an organization with room to move ahead. But they were weary.

'OK. It's a night,' I said.

'Yeah. Good idea. Get back at it first thing. Meantime we'll check all the motels, see if they've got the Tracy woman staying there. Shouldn't be hard to track her down if she's in town.'

Not if she was dumb enough to take a motel, I thought, but she wasn't. Either she would rendezvous with somebody and drive away or else she would check in at some guest house run by a widow who would have the lights out by now and wouldn't be checked.

'I'll look in on her house on my way home,' I said. 'Talk to you tomorrow.'

'Right, thanks. Oh, and the inspector says, can you send us a copy of the Fax, together with the source.'

'Will do, but don't call them, he's a cop too, working on a homicide in Toronto. He needs his sleep as well. Besides, he's my brother-in-law.'

'Small world,' Holland said and hung up.

I sent them the message, along with Elmer's name and rank in the Metro department, then closed up the station and drove back to Main Street, over the bridge and up the side of the lake to Ms Tracy's house. It was in darkness and there was no car outside but I was wary and drove by without slowing and stopped around the next bend in the road. Then I took Sam and walked back down there and checked the house. The padlock was in place in front and the back door was shut and didn't look as if it had been forced. I'd bolted it when I closed the house up and had not yet given Ms Tracy the key. She was still away.

I stood there and thought for a while, wondering what to do next. I hadn't thought to ask Holland the time she had checked out. Maybe she was still on her way down here. Maybe. And in the meantime I had nothing to do but sleep till morning.

That decided me. I've slept out a lot. Camping with my family as a kid, and most of the nights I spent in Vietnam. And I had Sam with me, he'd wake me if anyone showed. I would rest here. I moved out into the bush beside the house, close to the road, took off my cap and stretched out on the dry duff of needles and debris from the pine trees overhead. Sam settled beside me and I lay there and relaxed in the warm night, glad that the mosquitoes had given up, as they do after midnight. Pretty soon I was asleep.

Sam woke me, stirring slightly, and I opened my eyes and sat up, wide awake, the way you are in the boonies when the guy on watch nudges you. A car was coming up the road towards us. I checked my watch, it was three-eighteen.

I crouched up as it pulled into Ms Tracy's driveway.

Someone got out of the passenger side. Her car! And she was not alone! I had them!

I pulled my gun and stepped out on the driveway with Sam beside me. I was thirty yards from the car and edging closer when I heard Ms Tracy swear. 'There's a goddamn padlock on here. Help me.'

I stopped as the driver got out of the car. There were two other people inside I saw, and then, outlined against the glare of the headlights I saw that the man was carrying a long gun. 'Police. Drop the gun,' I shouted.

He whirled towards me, levelling the gun and I fired twice and dived sideways into the trees as the orange muzzle flash from the shotgun bloomed towards me, round and bright as the sun.

Shot crashed into the branches over my head and I heard Ms Tracy scream. Then the car roared back towards me and past, the driver's door open with the driver craning up over the roof. He fired again, too high and I fired back, emptying my pistol at the tyres, but he wheeled back and slammed the door as he raced off up the side-road, back towards the highway.

I shouted 'Fight' at Sam and he bounded to the step where Ms Tracy was still screaming, his barking blending with her voice.

'Guard,' I shouted and he fell silent, crouching in front of her, baring his teeth as I sprinted for the scout car.

I was almost a minute behind them but I roared after them, staying in second gear, siren blaring, hoping one of my good citizens would hear and phone the OPP. There was no sign of the car ahead but I drove flat out, pushing the car to the limit of my skill. Back I raced, to the north side of the bridge opposite Main Street, alone in the darkness. And then, far ahead at the edge of the highway, I caught the flash of their headlights in the trees as they slowed there before turning north. I followed, driving one-handed now, frantically adjusting the wavelength on my radio to the OPP frequency . It was hard at the limit of the car's speed, watching for oncoming traffic, trying to catch a smaller, faster car screaming down the middle of the road, but at last I got close and bellowed into the microphone.

'Bennett, proceeding north from Murphy's Harbour. Hot pursuit of a blue Mercedes. Shots fired. Do you read?'

There was a squawk, broken up. I was far enough off frequency to be unreadable, I guessed, and gave the knob a tiny flick. I repeated my message three times, flicking the frequency each way, bracketing the OPP wavelength the best I could. Then I came over a hill to look down at a mile-long slope on the highway ahead and saw no car. I'd lost them.

I kept on, adjusting the set again until finally the OPP man answered. 'Bennett, location please? Location, over.'

'Seven kilometres north of the Harbour. No sign of the car ahead. Car may have pulled off into Honey Harbour or along side-road 513. Have my dog holding Ms Tracy at her house. Send a PW down for the interrogation. Will proceed as far as Wildhaven Lodge and then return to the Harbour.'

'Roger, hold, Bennett.' The dispatcher said anxiously. 'Here's the inspector.'

It was Dupuy. I briefed him in two sentences and he told me to return and hold Tracy at her house. A policewoman would join me in twenty minutes.

So I killed the siren and turned back, taking time now to check a few hundred yards into the Honey Harbour exit from the highway, finding it as peaceful as my own community was, on good nights. No Mercedes. Then I sped back to the Tracy house.

She was standing on the porch, motionless, Sam in front of her. I shone my flashlight over her and saw the terror in her eyes. I told Sam, 'Easy boy. Good boy,' and made a fuss of him before telling her. 'Sit down, Ms Tracy. I have a policewoman coming and then we'll take you to the station. You're under arrest.'

I hadn't worked out what the charges would be and she didn't cut me any slack. 'What for, for God's sake? I get a ride home from Parry Sound with some people and you come out of the bushes shooting at them. What's going on? Tell me that.'

'Who were they?'

'I never saw them before.' Her voice was clear and confident. She was going to lie. I gritted my teeth and hoped the OPP would trace the other car. She was only a minor part of the mystery. She hadn't done any of the killings and it was the killers I wanted.

'Make yourself comfortable. We have about ten minutes to wait,' I said.

'I need to use the bathroom, you bastard.'

'Ten minutes,' I repeated.

'I can't wait that long. I was terrorized by your goddamn dog.'

'Then step down into the side somewhere. He'll come with you. I'll wait here.'

She swore angrily and sat down, her back against the door with its padlock still in place. I ignored her, reloading my revolver and glancing around. There were maybe half a dozen places within a couple of hundred yards each way but there were no lights showing. People were asleep or didn't want to get involved, which was good.

'Who was in the car with you?' I asked.

'How would I know?' she said angrily. 'I got out of the hospital and as I was walking down the street in Parry Sound they gave me a lift.'

It was too early to lean on her. I needed a woman there to remove any chance of her claiming I'd molested her. Tough as she was, she would do it automatically to discredit me and any evidence I got from her. But maybe I could trap her into something. 'How many people were in the car?'

She thought that was innocent. 'Three. Besides me.'

'Two men and a woman?' That had been my reading, although I hadn't had time to concentrate on the others once I saw the driver had a gun.

'They didn't talk, I don't know.'

'You're lying,' I said. 'That was your own car.'

She didn't answer for a moment, then sneered. 'I thought it seemed familiar. Small world, isn't it?'

'Either you help us or you're going to be in jail for aiding and abetting an escaped prisoner in the commission of a murder,' I told her. 'Now you sit there and think about that for a few minutes until my partner arrives.'

'I've got nothing to say, now or later. This is all ridiculous,' she said but there was fear in her voice. I said nothing, just stood and waited for ten long minutes until I heard a car coming.

It was an OPP cruiser and Elaine Harper got out and walked up to us. I did everything formally. 'Officer Harper, this is Ms Tracy. She is under arrest for aiding and abetting an escaped prisoner in the commission of a homicide.'

'Sounds like you're in a whole lot of trouble, ma'am,' Elaine said cheerfully. 'Where d'you want to do this, Chief, here or at your office?'

'At the station, please. Will you take Ms Tracy in your car?' Thank the Lord they're allowing women into the OPP. There would be no chance for our prisoner to allege misconduct.

'Fine. Come with me, please.' Elaine made an 'up' gesture with her finger and Ms Tracy stood slowly. 'Do you have any cigarettes?' she asked.

'Don't use 'em,' Elaine said.

'Then may I open my house and get some?'

'What do you think, Chief?' Elaine turned to me.

'If we go in there I'm going to conduct a search for drugs,' I said. 'Do you still want to open your house, ma'am?'

'Where's your warrant?' Ms Tracy demanded. Her voice was strong but it had a nervous tremor.

'I'm going to apply for one as soon as we reach the station. It will be issued while you're in the cells. This way I save time. What would save more time is for you to admit that you have drugs in there, if you do, and I won't have to turn my dog loose.'

In the starlight I could see the policewoman looking at me strangely. She hadn't heard about what the suitcase contained. She thought this was a fishing trip.

Ms Tracy said nothing for about half a minute. Then as Elaine reached out to bring her along she spoke. 'The hell with it, I need a smoke. Do you have the key for this padlock?'

I undid the padlock and she produced the front door key. 'Where did that come from? You had nothing with you when you left here?'

'It was under the mat,' she said angrily. 'Even with your dog after me I picked it up.'

Not an honest answer, but credible. We followed her through the verandah and she unlocked the inner door with the same key. 'I have to use the bathroom,' she said, switching on the light.

'I'll have to come with you,' Elaine said. I watched the tension between them. Elaine was smaller, only around five-six and slight, with the bulk of her gun incongruous on her slim waist. Ms Tracy was taller and older and her contempt was enormous.

'Afraid I'll hurt myself?' she sneered.

'Maybe. Or flush your dope down the john,' Elaine said. 'Let's go.'

They went into the bathroom and I looked around, wondering where drugs would be hidden if she had any. There were a thousand hiding-places but I knew Sam would find anything so I relaxed and waited.

When they came out again I asked Tracy, 'Do you have any drugs here, ma'am?'

'It's not ma'am. It's Ms,' she hissed. 'And no. I don't

have any goddamn drugs. But I have friends who use this place from time to time. Maybe one of them has put something somewhere that I don't know about.'

I smiled. 'There. Now you're golden. I'll get my dog to check.' I bent to fondle Sam, holding his head between both hands to get his attention. Then I told him Mei Kong and stood up.

The women watched, fascinated, as he stiffened and turned his head slowly, sniffing the air. Then he sniffed the couch and one of the chairs, growling softly. Someone had used dope in this room, sitting there. And at last he went over to the bookcase and sniffed up high, then stood on his back legs to claw at a shelf of books about four feet off the ground.

'Easy,' I told him and lifted the books down. There was nothing behind them but his head sank to one of the books and he barked again, scratching at its cover with one foot. I picked it up. It was old, red leather bound. *Supreme Court of Ontario Decisions 1899.* I read and opened it up. The centre of the pages had been hollowed out and there was a plastic bag of white powder inside.

'Is this your book?' I held it up to Ms Tracy.

'That belongs to John Waites. He left it here. Said he might have to consult it occasionally,' she said. 'Happy now?'

'Happier,' I admitted. 'Take your cigarettes and let's go.'

Elaine took her arm and we left, me carrying the book with its white cargo. It might prove something, I thought. She would get off a charge of possession by blaming Waites, but if the chemists could prove it was identical to the contents of his suitcase we might be able to find out more about its source. And the find put more pressure on her. Now, she might volunteer some help.

I watched Elaine put her in the cage of the patrol car and then whistled Sam and checked the driveway where the man with the shotgun had been standing. I couldn't see any evidence that I'd hit him but I found his shotgun shell, and then, lower down the driveway, where he had fired as he backed out, I found two more. I picked them up on the end of my fingers and put them into the windshield of the cruiser. Once we found the gun I could have ballistics check the cases and see if they matched. Then I'd have attempted murder to add to the charges. Good additional material if it got down to a plea bargaining situation.

Wearily now I drove around and over the bridge to the police station. All I could think of was that I should have shot out the back tyre before I challenged the gunman. That way I would have stopped the car. Dammit, Bennett, you're getting slow, I told myself.

Elaine was waiting at the station and when I unlocked the back door she got Ms Tracy out and led her inside. We booked her formally, Elaine charging her and reading her rights. Then I stepped out into my office while Elaine searched her. She opened the door a couple of minutes later. 'She's clean. Nothing but some cash and her cigarettes.'

'OK. Let's call the inspector, see if he can join us and we'll talk to her,' I said. 'And I'll put some coffee on. I can hardly stay awake.'

'Getting old.' She grinned. 'Let's put her in a cell and do it.'

We went back out to the cells and Elaine ushered Ms Tracy into the cell farthest from the door, the most isolated and therefore the most frightening. She said nothing and we left her there and came out to the telephone. Elaine phoned Parry Sound and the dispatcher told us that Inspector Dupuy was out, supervising the search for the Mercedes. He would try to raise him on the radio.

Elaine took over the coffee-making chores, laughing that she had tasted my coffee and wasn't going to set me loose with a pot ever again. It took a while to perc and we had some and offered a cup to Ms Tracy. 'Ready to talk yet?' Elaine asked.

'I want a lawyer,' she said. 'I get a phone call, don't I?'

'Sure. You said "no" earlier. Have you changed your mind?' They might have been college buddies, kidding, from Elaine's tone, no threat, no tension.

'I want to call,' Ms Tracy said and Elaine led her through to the office. I went with them and watched as Ms Tracy dialled, wondering how many people around know their lawyer's phone number without looking it up. She waited for about ten seconds, then said, 'This is Marcia Tracy. I've been arrested at Murphy's Harbour. It's now—' she glanced up at the clock—'four-fifty, Saturday morning. Can you help?'

She hung up and we led her back to her cell where she sat on the wooden board bunk and sipped her coffee. 'You haven't got long to plea bargain,' Elaine said quietly. 'Did you think of that? We're going to find that car, come daylight. And when we do, your help won't be worth spit. Act now and we might be able to bargain with the Crown Attorney.'

Ms Tracy set down her coffee cup and lit a cigarette from the little pile beside her. 'This has been the worst day of my life. I've been raped, beaten up, knocked unconscious, terrorized by a slavering dog and arrested. What can I say?'

'You lied about the rape,' I said. 'We found Waites' suitcase. It contained some interesting things, including your production file.'

'What's that got to do with my being raped?' She flung the question at me furiously.

'You told me this morning that Hanson did it when you turned him down for the part in your movie. But you've got him inked in.'

She looked at me grimly, holding a mouthful of smoke for a long time, then releasing it as she spoke. 'I was confused when you talked to me. You have to remember, I'd been knocked out. I didn't know what I was saying.'

'But now you're clear-headed. And here's a clear proposition for you. I will do my level best to have all the charges against you so far—' I held up my hand—'all the charges that have been read to you, dismissed, if you tell us who was in the car with you and where they were going.'

She looked at me for a long time. The she stubbed her smoke on the bowl of the toilet and tossed the butt into the water. 'You heard what he said.' She pointed at Elaine who nodded, not speaking.

Now she dusted her knees, looking down primly as if she were wearing a long skirt. 'Very well. They were going to snatch the kid and hold him to ransom.'

I knew who she meant but Elaine blurted, 'Which kid?'

Ms Tracy looked at her levelly. 'Phillip Freund,' she said.

CHAPTER 15

I ran to the phone and dialled George Horn's number. It rang three times and Jean Horn answered. 'Hello?' She sounded alert. Good, she was already up.

'Reid Bennett, Jean. I've heard that some guys are coming to grab young Phil. Is he there?'

'Still in bed. I was just getting up.'

'Is Peter there?'

'No. George and him went fishing.'

'You have a shotgun?'

'Sure. You know that.'

'Load it. I'll be there as soon as I can, ten minutes. If you see a blue Mercedes pull up, poke the gun out of the window and fire over their heads. Don't go out, they're armed.'

'Jesus Christ,' she said, startling me. She's a good Catholic.

'Be right there.' I whistled Sam and unlocked the chain

on the firearms, grabbing the Remington pump shotgun and a box of double-O buckshot and ran out.

Sam sat beside me and I raced back through town to the bridge, and up the side-road past Ms Tracy's house. The Reserve has an unmade road of its own, leading from their little private marina. I put the siren on and flew along it, juddering over the washboard surface, slipping on the corners as I jammed on every bit of speed the road would handle.

I saw no cars and there was no telltale cloud of dust in the air ahead of me, that much was good but I didn't slacken speed until I reached the Horns' house and cut the siren.

Jean came to the door. She seemed calm but her voice was a little higher pitched than usual. 'You sure about this, Reid?'

'We have a woman in custody. She told us.'

'Come in.' She stood aside and I came in. She had an old pump shotgun behind the door. I picked it up and unloaded it, working the mechanism four times, ejecting three shells and then nothing.

'You won't need this now.'

'Well, that's good,' she said easily. 'I leave the hunting to Peter. Want some coffee?'

I had an idea and I put it to her. 'Where could I hide the scout car?'

'Jim Buck's garage is empty. You could put it there.' She looked at me. 'You planning on staking us out here?'

'Yes. The OPP are in charge of the case. I've got an officer at the station and more are on the way.'

She gave a faint grin. 'So you're gonna lie in the weeds like a big old muskie waiting for a pickerel.'

'Makes sense,' I said. 'Call Jim, tell him I want to use his garage for a couple of hours. Could you do that?'

'He's out with the guys,' she said. 'Jus' do it.'

'Right. I'll be right back.'

I went out again into the first tinge of daylight and drove the extra hundred yards to the Buck house. Jim is a widower and lives alone. The place is run down but he has an old clapboard garage that houses his snowmobile. There was room alongside to squeeze the scout car in. I did it and shut the door, then took Sam and the shotgun and shells and walked back to Horns'.

Phil Freund was up and washed. He looked a little sleepy yet but was glad to see me. 'Hi, Chief. Mrs Horn says you're staying here a while.'

'Yes. We got word that a couple of guys were looking for you. I'd like to talk to them.'

'Talk?' He smiled crookedly. 'Never thought you'd need a shotgun to talk to someone.'

'One of the guys is on the lam from jail,' I explained. 'He may not want to listen.'

He was holding the puppy which was squirming in his arms, trying to get down and play with Sam. 'Easy, munch-kin,' he said and tried to stroke it.

'I'll set Sam outside the back door,' I said. Nobody would see him there from the road and I was certain that if they came it would be by car.

'Shall I take Blue outside, Mrs Horn?' he asked. 'He didn't wet in the night, he needs to go.'

'I'll take him,' she said. 'It's best if you stay in until this is sorted out.'

'Can I use your phone, please, Jean?' I asked and she nodded.

'Help yourself.'

She took her dog outside and I set Sam on the back step and then phoned the OPP. The dispatcher told me that all hell had broken loose. The helicopter was taking off at first light to search for the Mercedes, the inspector and every available officer in the area were down in my vicinity look-ing for the car, and a special team of investigators, with a superintendent no less, were heading up from headquarters in Toronto to talk to Ms Tracy.

I filled him in on my plans and gave him the Horns' phone number, then hung up. Jean was back in, putting a skillet on the stove.

'Pancakes and bacon,' she said. 'How's that sound?'

'Not for me, thanks, Jean. I'm going to hole up across the road where they won't look.'

'Take this with you,' she said firmly and gave me a cup of coffee, adding, 'You don't eat right.'

'Later,' I said. 'Thank you. When Phil's had his breakfast, let him work outside. Phil. I want you to hang loose, try and stay in front of the house where I can see you. Nothing's going to happen but I want them to see you if they show up.'

He laughed nervously. 'Hey, no problem.'

I gave him a wink, then took my coffee to oblige Jean, and crossed the road quickly. I found a rock to sit on, behind a birch tree. When I was installed I whistled Sam and he ran across after me and lay down at my side as I sipped the coffee, nursing the loaded shotgun in my right hand.

Morning came, grey first, then bright, burning off the dew and waking up a few late mosquitoes who buzzed around me hopefully. I hadn't thought to bring fly dope so I amused myself by keeping count of those I killed before they bit me. The score was mosquitoes seventeen, Bennett thirty-two by the time a car came down the road, moving slowly.

Phil Freund was in the front of the Horn house, repainting a window-sill. He looked up when the car passed but went on painting. A cool kid, I thought. He was going to be all right.

The car wasn't a Mercedes but I wasn't really expecting one any more. They would know it was hot and would have stolen something fresh, probably from a marina in Honey

Harbour, knowing the owner would be away and not report it missing for a couple of days at least. This one was a Chev, old enough that it didn't have an automatic lock on the steering. They had chosen well.

I watched as they tooled by. The sun was low and behind them so I couldn't see faces, but I picked out two people, both in front. They cruised on up the road a couple of hundred yards, then turned in a driveway and came back, on the same side as the Horn house.

They stopped and got out, both of them. The driver was short and trim, the passenger taller. Neither one looked heavy enough to be Kershaw but I couldn't have told anyway. They were wearing stockings over their faces.

They went through the gate and over to Phillip. He came down from the stepladder in a rush when he saw them but they grabbed him, the smaller one putting a hand over his mouth to muffle his yell. The puppy was yapping under their feet and the small one kicked it aside, sending it yelping for the door.

I let them reach the gate and come through on to the road, then stepped out, pointing the shotgun. 'You two. Down on your faces.'

They let him go and split, one going each way. I paused a moment to point at the big one and yell. 'Track' and Sam bounded after him. Then I took off after the small one. He was thirty yards ahead, making for a bare rock on the side of the road. From there he could break in any direction into the bushes. I shouted 'Halt,' then fired the shotgun, high over his head.

He took a couple more steps, then ran down like a broken toy and turned back, hands high. 'Don't shoot,' he screamed.

I trotted up to him and cuffed his hands behind his back, then called Phillip. 'Come and hold this one, Phil.'

He came forward nervously and I jogged down the road

the other way to Sam who was standing over the second guy, snarling into his face.

'On your feet and take that mask off.' I kept the gun pointed at his legs, looking businesslike.

'Don't shoot. I can explain,' he said and I recognized the voice, even before he pulled the stocking from his head and his features sprang back into their usual shape. It was Hanson.

'Hands on your head, walk back to your buddy.' I waved the gun muzzle and he came, moving as carefully as if he thought the road was mined.

Phil Freund was walking back, one hand on the other prisoner's arm. 'I know him. It's Cy,' he said excitedly. 'Why were they trying to grab me?'

'That's what I'm about to find out.' I took a moment to peel the stocking back from the prisoner's face and recognized him as one of the gang members I had seen in the first encounter. 'You're in a mess of trouble,' I told him, unlocking his left handcuff. I snapped it on to Hanson's right wrist, right hand to right so that they couldn't run freely. 'Stay here,' I said, and told Sam, 'Guard.'

He sank low in front of them, baring his teeth, and I went to Buck's garage and drove the scout car back to the prisoners. I put them both in the cage and told Sam 'Easy'. 'I'd like you to come with me, Phil. I'll just tell Jean what's going on.'

She was already at the gate and she waited for me to come up. 'Nice work,' she said. 'They never knew you were there.'

'I've been taking Indian lessons from George.'

She laughed. 'You get good marks.'

'Listen, I'm going to take Phillip with me. The OPP detectives will want to talk to him and I'd like to have him at the station anyway, keep him on ice until this is wrapped up. I'll bring him back later to finish up.'

'No problem,' she said. 'He's about done anyway. I'll clean the brush.'

I nodded to her and left, calling Sam to sit next to me, with Phil the other side of him. The boy was quiet, embarrassed, I guessed, at seeing what kind of guys he'd been associating with.

'It's just about over,' I told him. He looked at me, full of questions but I just winked. I didn't want to tip my hand to the guys in the back.

There were three more cars at the station, but they were unmarked. If they were police cars, I didn't recognize them. I let my prisoners out and led them to the back door. As I put the key in the lock the door was opened from inside by an OPP detective I knew, Walker, all the way from Toronto head office.

'Hi, Reid. Looks like you struck oil.'

'Yeah. Now we've only got two unaccounted for, Kershaw and Moira Waites.'

'Well, bring these guys in to join the party,' Walker said. 'Ms Tracy's lawyer just showed.'

'What's he saying to her?'

'It's a woman,' Walker said.

He stood back so I could bring the prisoners in. They were silent, frightened. Phillip followed them and as I stepped up through the door I heard him say, 'Mom!'

His mother was sitting at the desk in front of the cells, writing in a notebook. When she saw him she sprang up and hugged him, tears running down her cheeks. 'Darling. They wouldn't let me come and get you.'

'I'm OK, honest.' He was close to tears but gruff with teenage machismo. 'The Chief caught the pair of them.'

She let go of him, staring at the prisoners. Then she sprang like a tiger, slapping at them furiously. 'You rotten little bastards!' she screamed.

Walker grabbed at her and Elaine the policewoman took

her hands. 'Take it easy, ma'am. They're in custody. Your son's OK.'

Ms Freund went on shouting but I was watching the prisoners. Hanson handled it better. He looked at the floor, not blinking. I could see tears starting down his cheeks. An actor to the end. The other kid was angrier. 'Keep her off. We didn't do anything.'

'You tried to kidnap this boy,' Walker said. 'I'm going to read you the charge and tell you all the wonderful things you can do to get off them, then you can talk all you want.'

'I want a lawyer,' Cy shouted. 'I'm not saying a thing until I see a lawyer.'

'Not me.' Ms Freund was composing herself. 'I'm removing myself from this case. You find somebody else.' She turned and shouted back at the rear cell, where I could see Ms Tracy's hands through the bars. 'You too, Marcia Tracy. You're on your own.'

I spoke to Hanson. 'One question,' I said. 'Where's Kershaw and the woman? Answer that and I'll do whatever I can for you.'

'Thank you, Chief,' Hanson said. 'I don't need a caution. I'll tell you everything I know.'

'Where are they?'

'We left them at the cottage in Honey Harbour,' he said. 'I'll take you there.'

'Fine. We'll go in your car. Elaine, can you come with me to pick it up?'

She was about to answer when the door to my office opened and the superintendent walked through. 'Pick what up?' he asked.

I knew him, a stickler for the book but a good copper. 'The kidnap car. This prisoner is going to take me to where the other two are staying. I want to go in his car.'

'Is that necessary? Why don't we head over there in force and take them? Are they armed?'

'Yes. Kershaw's got a shotgun and he's not afraid to use it.'

'OK. You and Walker go with the witness and take the car. We'll have back-up two hundred yards behind you.'

'Good.' I unlocked the cuff from Cy and snapped it over Hanson's other wrist. 'Let's move.'

Walker came with me, checking the load on his gun as we walked out to my scout car. I took the shotgun out of it and called Sam and we drove Walker's unmarked police car over to the Reserve and collected the Chev. I stuck Hanson in the passenger seat and Walker and Sam took the rear. By the time we got back to the bridge the other police car was waiting for us and we headed out up the highway to Honey Harbour.

'It's in about two hundred yards,' Hanson said. 'We rented it this morning.'

'That was dumb,' I told him. 'Why didn't you just run when you got a new car?'

'Kershaw wanted to pick up the boy. He said his ex-wife had money. He said she'd pay to get the kid back.'

'How come you got sucked into a dumb plan like that?'

'I had no choice,' he said carefully. 'They had enough on me that I couldn't get out.'

'That doesn't wash, Eric. He had no clout. And he was the guy who loaded you up with angel dust, right?'

'Yeah. We were both staying at the motel. I joined him there after I went to dinner with Ms Tracy. We had a party, celebrating the shit I'd created at your town, and he told me he had some good stuff. So I took some. But there's more to it than that.'

'You mean you were running drugs?' It was the logical question. Drugs had to be at the bottom of the whole case, I couldn't see any other explanation.

'Not me,' he said miserably. 'John Waites and Tracy and the Jeffries were all running drugs. They used to bring them in at Sault Ste Marie. They had a deal with one of the

Customs guys. They used a special suitcase. Moira Waites would pick the case up when she came to visit and carry it back to Toronto.'

'And were you involved?'

'No.' He said it fervently. 'I've only been involved in this gang stuff as a favour to Ms Tracy. She said she would give me the part if I did it, to keep you busy. And to pick up Phil, get him involved.'

We were approaching the turn-off for Honey Harbour and I slowed and turned on the indicator. 'We'll talk some more later. When we get there, you run up to the door in a panic and tell them the kid's out cold, you had to hit him. Can he come and help carry him inside.'

'Right,' he said, then drew a deep breath, the way I've seen Fred do when she was rehearsing a part. I knew he was going over his business and said nothing as we pulled up at the door.

I got out quickly and pretended to be digging into the rear seat with the open door between me and the house. Walker took his cue and dropped down out of sight. He had his gun drawn and he was resting his head on Sam, who was looking at me expectantly. I waited thirty seconds and then Hanson came running out. 'He's gone,' he shouted. 'He's left the woman here tied up.'

'I'll check.' I called Sam and sent him ahead through the open door. He bounded in, barking. A woman was lying on the floor, her hands tied behind her, a tea-towel wrapped around her mouth. I left her there a moment longer while Sam checked each of the tiny bedrooms. They were empty. Then I holstered my gun and took out my pocket knife and cut her hands free. She fumbled with the cloth around her mouth and I checked her hands and undid the knot.

She was gasping with fright and anger. 'That bastard!' she screamed. 'He didn't have to do that to me.'

'Who didn't?' I knew but I wanted her confirmation.

'Kershaw,' she said, gasping, out of breath but becoming

calmer. 'George Kershaw. He's the man who killed Moira.'

'You're not Moira Waites?' Now she had surprised me.

'No. I'm Carolyn Jeffries. Kershaw killed Moira and put her in the trunk of her car.'

CHAPTER 16

I looked at her stupidly. 'Waites told me that the woman in the trunk of his car was Carolyn Jeffries.'

'I'm Carolyn Jeffries,' she sobbed. 'They told you I was dead so that nobody would know Moira was dead. Waites would have said she ran away with Stu.'

'Well, why did you run away? And who helped you when you left your car up that side-road?'

'Questions,' she said bitterly. 'I've been terrorized and abused in every kind of way by an animal since last night and you ask me questions.' She was weeping uncontrollably. 'A man has been in prison for six years. Can't you see how horrible it's been?'

'I'm sorry. I'll get you to a doctor.'

She would talk later, she would tell us everything, but this wasn't the time to ask questions. I went to the kitchen for water and as I returned, Walker came in, breathless. 'I've looked all around outside. He's gone,' he said.

'Meet Mrs Jeffries. She's just telling me what's going on.' It was his cue to nod and say nothing while she talked.

Now, with a glass of water in her hands and the knowledge that the worst was over, she did. 'Waites got Kershaw out of prison. I don't know how. He brought him up here to kill Moira. Then we got a phone call, Stu did. We were just finishing dinner. And he said we had to leave right away. I wanted to know why but he just said we were in terrible danger. So we left. Then some woman lent us a car and checked us into a motel. And that's where that bastard found us.'

'But what were you scared of? Why didn't you just go to the police?' I knew the answer but I wanted confirmation. Walker and I listened intently wanting to hear and remember every word she said.

'Drugs,' she said bitterly. 'Waites and Stu had cooked up this scheme to bring in cocaine over the border at the Soo. I never realized until the last time Moira visited. She had begun to wonder why her husband encouraged her to come and see us so often. Then, last time, I found Stu repacking her case, putting her clothes into the duplicate case he had in his closet, the one he used when he crossed the border.'

That was enough for a start. It was time to do the difficult thing. 'Mrs Jeffries, I'm afraid I have some bad news for you,' I said.

She turned and picked up the tea-towel she had been gagged with and wiped her eyes angrily. 'Not news,' she said. 'I was there, wasn't I? I saw him doing it, killing Stu for that goddamn suitcase.'

She sat on the couch, sobbing. Walker looked at me. 'I'll get the superintendent. He can take over.'

The superintendent wasn't much bothered about public relations. He came into the room and spoke to Mrs Jeffries. 'We'll find this guy, he can't have got far.'

Not a word of sympathy for her loss or for the ordeal she had been through. Just business. It rang as clumsily as the old gag about 'Are you widow Jeffries?' but she took no notice and it reminded me that I had personal priorities of my own. I checked my watch. It was nine o'clock. I was supposed to be at the hospital, collecting Fred.

I spoke up. 'I've got to pick up my wife from hospital, sir. I'd like to leave my dog guarding my place in case Kershaw is after me. He threatened to try.'

'No need for that.' The superintendent was playing by

the rules now, his rules. 'I'll send an officer to watch your place until you get home.'

'There's a neighbour woman coming in to tidy up for me. That's why I can't leave the dog on watch. Can you get someone over there right away?'

'I said I'd do it.' He was imperious now. I was nominally a chief but if I'd been in the OPP I would have been at best a sergeant. He didn't want discussions he wanted obedience.

'Fine. Thank you. I have to get her. When she's settled in, I'll come down to the station and we can tidy things up. Right now I need a ride back to my car.'

'Good.' He nodded to Walker. 'We'll take these people back to Murphy's Harbour for now. You look after Mr Bennett.'

So that was me, a mere citizen in his eyes. Walker said, 'We'll take the detective car, Reid,' and we went out to it and got in, with Sam in the back seat.

'Make sure he sends somebody,' I told Walker. 'This guy Kershaw swore he was going to get me and I don't want my wife and kid in danger.'

'It'll be done,' Walker said. 'I'll make sure of it if it should slip his busy mind.' Sarcasm dripped off the word 'busy'. I was glad once again that I didn't work for a big department. The politics are endless.

He let me off at the Horn house. Jean had already gone so I couldn't turn Sam over to her, which would have been the perfect answer. Instead I stuck him in the front seat and set off for Parry Sound.

Fred was dressed and waiting, with the baby asleep in her arms. She beamed when she saw me. 'I thought you'd forgotten us.'

'Sorry, love, it's been a busy morning but we've wrapped things up now, we can relax.' The OPP would soon find Kershaw, I thought, no need to alarm her.

She kissed my stubbly cheek. 'You're looking kind of

lived-in, old thing,' she said. 'Been up all night carousing?'

'You're half right,' I kidded. 'Except the carousing part.'

She wrapped the baby a little tighter in her shawl and I went for a nurse. That meant we had to take a wheelchair which made Fred a little impatient. 'I'm going to have to walk when I get home,' she protested cheerfully.'

'All the more reason to sit while you can,' the nurse said and we all went out to the front door.

The nurse laughed when she saw the scout car. 'Hey, wonderful limousine service you've got.'

The one thing I'd forgotten was a car seat for the baby, so I took five minutes to drive into town and buy one. Then we strapped it in place and set the baby in it, her head close to the shotgun in its front seat bracket. Fred smiled. 'I'll tell her about this when she's older. Her very first ride was in a police car.'

I strapped Fred in neatly and set off down the highway, travelling at the limit, scaring a whole line of drivers into unusually good driving manners. It was a beautiful morning, blue skies, warm, perfect high summer and I tried to relax. The only missing link in the chain was Kershaw and he wouldn't stay loose for very long. But his threat still bothered me. And he was in striking distance of the house. It made me cautious as I drove up the last half mile from Murphy's Harbour to the house. Fred was sitting up, bright and talkative. If she sensed I was on edge she said nothing about it. And then we reached the house and I saw Elaine Harper's OPP cruiser in the yard, next to Horn's pickup.

'Company so early?' Fred said. 'What's the occasion?'

'Jean Horn offered to come over and freshen the place up,' I said. 'And the OPP car is Elaine Harper's, you've met her. I guess she's stopped off to see the baby.'

I pulled in on the far side of the other cars, still cautious.

'Stay here a moment, I'll get the camera,' I lied. Something wasn't right. Two women in the house and a baby arriving on the doorstep. One of them should have come to the door.

'We can get pictures later,' Fred said, but I said, 'Please, I want to catch this moment.'

She leaned over and kissed me. 'You're a sentimental s.o.b., Bennett, and I love you.'

I patted her hand and got out, letting Sam out of the car. I whispered 'Seek' and pretended to tie my shoe lace as he ran around through the bushes, finding nothing.

I straigtened up then and headed for the house. Nobody came to the door and I felt my skin draw tight with tension. Something was wrong, I was sure of it.

At the door I hesitated. If Kershaw was inside, threatening the women with his shotgun he would kill me the moment I opened the door. If he wasn't, I was being a fool. But I had to be sure.

I thought for a moment, then pretended to fumble in my pocket for keys. I turned to look at Fred who was craning down to see through the window of the other cars to the door. I made a turning motion with my hand and mouthed, 'Forgot my key.'

Then I stopped off to one side of the door and reached across to tap it with my knuckles, withdrawing my hand at once.

Instantly the door blew apart, the shotgun load shredding it in a shocking burst of sound. I gave a shout and slammed both feet hard on the floor, like a flamenco dancer, still standing off to one side.

It seemed like a year and then the muzzle of the gun stuck out through the hole in the door, pointing down to where my body should have been lying.

I grabbed the muzzle, feeling it hot in my palm, and snatched it towards me. He hung on but I wrenched him against the inside of the door and I had the muzzle turned from me. Still holding it with all my strength, I threw my weight against the broken door and it gave, sending the door back against the wall. He was in there but not trapped. He let go of the gun and tried to get out. I didn't hesitate. I drew my revolver and reached around the door to shoot him through the body. He gave a grunting cry and went slack. I hooked the door away from him with one foot and stood over him, gun trained on the middle of his chest.

It was Kershaw. His hair was greyer then in his photograph but unmistakable. He was holding his side and blood was oozing through his fingers.

'Jean! Elaine!' I shouted, and heard a muffled half scream. I stepped away from Kershaw, carrying his shotgun in one hand, my service revolver in the other, and crouched to look around the door jamb into the kitchen.

Both women were lying face down on the floor, hands and mouths tied with strips of tea-towels. Elaine looked up at me. 'Is there anyone else?' I shouted it, in case the shots had deafened her. She shook her head and I took a quick look back at Kershaw. He hadn't moved and I pulled a knife off the magnetic strip and cut her hands free, then Jean Horn's.

'He's down. Watch him,' I said as they untied their gags. I grabbed the phone and rang the station. Walker answered and I filled him in. I was trembling with tension and fury. 'The bastard could have killed my family,' I shouted.

'Be right there. Take care of the women.'

Walker hung up and I turned to the women. 'Did he hurt you?'

Jean spoke first. 'No. He said he was going to have some fun when you were dead. He didn't want to take the time until then.' She was calm but pale.

'Sit down,' I told her. 'You too, Elaine.'

Elaine sat, weeping. 'I'm sorry, Reid. I was sitting having a coffee with Jean and he just walked in on us with that gun. I should have been doing my job.'

'Forget it. Sit down. I'll get my wife and baby in.'

Elaine stayed where she was but Jean came out to the

living-room where Kershaw was sitting, blank-faced, pressing his hands uselessly against the wound in his side. 'He's hurt bad,' Jean said. 'Leave him. Get Fred. Take her in the back way.'

I touched her on the shoulder in gratitude and ran back out to Fred. She was in the front seat of the car, the baby in her arms, talking softly to her. 'It's over,' I said. 'You can come in now.'

She looked up at me, rocking gently with the baby, her face chalk white. 'I can't take this,' she said softly. 'I love you. You know that. But I saw that door explode. You could be lying there now, dead.'

She began to weep, tears spouting from her open eyes. I bent and held her very close and she forced her head into my shoulder, wiping her eyes to and fro against my shirt front. 'It's over,' I told her. 'I'll quit this job if you want.'

'It's never over,' she sobbed. And then Jean Horn came out of the house. She came over and touched me on the back and I let go of Fred and stood up.

Jean knelt beside her. 'What a beautiful baby.' She held out her hands and slowly Fred gave up Louise and Jean took her, crooning to her in Ojibway.

Fred wiped her eyes on her sleeve and got to her feet. 'Let's get inside,' she said.

Jean straightened up, carrying the baby, and I took Fred's arm and led her to the back door. Elaine Harper opened it without speaking and Fred stepped up inside. 'Where is he?' she asked me.

'In the front, by the door. Stay with Elaine, please.'

Elaine steered her to a chair and I went to Kershaw. His head had slumped forward and his jaw had dropped. I knew he was dead.

I was crouching there and I heard a car pull up outside. Walker and the other detective came up the steps, the superintendent behind them. Walker bent and felt Kershaw's throat. 'Well, he won't make any more trouble,' he said softly.

The superintendent was puffing. 'What the hell happened here?'

'I'll tell you in a minute. Right now I've got to look after my family.'

The superintendent looked at me sharply. 'You can't just walk away,' he began.

'Watch me,' I told him.

I went back to the kitchen. It was empty. Fred and Elaine were standing outside with Jean Horn who was still holding the baby. 'You can't take her into the house with that thing in the door,' Jean said. 'I'll take them home with me until it's cleared up.'

Fred protested but Jean clung to the baby, crooning. 'It's better,' she said.

I took Fred's arm. 'It really is, dear. I won't be long here. Then I'll pack us a bag and we'll take right off for your folks.'

'Maybe,' she said and I was happy to see the first of the steel coming back into her voice.

I drove them over in the scout car and came back to find the ambulance crew taking Kershaw's body out of the house. The superintendent was talking to Elaine Harper and he looked at me as I came in.

'I hear you were too smart for him.'

'Seems that way. I hope you've got all the pictures you need. I'm going to scrub that blood out of the walls and get a new door put in.'

'We don't need pictures. We have first-hand evidence from PW Harper,' he said. 'Go ahead.'

And so I did it, changing the cleaning water four times before every trace of the blood was gone. Then I called the lumber yard and got them to send a new door right away, and a handyman. After that I sat down and made a formal statement to the OPP.

'You're free and clear,' Walker said. 'Clear case of self-defence.'

'Good.' I was still not talking much. 'Now I want you to take the prisoners away. I'm through. Right now I'm hanging up my skates.'

'For keeps?' he asked in surprise. 'Hell, Reid, don't be too hasty on this. You've got a good little place here.'

'If my wife wants me out, I'm quitting. Right now I'm taking time off.'

'Good idea.' The superintendent had come out of the house and was listening. 'We'll tidy up the ends.'

And take whatever credit was around, I thought without bitterness. 'We got statements from everybody,' Walker said. 'What a bunch of whiners, they were all so eager to get off that they've incriminated the hell out of one another.'

'What did they do about a lawyer?'

'Hell, shysters came down like flies on honey,' Walker laughed. 'Two from Parry Sound, three from Midland, phone calls from as far away as Toronto.'

'But the suspects all talked?'

'Yeah. Sang like birds,' Walker said happily. 'We got everything. Bill Holland came down with Inspector Dupuy from Parry Sound. He says you called the whole shot on it.'

'Walk me through it,' I said and the superintendent stepped in. 'You're still in shock,' he said. 'Do you have a drink in the house?'

'Yes. Good idea. I'm off duty now.'

I got my bottle of Black Velvet rye and after a little polite headshaking they all joined me. I poured myself a solid double, the others took them lighter and Walker relaxed with his drink on his knee.

'Waites was at the bottom of everything. Him and Jeffries. They were running coke over the border at the Soo and down to Toronto. They were working for some sleazebucket Waites defended one time in court. Jeffries was the pipeline.

He'd pick it up and bring it this far, then Waites' wife would bring it down. Only she didn't know what was going on until a couple of weeks ago when her friend Carolyn found Jeffries changing the suitcase Moira had brought up for a new one, full of junk. The women talked about it and Moira Waites was going to blow the whistle.'

That all made sense and I nodded. 'And Waites sprung Kershaw to kill her?'

'Right. He set her up, Kershaw killed her and put the car in the lake, slashing the seats so you'd think it was a gang thing. Then Waites rang the Jeffries and told them what had happened. They panicked and ran. Ms Tracy met them on a side-road and put them into a motel. Kershaw and Hanson were already staying at the other place, where you found Hanson.'

'What was Tracy's angle? Money for her movie, what?'

'Yes. Waites promised to get her the money she needed if and when the murder came off as planned. Her end was to create a disturbance and take care of Kershaw. That's why she organized young Hanson to fake this gang crap.'

'What went wrong?' They'd all got what they wanted, I thought.

'Kershaw wanted more money. He'd been paid ten grand but he knew he had Waites over a barrel. He went after more. And at the same time Jeffries made trouble. He had money in a safety deposit box in the bank but he couldn't get it. So he went to Pickerel Point to have it out with Waites and they fought and he killed him and took the case, knowing it was loaded with coke and he could get money on that.'

'And Kershaw went after the case.'

'Right. Ms Tracy helped him, told him where the Jeffries were hiding and lent him her car. Only she acted too fast. She realized you'd come asking questions when you saw her car was missing. That's why she banged her face up and said she'd been assaulted.' Walker raised his glass triumphantly. 'But we got 'em.'

The superintendent sipped his rye slowly. 'Kershaw's been up here ever since he got away from Toronto. When you found Hanson at the motel he got out of the back window and ran. That night he hid out, stole food from the grocery. He didn't want to kill you until he'd got more money to get away. He figured he'd get more from Waites, he was counting on it. He didn't know Waites was going to be killed.'

'And Ms Tracy set him up to kill me?'

'Yeah,' the superintendent said. He didn't like telling this part of the story, but maybe the drink had loosened him up a little. 'She figured by then that you were pretty good at your job. That's why she'd had Hanson pull this gang caper. But when you were right behind her, stepping on her heels every move she made, she figured you had to go.'

It was as close to a compliment as I would ever get from this man. I changed the subject. 'Why did she involve young Freund?'

Walker explained it. 'She had Hanson pick up Kershaw's kid in the beginning, so she would have something to hold over Kershaw's head. Apparently he wanted to see the boy, despite the divorce.'

'But in the end he tried to have him kidnapped,' I protested.

'When he didn't get the coke and didn't get any of the money Waites had promised him, yeah. He figured, kill two birds with one stone: spend time with his kid, have his ex-wife pay him as well.'

There was a tap on the door and I went out to find the guys from the lumber yard there. No carpenter. They were sorry but he was sick.

That did it for me. I shoved the OPP guys out and spent an hour hanging the door and fitting a new lock. Then I drove over to the Horns' place.

Fred came to the door when I got there. She said nothing for about half a minute, we stood and looked at one another and then she kissed me, gently. 'Let's go home,' she said. 'I'll get Louise.'

So I thanked Jean and drove my wife and baby back to the house. She looked at the new door. 'Pretty neat. Ever think of taking up carpentry as a career?'

'I can do,' I said carefully. 'I'm off now and I'm not going back.'

She undid the straps around our daughter. 'Not for a month anyway,' she said. 'We'll go out west first, think things over from a distance.'

'OK.' I put my arm around her shoulders and we walked slowly up the steps to the house, feeling my way back into my life, wondering if anything would be the same from here on.